Praise for D

Overall, Parker has written a fun mystery, one that not only challenges us in our detective capabilities but also morally, questioning how our justice system isn't always as equal as we like it to be. **Deadly Darkness** is a great mystery for any fan of the genre.
Tierney for Novels Alive

The historical details, such as blackout drills, add to the rising tension and intensity of the story as well as the inevitability of war. But with darkness there is also light, found here in the antics of the boys along with enough humor to alleviate the gloom. The characters bring the story to life and give it heart.
Cozy Up with Kathy

Historical fiction readers as well as mystery lovers will appreciate this incredible series. This book stands alone but will entice you to go back and read the series from the start. Prepare to sit a spell because you will be drawn in with danger on every page.
Laura's Interests

I especially like how realistic the characters feel as the deal with the effects of an upcoming war looming on the horizon as Parker captures how it felt along with the charm of England. Makes for quite a fun read for fans of historical cozies.
Books a Plenty Book Reviews

Also from Kate Parker

The Deadly Series

Deadly Scandal

Deadly Wedding

Deadly Fashion

Deadly Deception

Deadly Travel

Deadly Darkness

Deadly Cypher

The Victorian Bookshop Mysteries

The Vanishing Thief

The Counterfeit Lady

The Royal Assassin

The Conspiring Woman

The Detecting Duchess

The Milliner Mysteries

The Killing at Kaldaire House

Murder at the Marlowe Club

The Mystery at Chadwick House

Deadly Cypher

Kate Parker

JDP PRESS

This is a work of fiction. All names, characters, and incidents are products of the author's imagination. Any resemblance to actual occurrences or persons, living or dead, is coincidental. Historical events and personages are fictionalized.

ISBN: 978-1-7332294-7-0 [print]
ISBN: 978-1-7332294-6-3 [e-book]

Published by JDPPress
Cover Design by Lyndsey Lewellen of Llewellen Designs

Dedication

For all lovers of good tales

For my children

For my parents who are cheering me from beyond

For John, Forever

Late November, 1939

Chapter One

"Yesterday morning, a German linguist named Sarah Wycott was reported missing when she didn't show up for work." Sir Malcolm Freemantle, the ferocious British spymaster I neither trusted nor liked, glared at me from under his bushy eyebrows and added, "They found her last night. Along a country lane. Dead."

I continued to watch him, knowing I was the rabbit to his hawk, and waited for him to continue. We were at war, although no one was shooting at us yet. The declaration of war on the third of September meant tall, bulky Sir Malcolm owned me, and many others, for the duration.

"Miss Wycott worked at a government facility in a railroad junction town fifty miles northwest of London. A Most Secret Facility. The Government Code and Cypher School." Sir Malcolm seemed to speak in leading capital letters. "If her death was a random event, or due to a jilted lover or angry neighbor, then it is sad, but none of our affair."

When Sir Malcolm didn't continue, I said, "And if it's not?" The wooden chair across his desk from the spymaster hurt my rear, and I didn't want to spend any more time there than necessary.

"If it's not, and we don't find out who killed her, Mrs. Redmond, we may have already lost the war."

Oh, good grief. Sir Malcolm had a tendency to make pronouncements of massive weight, delivered in his bass voice. Unfortunately, I'd learned that he rarely overstated the case.

I was curious despite myself. "If you want me to find her killer, you need to tell me as much as possible about Miss Wycott and why she's at the center of our war effort." Then the name sank in. "She attended my college, didn't she?"

"She was two years behind you, but yes, she went to Newnham College."

"I knew little about her then, and nothing since," I told him.

He opened a file on his desk. "She was a linguist at the Government Code and Cypher School at Bletchley Park and billeted at Bloomington Grove."

"I've heard of Bloomington Grove. I've never been invited to any of their parties," I added wistfully. Bloomington Grove was the home of the Earl and Countess of Haymarket, who entertained lavishly and recklessly. In the process they burned through money. I'd heard their estate on the Buckinghamshire-Bedfordshire border was offered to the government shortly after war was declared. No doubt they needed the rent.

I looked past Sir Malcolm out the window that overlooked rooftops and the nearly bare top branches of trees and wondered how living in a grand house would feel.

"Your assignment is to take Sarah Wycott's place at work and in her room."

I jerked my attention back to Sir Malcolm. "Am I supposed to take over a dead woman's identity?" I didn't see how that could succeed, since her colleagues there would know her.

"No. Of course not, Olivia. You're her replacement in both her work and her housing assignment. Everyone there knows others working there through family connections or university ties. Due to the need for absolute secrecy, recruitment has been limited so far on the basis of personal knowledge of the character of each person assigned to the Government Code and Cypher School at Bletchley Park."

"Why?" That sounded as if it were an odd requirement.

"We have to be certain of everyone's silence. You will keep your own identity as Olivia Redmond, who left her job as a newspaper reporter to work there. Especially since you've already demonstrated how good your knowledge of German is."

Last spring, he'd sent me on a Kindertransport mission due to my fluency. I'd been happy with the outcome, especially rescuing two young boys, sons of a German government employee working as a British spy. I hoped I'd be as successful this time.

"Do I get the countess's bedroom at Bloomington Grove?" I gave him an eager smile, not able to resist a little sarcasm.

"No. Women are billeted on the ground floor of the

servants' quarters. The main part of the house has been taken over by the army for training recruits." As my shoulders sagged in mock disappointment, he added, "The countess's bedroom now houses a classroom."

I doubted a parlor maid had been housed in anything more than a dinky, cold little room. I was going to miss my modern flat in the middle of London. "And my work assignment?"

"I'll let you experience that the same way everyone else does. At least you've already signed the Official Secrets Act, so you understand the importance of strict silence about anything and everything that has to do with your work at this location." He leaned forward. "Complete strict silence. Except to me, of course."

"There is nothing about this assignment that will be any use to Sir Henry." Sir Henry Benton, publisher of the *Daily Premier,* was my employer and had "loaned" me to Sir Malcolm on occasion in exchange for the ability to write feature stories about places and people I encountered during my investigations.

This time, he'd get nothing in trade.

"You can't even tell him where you've gone. You'll have a Foreign Office box number where all correspondence will be sent."

"Who's going to pay me?" The government didn't pay women anything near as much as what Sir Henry paid me. I couldn't afford to live on a government salary.

"Sir Henry will pay you. We will reimburse him for your

time away from your pressing duties at the newspaper." He said this as if he found it humorous.

I didn't see anything to laugh at. It was my profession and my salary. And I didn't trust him.

I needed information from him if I had any hope of learning who killed this woman, so I asked, "What can you tell me about this woman and the circumstances surrounding her death?"

"Monday night, Sarah Wycott returned to where the transport from Bletchley Park—shall we call it BP?—dropped her off after work. This was down the lane from the drive to the manor house, not overlooked by any dwellings. She was never again seen alive.

"Yesterday—that is, Tuesday morning—she was reported missing by her supervisor, both to the local police and to us. We could get a great deal farther than the local bobbies when it came to BP. They can't get past the gates." Again, that cat smile.

"However, her body was found late yesterday by a dog walker who reported his finding to the local police station, who told BP, who told us."

"How was she killed?"

"Strangulation. We sent out one of our pathologists to take a look, and he says he believes someone with medium-sized hands, quite strong hands, killed her. Up close and personal."

Interesting. "The size of the hands means this could have been done by a man or a woman."

"I thought you'd notice that. This murderer could get close enough to reach out and strangle her. There were no signs of defensive injuries, as if she were taken by surprise. Either it was done by sneaking up behind her, or by someone she trusted."

To me, it sounded as if it were a silent attack used by Fleur Bettenard, the Nazi assassin I'd first met in London over a year ago. *Wonderful.* I had no idea if Fleur was still in the country, but if she was, I didn't want to meet up with her again. On our previous encounters, I'd barely escaped with my life.

"When did Sarah die?"

Sir Malcolm consulted a file on his desk. "Monday night. Before she was reported missing. The body was shoved back in the hedgerow, and since the harvesting's already been completed, no one was too close to the spot where she was found until the dog sniffed it out."

"Was this spot between Bloomington Grove manor house and the bus stop?"

"Oddly enough, no. It was along the lane beyond the drive in the opposite direction. In terms you would understand, if this distance were in London, it would be several streets away."

"Was she robbed? Was she—assaulted?"

"You mean sexually?" Sir Malcolm was blunt. "No. A bracelet she often wore was missing, and there was no money in her bag. Other than that, she had nothing worth stealing. It looks just barely as if it might have been a robbery."

"What do the police think?"

Sir Malcolm looked as if he'd tasted the chicory coffee that was showing up in more and more places and found it unacceptable. "They think some personable young man sweet-talked her into walking along with him, and when she wouldn't do what he wanted, he lost his head, killed her, grabbed any valuables, and hid the body."

"As I recall, it was too cold outside Monday night to think about sparking, let alone trying it on," I told him. I doubted Sir Malcolm was that practical.

"I doubt that has occurred to the police," he replied drily.

"Do they think it was someone she knew?"

"They've questioned some young men at the army training facility known to frequent pubs in the area, but they were all alibied by their program. All of the young men she worked with were alibied by each other. They've run out of ideas and suspects, and with the call-up, the police don't have the manpower to pursue this." Sir Malcolm watched me closely.

"You're being called in, Olivia, because we have a greater need to find her killer than only to see justice done for Miss Wycott."

"What aren't you telling me?"

"You remember I mentioned the Government Code and Cypher School?"

I nodded.

"You must keep silent about this until your dying day.

They are trying to break the German army, navy, and air force codes. Messages in codes we need to read to know what the enemy is planning."

"Yes, sir."

"The codes are created on the Enigma machine. Most people, including the Germans, think they're unbreakable. We've had brilliant minds working on this for the past year, and we've had help from the French and the Poles, who've received information from back channels."

"Stolen or sold."

He smiled. "If you prefer. Miss Wycott was a German linguist who finished at Cambridge two years ago. She's been helping with these efforts."

"Why German linguists?"

He laughed. "My dear Olivia. The messages are in German. These brilliant minds are looking at this as if it's a chess match or a crossword puzzle. In English. Someone has to tell them if they actually get useful German from their solutions."

Sir Malcolm didn't have much more to tell me about the murder. I was given a rail ticket to Bletchley for the midday train the next day and told someone would meet me at the station. My cover was I would be working a temporary slot at the Foreign Office and given a Foreign Office box number for an address.

When I told Sir Henry, my boss and the publisher of the *Daily Premier*, about my new temporary position, his immediate reaction was, "Sir Malcolm is at it again. How long this time?"

I should have known Sir Henry would immediately look at the practical issues. "I don't know. But he did say this time he would reimburse you for my wages while I'm away."

Sir Henry laughed aloud. "That will be the day. Well, come back as soon as you can. And be careful. We'd like you back in one piece. Especially with many of our reporters getting their call-up papers, we can use your talents."

He must have meant my talents for sniffing out stories. My writing had not improved. But maybe, with male reporters being called up, I had a chance to do real reporting. Something more than fashion shows and wedding notices. But first I'd have to get back to London.

I wrote my husband, Captain Adam Redmond, at the address I had for him as well as leaving him a note on our kitchen table in case he was able to get into London in the next few weeks. I didn't know where he was except for an army box number. Now he wouldn't know where I was, either.

Finally, I needed to break the news of my leaving town to my father. At my request, we went out to a hotel dining room for dinner where they still did things to a prewar standard. I wore my blue evening gown with my silver earrings and bag, knowing I wouldn't have a chance to wear them again for some time.

Once we'd ordered, my father asked, "Have you heard from Adam?"

"Not for at least a week. I'm sure the army is keeping him

busy."

"From what we see in the Foreign Office, the army is keeping everyone busy."

I didn't think it would be this easy to find an opening in our conversation. "I've been asked to take a temporary assignment for the Foreign Office."

"Really? Why you?"

I would have left the table and gone home if I hadn't known this would be the best meal I would have for weeks. "You seem to forget I have some talents and skills that have been used before."

My father shut his eyes and his mouth. Seen this way, in evening clothes, with his silver hair and lean build, he was quite attractive. Then he opened his mouth and his words ruined the image. "Is this one of Sir Malcolm's plans? I told you a year ago not to get involved with that man."

"I was supposed to let you rot in some secret prison last year, was that it? If you hadn't been suspected of your friend's murder, I would never have met Sir Malcolm while I was trying to get you released."

"It wasn't a secret prison. It was run by the British government. In Britain."

"Yes. It was, shall we say, clandestine?"

"Possibly to you. Not to me."

I'm certain by this time my face was red with anger and my hands were clenched. Fortunately, that's when the soup arrived.

We ate dinner in silence while all those around us

chatted amiably and laughed loudly. The silver, the crystal, the sparkling white table linens all looked as they had throughout peacetime. There was peacetime variety and quality in the food and the wines. No one in this restaurant seemed to have a care, except for me.

After our coffee arrived, my father said, "I don't want you to do this, whatever Sir Malcolm has in mind."

"Neither of us has any choice. No one in the country has any choice." I was hissing my words at him.

"You should have resigned and become a housewife four months ago when you married."

"I told you that wasn't going to happen." My father's plans for my life were diametrically opposed to my plans or Sir Malcolm's plans, or even Sir Henry's. "Even if I had resigned, Sir Malcolm could have simply called me up."

"Could have, yes. But why would he? You're just not that special."

That was typical for my father. "You've certainly never thought so." I'd helped Jews escape the Third Reich and hunted down murderers and spies, but my father ignored any mention of my successes.

"You're my daughter. My only close relative. I love you, but even I can see you're not in any way special."

I set down my coffee cup, still half full of real coffee. "Then it's a good thing my darling Adam, and Sir Malcolm, and Sir Henry don't agree with you. Good night, Father." I rose and walked away from our table.

Chapter Two

Early the next afternoon, lugging two heavy suitcases, I left the train at Bletchley station and found a middle-aged man in brown trousers and a tweed jacket on the platform. "Mrs. Redmond?" he asked.

"Yes."

"We're waiting for one more, and then we'll walk up the hill. I'm—oh, here we are."

A young man about my age with two suitcases of his own walked up to us. He wore a heavy gray coat over navy blue trousers.

"Mr. Townsend?"

"Yes." Townsend smiled and I immediately guessed he was a heartbreaker. He had a square face and twinkling blue eyes that made him appear pleased with all that he saw. All I saw was a grimy railroad station with a tall barbed-wire fence running along the tracks on the opposite side from us.

"I'm Captain Wellesley," the man in the tweed jacket said. "Ready? Let's head up the hill." He started off on a pace I couldn't keep up with. Mr. Townsend was managing, just barely, to stay with our guide. The captain seemed to forget that both of us were weighed down with luggage.

I finally reached the gate in the forbidding wire fence placed alongside the road to find the two men standing in wait as if they'd been there all day. They looked relaxed, while I felt sweaty and disheveled. Two guards in army uniforms stood inside the gate, grinning.

"Ready, Mrs. Redmond? Good. Go through here."

We walked down what felt as if it was an impossibly long path around a pond and past some flimsy-looking, squat wooden buildings. Finally, we entered a Victorian manor house that displayed several architectural styles smashed into each other and were led into a small room just inside the main door. Winded, I walked in, dropped my suitcases, and collapsed into a seat. My arms ached from the distance I'd lugged all that weight.

Captain Wellesley gave us a lecture about how revealing anything that we would see, hear, or learn here would put us in jail for thirty years, if we weren't shot. Everything here was a secret that we had to take to our graves.

I had already been threatened with evil consequences by Sir Malcolm, who was truly frightening. With this man, I wanted to say, "I understand. Now, may I please have a cup of tea?"

Mr. Townsend looked startled at my lack of response.

I noticed neither of us were handed the Official Secrets Act to sign. I wondered when Townsend signed his.

That done, we went to the administration office and

received our passes, filled out piles of paperwork, and were told to leave our cases there while we went to tea in the canteen.

Mr. Townsend asked me to join him. We went into a large room, possibly the large drawing room in earlier days, where most of the tables were empty since lunchtime was over. We both chose tea and pasties.

"I'm Simon," he said, holding out his hand.

"Olivia." We shook hands.

"Where are you from?"

"London. And you?"

"Cambridge. Jesus College."

"Did you just graduate?"

"Five years ago. I've been doing post-graduate work on mathematical theory since then and lecturing."

"I was in Newnham College, and I've been working for a London daily for the past two years." My goodness, had it been that long? More than two years, really, since Reggie was murdered and I had to get a job. I took a sip of tea to cover my feelings of sadness.

His face lit up. "That sounds as if it's an exciting place to work. Which paper?"

"*The Daily Premier.*"

"I read that. Have I read any of your articles?"

I couldn't resist deflating him a little. "Do you read the women's section or the society pages?"

He shook his head, looking a little embarrassed. "Were you an English major?"

"Modern languages. And you studied mathematics?"

"And lecture in it now."

That made sense, since we were at the Government Code and Cypher School. Math would be a handy thing to study if you wanted to break codes. I gave him a small smile. "Where are they billeting you?"

"With my aunt and uncle. He's the vicar at St. Stephen's in Little Rowanwood. And you?"

"In the servants' quarters at Bloomington Grove."

"My. You fell into a pot of honey."

"I doubt the servants' quarters are a pot of honey." But they should tell me a great deal about the murder victim.

We soon ran out of neutral topics, finished eating, and headed back to the administration offices. Captain Wellesley reappeared and led us outside. "That is Hut Six, where you both will report tomorrow morning. Now get your cases and we'll go down to the gate. Your ride should be here in a moment."

Our ride was an estate car, probably once a shooting brake at some estate, driven by a young woman in uniform who whizzed down lanes much faster than I would have thought wise. It was already growing dark by midafternoon this late in the year and shadows hid the road in places.

This was earlier than Sarah Wycott had been dropped off when she disappeared. Why had she walked off in the dark along an empty lane? I wouldn't without a good reason. What reason would she have had?

We dropped off Simon Townsend in the center of Little

Rowanwood and continued on. The driver stopped at a crossroads a few minutes later. "This is where the bus will pick you up in the morning. The house is just over there." She pointed down a dark lane to the right.

I climbed out with my cases and she zoomed off.

I hoped she was right about the location of my billet, because I couldn't see any sign of life in this gloom.

Again, I had a long walk with my suitcases. It was a good thing no one tried to attack me in the darkness, because I was tired and sore and annoyed. I would have killed them.

Finally, I turned a corner in the lane and saw a huge house with lights on ahead of me up the drive. It was almost curfew time. I hoped I arrived before all the lights were blacked out.

As it turned out, I reached the main door shortly after all the blackout curtains had been lowered and any outside lights had been extinguished. The person who answered the door, a young sergeant in army uniform, gave me directions to the servants' entrance and quickly shut the door. Now I had to get down the stairs and around the side of the house while carrying my cases. In the dark. Without twisting an ankle or tripping over anything.

Somehow, I managed to do it successfully, only to stand at the door in the cold for two minutes. The door was finally answered by a heavy-set woman in a maid's uniform.

"I'm Mrs. Redmond and I understand I am to be billeted here."

"Taking Miss Wycott's room?"

"Yes."

She opened the door fully so I could get in with my cases. "Down the hall there, third on the left. Facilities are first two doors on the right."

That sounded as if this would be modern living at least. Until then, I hadn't thought of the possibility of outdoor facilities. Relieved, I gave the middle-aged woman a smile.

"When you're ready, we'll have the kettle on in the kitchen."

"That sounds wonderful." I meant it, and my gratitude came out in my tone.

When I walked into the room that had been Sarah Wycott's and now was mine, I discovered it held a narrow bed, a wooden chair, a small table with a lamp, and a wardrobe. The window was covered with a heavy blackout curtain. I set down my cases and looked in the wardrobe. Nothing had been left. Pulling the chair over, I found there was nothing left on top of the wardrobe but an even coating of dust. Nothing was hidden under the thin mattress.

Not a single clue as to what happened to Sarah Wycott.

I walked down to the servants' hall and found there was a long farm table and a dozen chairs. I could see a huge kitchen through a doorway. "Is there a chance of a cup of tea?" I asked the two heavy-set women in maids' uniforms seated at the table.

"Of course. Sit down. The countess says we need to take good care of you girls. Not the way we treat that lot in the main part of the house."

I saw now the woman who answered the door and had spoken was the younger of the two. She went into the kitchen to pour a cup of tea while the older rose stiffly and went to work at the stove, stirring something that smelled delicious.

"Where is the countess living these days?" I stood in the doorway watching them. I was curious, even if the knowledge wouldn't help me solve this murder.

"Upstairs. The family, and the two of us, now occupy the first and second floors in this wing. And you'd better believe they moved over the best of the furniture away from those army boys," the maid said. I had to step back so she could move past me to set a cup of tea at a place at the table.

"I'm glad we haven't entirely kicked them out of their home. Their dinner certainly smells good," I added as I sat to drink my tea.

"This?" the cook called out. "Oh, no, this is for you girls and for Betty and me. They won't eat stew. I'll roast them a chop and some vegetables later on."

"If it tastes as good as it smells, they don't know what they're missing," I told her.

The cook smiled at me. "What's your name? I'm Elsie, and she's Betty."

"Mrs. Redmond. Livvy," I added.

"Your hubby been called up?" the younger one, Betty, asked, sitting down with her knitting. A khaki sock.

"He joined a few years ago. He's a captain in the army."

"So, you must be knitting, too. This is for my nephew. He got his call-up papers last month."

I shook my head. "I never learned."

"Your mother has a lot to answer for."

"She died when I was six. It was just my father and me, and a string of housekeepers who didn't have time to teach me anything like that."

"Poor mite. Get yourself some khaki wool and needles, and we'll be glad to teach you."

"What should I start with?" Everyone was knitting these days for servicemen, either for their own family members or to be delivered by the Women's Institute.

"Try a scarf first."

"Hasn't done Miss Carter any good," the cook said. "She's on her third or fourth scarf, and still has mistakes all over it."

"Just as warm, even if it's not as good looking. Miss Carter, next room down the hallway from you, has been doggedly trying to learn to knit. With no one in her family to knit for, she turns hers in to the WI."

"Is it hard to learn?" I'd never tried this before.

"No, but I've been knitting since I was a child."

"Things are always easier to learn as a child." Maybe I'd try to learn, but I didn't expect anything.

When our conversation faded out, I asked, "Was Miss Wycott a knitter?"

"Yes. She turned hers into the WI, too. The same as Miss Carter and the Allen twins."

"The who?"

"You've not met your housemates?" the cook asked.

"No."

"You'll like the Allen girls. Talk nonstop, but real helpful. Marianne is a year older than Maryellen, but they look the same as twins. Sound identical, too. They'll make sure you get where you're going in the morning."

By the time I finished unpacking and explored my new living quarters, there were several young women talking, laughing, and rushing up and down the hall. I followed the noise to the servants' hall and found them sitting down at the long farm table. Betty was setting out ten flat bowls of stew with cups of tea and a bread basket. Then she and the cook sat down at one end of the table.

I took an empty seat about halfway down the table and nodded to everyone.

"This is Mrs. Redmond, come to take Miss Wycott's place," Betty said. After a redhead glared us all into bowing our heads for prayers, I received several greetings before everyone began to eat the hot stew. It smelled heavenly. It was hot and flavorful, although it was mostly potatoes and cabbage with a few shreds of pork. I found I was famished.

We all complimented the cook, who two different housemates informed me was called Elsie. There wasn't a break in the conversation for me to tell them I'd already learned her name.

"Is this the time we get back and have dinner every night?" I finally asked.

One of the two identical blondes sitting on the other side of the table said, "Pretty much, yes. Unless you have extra work to finish. Oh, I'm Maryellen Allen."

Her mirror image sitting next to her farther down the table added, "That's why we didn't think it strange Sarah was missing the night she died. She had some work to complete and would have come in after we finished dinner. I'm Marianne Allen." She looked at her sister and said, "We're not twins."

"The bus picks us up promptly at seven-thirty. Breakfast is at seven, so be ready to leave immediately after," Maryellen said.

"The queue for the wash-room starts at five-thirty," Marianne said.

"So we knew by seven the next morning something was wrong," Maryellen said.

"Sarah would never have stayed out all night," Marianne added. "She was a well-brought-up girl. Her family was chapel."

Then what was she doing down a country lane, alone, in the dark?

Chapter Three

After dinner had been cleared away by Betty and two of my housemates, four of the women came back to the table with their knitting. The two Allen girls I'd been introduced to at dinner, the short redhead with a covering of freckles who'd insisted on saying the grace before dinner and who now introduced herself as Aileen MacLeith, and a brunette who was the knitter with the odd-looking scarves named Fiona Carter. The other women from dinner didn't make an appearance.

Marianne went over to the console radio along one wall and turned it on. The BBC orchestra was giving a concert.

"Rosalie had this sent a few weeks ago from her home in Lancaster. She said they'll never miss it. Rosalie's a good egg," Marianne said.

"Or has some light-fingered relatives," Maryellen added, "to pick this up."

I'd met Rosalie at dinner, but I couldn't remember which one she was. I wondered if there were thieves in her family and if it made any difference to my investigation.

"Do you want me to fix that, Fiona?" Maryellen asked, gesturing to Fiona's knitting.

"No. The WI is happy with them and they hold up well. The soldiers are glad to get them. They're just—different," Fiona said, working away on her scarf that had more than its share of lumps and bumps in the pattern.

"I've never knitted," I admitted. "Is it hard to learn?"

"It's not hard to learn," Fiona said. She glanced down. "It's hard to do well."

"It can be taken out and done again to do it right," Maryellen said.

"I'd rather just keep going. I'll get it right eventually if I keep trying. And in the meantime, the scarves are usable." Fiona was looking down at her knitting, but she seemed to be pouting.

The sisters looked at each other. Marianne said, "I'm glad none of us had to work late tonight. It's making me uneasy, thinking about walking back from the drop-off point in the dark. I wasn't too worried about it before."

"Is it always only one who has to work late?" I asked.

"There's not so much work that any of us need to stay after," Fiona said.

"Lately, Sarah had stayed late more than a few times. Someone will have to pick up that work," Maryellen said.

"If it was work," Marianne said.

The sisters looked at each other and grinned.

I looked from one to the other. "You mean she was staying after because of a man?"

Both sisters gave me innocent looks.

Aileen looked up from the winter cap she was finishing and glared. "They're making things up. I'm sure Sarah had work to finish. She was never long behind us. Until Monday night..."

Everyone fell silent.

Eventually, they explained the complicated system they'd worked out to get eight women through bathing, makeup, and doing hand laundry with facilities that weren't easily shared. I was to get Sarah Wycott's slot. As much as I was accustomed to having my own flat and using my own facilities, I didn't mind. I knew I wouldn't have to deal with it for long.

If I could quickly find a killer.

"Did she have a special young man?" I asked.

"I don't think so," Maryellen said.

"Not around here," Marianne said. "That's why she did so much knitting. There's nothing else to do here now that the weather has turned bitter."

"And she was good at it. That was why she kept asking Fiona if she could fix all her mistakes," Maryellen said.

Fiona gave a small sound between a growl and a scream.

"She was chapel. Strictly brought up. No frivolity on the Sabbath. No dancing anytime. No men friends," Aileen said.

"The same as you," Fiona said. "You're chapel, too, aren't you?"

"Of course. I'm from Edinburgh," Aileen replied with a hint of pride in her voice.

"Where are you from?" Maryellen asked me, and after that, we talked about the towns where we grew up.

The next morning, I overslept and missed my slot for washing up, so I just managed my face and hands after dressing while the others headed to the breakfast table. By the time I put on my lipstick and hurried in, there was little time left. I managed the last cup of coffee in the pot and the three spoonsful of porridge scraped from the bottom of the pan before I headed out with the others.

I carried my gas mask, required to be carried by every man, woman, and child in Britain since the war began, in my new oversized shoulder bag, which earned me the envy of my fellow boarders who carried theirs in a separate case from their small bags. I'd found while reporting for the *Daily Premier* that toting two bags while trying to take notes was too cumbersome. While I could return to carrying a small bag and a separate case for my gas mask as long as I was here, I didn't want to.

We walked down the drive to the lane, quickly out of sight of the ground floor of the manor house behind large evergreens. The pastures from the front of the house to the lane were kept for animals, sheep mostly. The army facility was inside the house and on the grounds behind and on the far side, I was told.

"What is that on your coat?" Maryellen asked.

I started looking at as much as I could see, when Marianne said, "No, that strip of—what is that?"

"It's reflective material, so autos can see you at night in

this blackout. Keeps you from getting run over," a dark-haired girl with the short, quick stride of a city resident said. "You must be a London girl. So am I. We didn't really have a chance to talk last night, but I'm Helen Preston. I have that on my coat as well."

I looked at her coat as I introduced myself.

The other women examined Helen's coat and mine before we all began to hurry once again to where we'd meet the bus.

We didn't pass any dwellings until we reached the crossroads and waited for our bus. Promptly at seven-thirty, a twenty-passenger bus arrived and we all climbed on. We took off down a lane away from the manor house that led, after a few minutes, to the village of Little Rowanwood. We picked up four men near a large pub in the village and then three more at the far side of the village, including Simon Townsend, before we rode to Bletchley Park.

Lining up with the others when we got off the bus, we walked through the gate and showed the guard our stiff cardboard passes. Then I headed for Hut Six in the chilly sunshine along with the other women from Bloomington Grove and some of the men on the bus.

Once inside the wooden one-story building, I saw it was larger than I first thought. As we entered, a few of the girls went into rooms to the left or right of the hallway, while others walked down the hall. I lingered, not certain where to go until a short man of nearly forty came toward me, hand outstretched, and said, "Mrs. Redmond?"

"Yes."

"Welcome to Hut Six. We're going to do wonderful things here that we can never tell anyone about. Ever. Is that clear?"

"Crystal, sir."

"Not sir. Just John. John Wiggins. We're very informal here. I'm the supervisor for this room, but officially I work in the Machine Room next door."

He wore a hand-knit sweater in bright reds and blues with a green and orange plaid tie that clashed with the sweater and probably everything else in his wardrobe.

"In that case, I'm Livvy." We shook hands, and then he led me down the hall to a room at the end.

He sat me down in front of a large typewriter-looking machine. "This is a TypeX machine modified so that when you put in the settings you are given for these three wheels here and type in the letters on the paper you are given by the Machine Room, a message comes out on the tape. What we want to know is whether what comes out on the tape is German, and if it is, what it says."

I nodded. "Is this where Sarah sat?"

"Yes. Where did you hear...?"

"I've apparently stepped into a dead woman's shoes." I made it sound creepier than it felt.

"Well, we don't want to dwell on that, now do we? Plenty of work to be done." John's voice was full of heartiness and bluster. It all sounded false. Either he didn't care at all and thought I was overemotional, or he really liked the woman and was upset by her murder.

"Then I should get to it."

He showed me how to set up the three wheels to the exact positions and handed me a stack of "messages," rows of letters on white tape glued to paper not unlike telegrams. The thought of a telegram made the very little porridge in my stomach churn. I knew now that we were at war, I might someday receive a message from the War Office, telling me Adam was dead or missing. I shivered, shook off the feeling, and got to work.

By lunchtime, I hadn't found a single message that had any similarity to German. From what I saw around me, neither had anyone else.

There were three other women in my section doing the same task as me who were also billeted at Bloomington Grove. Aileen MacLeith, the redhaired chapel-goer from Edinburgh, was one. The other two I'd met at dinner the night before. One was a very young-looking, delicate, rather vague blonde named Gwen Ellison. The other was a woman in her late thirties with very blue eyes and thick, shiny brown hair with a long face that gave her a striking appearance. She had to remind me her name was Mrs. Rosalie Billingsthorpe.

Rosalie and I were paired up to take the first lunch break. "The canteen has good lunches," she told me. "That's fortunate because there's no other source for food here."

"So, if the food were bad…?" I asked. We dashed out of the relative warmth of the hut into the cold winter air.

"There'd still be no other place to eat since Bloomington Grove doesn't supply lunches and we're not supposed to leave here during our shift."

I had to smile at her description of our situation. We introduced ourselves again as we rushed out of the cold into the main house and into the canteen.

We both took the lunch of the day, chicken stew and coffee with pudding for afters. She asked about my husband, and I told her we were newlyweds and he was off with the army. "And you?"

"Billingsthorpe is the heir to a fortune that didn't completely fail during the Depression, although he did. We were married in 1934 and the next year he was in a skiing accident that has left him in a wheeled chair."

"Oh, I'm sorry." Whoever suggested Rosalie's family had to be thieves to provide a radio for our living quarters was wrong. I guessed the residents of our wing of the house didn't know Rosalie well.

"Don't be. He's congenitally optimistic, so he's quite jolly. We get along well. And I don't have to worry about where he is, as you must." Her very bright blue eyes probed mine.

I admitted she was right. "But he must miss having you nearby. And you must worry about his care while you're gone."

"All of that is true. Fortunately, we get the weekends off. At least until this war starts to heat up. I'll be going home to Lancashire later on tonight."

I hadn't thought about that. Would I go home for the weekend, only an hour's train ride away, or would I spend the weekend investigating? At the very least, if I went home, I should get some yarn, knitting needles, and a pattern for a scarf. There appeared to be little else to do, and it would make good camouflage while I listened in to conversations.

"Do we get every weekend off?"

"Unless someone needs some translation work done and then they take whoever's available. If and when we get out of the phony war and into a real one, we'll be working a lot harder. We'll have to. Everyone else will be as well. And then who knows what our schedule will become." Those bright blue eyes searched my face again.

"I wouldn't be here if someone hadn't killed Sarah Wycott. But why? Who? It's so puzzling, and more than a little frightening."

Rosalie shook her head. "I don't know. It makes no sense. She was quiet. I wouldn't have thought she had an enemy in the world. She wasn't the sort to inflame anyone's passions."

"And you need to make someone passionately angry, or frightened, or jealous to murder," I replied.

"It must have been some random attack," Rosalie said. "Except..."

"What?"

"Sarah was unremarkable. Not particularly outgoing or bold or beautiful. She was smart enough to win a full scholarship to Cambridge and her hard work made her fluent in German and won her a first. She knitted well. She didn't take too long in the bathing room," she added, her blue eyes flashing with humor at the last. "All that says is it was random.

But she wasn't assaulted. Not sexually, and why else would a girl be killed on a lonely lane? She certainly had nothing to steal. A girl from a fisherman's family? They were poor."

"How do you know all this?" I lowered my voice, hoping she'd confide in me.

"Billingsthorpe's legs are ruined, but his status in the county isn't. He had the chief constable for Lancashire call the chief constable here to find out what was known. He didn't want me in danger if some rapist was loose in the area."

"He takes good care of you." I was impressed with this unknown man.

"He tries. And I try. As I said, we get along well."

"Therefore, there must have been a reason why Sarah Wycott was killed," I said, "and one that isn't obvious. Is everyone certain she wasn't involved with a man, particularly one in the office?"

"I don't think so. And no woman either, before you ask."

I looked at her, stunned. That wouldn't have occurred to me.

Rosalie smiled at my surprise. "You're as innocent as Sarah was. I shared lunch with her most days, and she was an innocent. The chief constable said she was a virgin."

The chief constable certainly shared more details than Sir Malcolm. "So, we don't have a rapist in the area, unless he was frightened off and killed her to keep her quiet. Although you'd think the weather must keep rapists indoors. Then why was she killed?" I asked rhetorically.

"Think about it." She stared at me.

I studied Rosalie for a moment. "What?"

"We're sitting in the middle of a huge reason. Perhaps she was killed to get someone else in here. Someone who would divulge our secrets."

When her words sank in, I rocked back in my chair as if she'd slapped me. "No. They know they can trust me."

"As much as anyone can trust anyone."

She was sharp. Everyone around BP probably was. I'd have to be careful how I worded things. "They asked a lot of people about me. I must have come well recommended to be sent here."

She nodded as she stared at me. "I believe you."

I'd have to watch the way I asked questions, or no one would tell me anything. And so far, I didn't have any idea why Sarah Wycott was murdered or who killed her.

Chapter Four

After lunch, the system worked better and with a final change in the three wheels on the TypeX, the messages I typed in came out in German. Some weather readings for who knew where. By midafternoon, my eyes were starting to cross.

I excused myself and hurried out into the cold to the annex where the toilets and washbasins were. At least it felt warmer than our badly heated hut, but I definitely didn't plan to linger.

I heard a man's voice say, "John's certainly taking her death hard," and I nearly jumped out of my shoes. Given my assignment, I stayed still and listened.

The voice had come from the other side of the dividing wall, where holes for pipes to go through weren't completely sealed. This could be a good thing for my investigation.

A second male voice said, "What do you expect? He wanted to train her to—" Any other words were drowned out by rushing water.

When the gurgling water sound stopped, the first voice

said, "Would it have worked out?"

The second said, "He'd have been disappointed. She was smart, but she'd have been no good at that."

Whatever was said after that was faint for a few seconds and then silence. They'd obviously walked outside. I washed my hands and went back to work.

I realized I didn't know the men in the next room and I had no reason to go in there. There was no way I could tell who had been speaking.

I'd have to get lucky or I'd never learn who killed Sarah. If her death involved espionage, then Sir Malcolm and the government needed to know quickly.

When it grew close to quitting time, John walked over and bent over to speak quietly in Gwen's ear. She nodded and then began to put away the things on her desk.

Was he reminding her she was to work this weekend, or was he telling her he wouldn't be keeping her late tonight the way he had Sarah at the beginning of the week? Whatever reason she had stayed late for.

As we closed up work for the night and for the weekend and went out into the cold and dark, a male voice said, "We're going to the Wren and Dragon. Anyone want to join us?"

His was the first voice I'd heard through the wall. "I'd enjoy that, but this is my first day," I told him, turning around. I recognized Simon Townsend, my fellow arrival at BP from the day before, as the speaker. "I have no way of knowing how to get to my lodgings afterward. Especially in the dark."

"That's right. You're at Bloomington Grove."

I nodded.

"I think some of your fellow lodgers are coming. It's less than a half-mile from the pub."

"I'm going, and I think the Allen girls will be there," Fiona said. "We know our way home."

"Will supper be waiting for us at the manor?" I asked.

"A bit cold and dry, but it'll still taste good," Fiona said. "Rosalie? Gwen? Are you coming?"

"I have a ticket to Lancaster on the nine o'clock train tonight. I'll have dinner in town and then go to the station," Rosalie told us, holding up her luggage to show us. "But thanks anyway."

"No, thank you," Gwen said quietly.

"We'll take the bus we came in on this morning and get off in Little Rowanwood," Fiona told me as she hurried toward the gate and the bus.

The hut, and the entire area inside the tall wire-fenced compound, was emptying out, with everyone heading for the town or the vehicles waiting to transport us to nearby villages. I followed Fiona and the Allen sisters onto our bus. We bounced along for a few minutes and then got out in front of the pub along with several men I recognized from the hut. Aileen and Gwen stayed on the bus to ride to Bloomington Grove.

I'd never have a better time than now to start interviewing the men. Before we went in, I pulled Maryellen aside. "Did Sarah come here with you, or was she strictly chapel?"

"She came here with us often enough. I don't think she was as chapel as some people are saying now. It's all 'Don't speak ill of the dead.'" She walked inside, and I followed.

Inside, the pub was dark paneled, smoky, with a low ceiling and several heavy scarred wooden tables and chairs scattered about. There was a dartboard on one wall away from the chairs, probably with good reason. When it was my turn, I got a half pint of ale. The ale was watery but at least the glass was clean.

Simon was talking to two other men, and one of their voices sounded as if it were the man he had been talking to in the facilities that afternoon. They were only a few steps away from where I'd picked up my ale, so I moved over and joined them.

Simon was as well-mannered as I thought he would be, and he introduced me to George Kester and Peter Watson. I was pretty sure I'd passed both of them in the hut that morning.

I asked Simon if he was settling in well with his relatives. "Yes. My aunt and uncle. They're glad to have me. And you?"

"Yes. There are eight of us being looked after by the last two of the Earl and Countess of Haymarket's servants. The food is excellent. Of course," I said, and glanced at the other two men, "I've moved into a murdered woman's shoes. It's just a little creepy."

George Kester, who other than his balding top looked to be in his early to mid-thirties, said, "Then don't make her mistake."

"What was that?" I'm sure I sounded gullible.

"Don't go wandering about alone at night." He grinned at me.

"Too late now. It's dark out and it's a half-mile back to the manor house."

"I said alone," George said. "You'll be heading back with several of your housemates." Without looking around, he added, "I hear the Allen twins."

"I thought they aren't twins."

George shrugged. "We call them that. They're close to identical."

"Sarah didn't go out by herself at night. She was afraid to," Peter Watson said. He was tall, dark-haired and, the same as me, a couple of years shy of thirty. His was the voice I'd overheard talking to Simon.

"But she must have. She was down the road from the manor house when she was found." I looked at him and frowned. I was confused.

Peter glanced at Simon. "She wouldn't go out at night except in a group or with an escort."

"Makes me wonder who her escort was that night," I said with raised eyebrows.

"I wouldn't know." Peter half turned away from me.

"If she came down here to the Wren and Dragon, it might have been any of you," I said with a smile. "I better watch out with you fellows."

"She wasn't down here that night," George said, shaking

his head. "She'd still be alive if she had stopped in here. We'd have seen her home safely."

"Your transport only takes you to the crossroads. We have better manners than that," Peter added.

"I want to avoid doing whatever she did that led to her death, but I haven't a clue as to what it was." That was true, and it didn't mention that I was on the hunt for a killer.

"She didn't keep her thoughts to herself," Peter said, still not looking at me.

"To be fair," George said, "you two had a run-in at Cambridge, but I saw no sign that she was still sticking her nose into your business here."

"Golly, was everyone here at Cambridge?" I asked.

"You too?" George asked.

We mentioned our colleges, but I hadn't known either Peter or George or anyone they might have known, because both of them were mathematics lecturers. That was definitely not my subject.

Then Peter grumbled the name of a girl who was in her first year at my college when I was in my last. She wasn't particularly remarkable to my mind. I mentioned that I knew of her.

"We were friends," Peter said. "Then Sarah jumped in and ruined our friendship by meddling."

"What happened to 'Don't speak ill of the dead'?" Simon asked.

Peter drained his glass. "Sarah poisoned her against me. She didn't bother to see things from my side. Ruined our friendship. Ruined my life."

He walked up to the bar to reorder.

"What happened?" Simon asked.

"I don't know. It must have happened after I finished and went back to London." But it might be a good thing to check. "Was Sarah seeing anyone here?"

"That is a very good question," George said.

"Well?"

"I don't believe it's my place to say."

"Then there was someone?" Simon asked.

Why was Simon taking my position? Why would he care? I waited for George's response.

"John was keeping Sarah after hours a few evenings, but it must have been due to training. She had an interest in the math side of things. But she wouldn't stay for extra training on certain nights, which makes me think she had a male friend. John's happily married, for Swithin's sake. It certainly wasn't him. He can't wait to get home to his family on those weekends when he can."

George looked from one to the other of us, handed Simon his empty glass, and continued, "I think everyone can manage their lives quite well without anyone sticking their long noses in, but I could do with a refill."

Simon glanced at me, I shook my head, and he went up to place their orders.

"I'm all for women getting more training and raising their pay grades," I told George.

"Even if they had no interest in moving ahead?"

"Sarah was happy with her pay?"

"She was living in the manor house with most of her pay left over after she paid the standard amount for her room and board. She could buy all the yarn she wanted. There isn't much else for you girls to buy these days, is there?"

"What do you mean?" He seemed to have a fixed idea of Sarah's preferences. Was it accurate? It certainly wasn't accurate for most young women.

"There aren't many clothes in the shops, or shoes, or makeup, or hair clips. Sarah, the same as any girl fresh out of university, was interested in these things and attracting a man, and not much else."

"Where did you get that idea of what women want? Especially on three pounds a week." I sounded huffy, possibly because that description was too close to the truth if he were talking about me when I left Cambridge. Now, I couldn't survive in London on that salary.

Thank goodness for Sir Henry and the *Daily Premier.*

"I was living and working in Cambridge until the war started. There are always young women to observe there, even if there is one special woman in Yorkshire who has all my devotion."

I considered him for a minute. "Did Sarah have a special man somewhere?"

"Who knows?" George gave me a smile. "I think there must have been, but I don't know who or where." Simon returned then and handed him his pint. "Thank you."

"Were any of the men interested in her, whether she was

interested in them or not?" Spurned lovers had been known to kill, and that would make Sir Malcolm very happy if that was the motive for her murder.

"We teased John about it, but there was nothing there. Just some extra training for some project John had in mind. I think Sarah's death has put that project firmly on the back burner." George shrugged. "We all enjoy the scenery, as it were, but nothing more than that. So, what's your interest?"

"I seemed to have stepped into the position of a murdered woman, and I don't want to make her mistake. Being married, I can only dream about having young men follow me around," I added with a grin. "What about you, George? Are you married to that someone in Yorkshire?"

"Oh, there's someone, all right, but we haven't set a date. If you want a young man following you around, you'll have to look to Simon."

Simon choked on his beer, and George pounded him on the back.

"Wow. I'll take that as a 'No,'" I said and laughed.

"No offense, but I haven't been thrown at someone that way since a first-year dance." Simon then gave me his cheery grin. "Can I get you another?"

"Another half, if you don't mind," I told him.

When Simon walked off, I asked George, "Do I need to apologize to Peter? He must have been angry with Sarah to have brought up whatever happened, and I said the wrong thing."

"No. He'll have forgotten it by tomorrow, and you can

start again. Oh, look," he said, glancing over my shoulder, "they've brought out the darts."

Peter and another man I'd seen around were on one team, and I recognized John although not the other man on the other team. There was cheering for good throws, and some good-natured teasing for badly placed darts, including a few that bounced off the paneling.

The door to the outside banged shut, sounding as if it were a shot. John, apparently not a good darts player at the best of times, was just letting go of his dart. He jumped and turned the same way as the rest of us, letting go of his dart at the worst moment.

The dart flew past Peter's head, making several of us gasp, and hit the wall behind him.

Peter, murder in his eyes, rushed John, his hands up to choke the shorter man. In a moment, they were in each other's faces, hands grabbing and shoving at necks and collars.

Could Sarah's death have been caused by a momentary flare of temper by a hothead such as Peter?

Chapter Five

Three or four men, including Simon, stepped in to separate the two combatants before the landlord threw us all out.

Once the two were at a safe distance apart, one of the men stepped between them. "John, what did you think you were doing?"

"I was startled by that bang. It was at just the wrong moment as I was letting the dart go. It was an accident. I hope I didn't hurt you, Peter." He sounded genuinely concerned.

"They shouldn't let you loose with sharp instruments, John. It was just by luck I wasn't hurt," Peter grumbled. His hands were down at his sides now and the two men holding him back decided to release him.

"I really am sorry. That was entirely my fault. Here, someone take my turn with the darts," John said.

"No, I think we'll put these up for a while," the landlord said, putting everything back into a small wooden box.

"Don't play darts again. You're a menace," Peter said, one finger raised to shake in John's face before he walked outside.

People went back to talking in small groups. I turned to George. “Has Peter always had that quick temper?”

“Yes. Fortunately, it cools off fast, too.” He turned the conversation to the newest Dorothy Sayers mystery and I didn’t get an opportunity to ask any more questions that evening.

* * *

The next morning at breakfast, I mentioned that I was hiking over to Bletchley to catch the train into London, but that I felt uneasy at the end of the drive. I was certain that when I reached the lane, I passed the spot where the woman I replaced was murdered.

“No,” Maryellen said, “it was down the lane quite a bit. It’s a spot you can’t see from the house or the army camp.”

“Do you want us to show you?” Marianne asked, sounding more kindly than ghoulish.

“You know where it is?”

“We all know where it is,” Maryellen said, as if I were mentally defective to not realize that everyone knew all the interesting gossip.

“If you’re finished, we’ll show you. We call it the spookiest spot in Bloomington,” Marianne said.

“You’re a bunch of ghouls,” Gwen said, letting her fork clatter onto her plate.

We finished, cleaned up, and then the sisters and I put on our coats and left for a walk. When we reached the end of the drive, we turned right, away from our bus stop.

The trees over our heads had bare branches, but the hedges along the lane were still thickly leaved. And it was the hedges that would keep the army camp, the manor house, and anywhere on the other side of the road from seeing a murder committed. Since the murder took place after dark on a cold night, it was unlikely anyone would have been around to see the act even without the hedges blocking the view.

The spot that the sisters pointed out was near a sharp bend in the road, keeping anyone from seeing far past that point in either direction. "Why does the road turn this way?"

"There's a beck on the other side of the hedge that cuts a sort of S-shape around some trees. The lane follows the same pattern as the beck, which is an old boundary line," Marianne told me with a note of authority in her voice.

"How did you find that out?"

"Talking to an old man in the pub in Old Bricton. That's the village if you keep going in that direction." Maryellen pointed down the lane.

"That's where the local Women's Institute meets," Marianne said. "That's where we take our knitting for the soldiers. They have lectures sometimes. Most of their programs are during the day, though, so we can't attend since we're at work."

"We do a lot of things with the WI at home. Otherwise, the countryside gets pretty boring in the winter," Maryellen said.

"That's why we can knit so fast. We used to race at

home," Marianne said.

I was suddenly very glad I grew up in London. "Is that why you volunteered for war work? To go someplace where there was more going on?"

"Of course. Plus they pay us. The salary here is good. There are few jobs in the countryside up north, and it's time we earned our own way," Marianne said.

"Our neighbor, a big landowner who was a colonel in the Great War and worked with some of the men here, suggested we get in touch with the Foreign Office, even though we don't speak a bit of anything but English," Maryellen told me as they stopped.

"He quite turned Maryellen's head with talk of glory and excitement," Marianne said.

"It makes a change from home. Nothing exciting or glamorous happens there," her sister grumbled. "I've been bored out of my head since I finished university. I don't know how Marianne stood it the last year I was away."

"I was bored silly without Maryellen. There are so many people here, it's as if it were Paradise," Marianne told me.

There was nothing to see to tell us there had ever been a crime committed there. The dried grass and low branches of the wintery landscape looked undisturbed. "There must have been quite a scene with the police all over the road," I said, looking around.

"When we heard the first siren go by, we thought something happened in Old Bricton," Maryellen said.

"When the second went by, we went out to take a look.

We had no idea, even when we got there, that it was Sarah. The constable kept us far away," Marianne said.

"If you were all there except Sarah...?" I asked.

"Oh, no. Rosalie and Gwen and Aileen wouldn't go out. And this was a day after Sarah had really disappeared, as we found out," Maryellen said.

"It's sad, really," Marianne said. "We all got along with Sarah. She was quiet and sweet, and she never bothered anybody."

"She was just there," Maryellen said.

What an epitaph.

"She was nicer than 'just there,'" Marianne said.

"She was sneaky. We all had the feeling at one time or another that someone had been in our rooms going through our belongings, and we came to the conclusion it was Sarah. She denied it, but I think she was a thief," Maryellen said.

"That's not fair," Marianne said.

"I wasn't the only one who had money disappear. Money disappeared when Sarah was around to take it," Maryellen said.

"Well...," Marianne said. "Maybe...but I don't think she was really..."

We walked back in the biting air, and then I readied to walk to Bletchley to catch a train to London. As I was about to walk out the door, Helen Preston asked if she could walk to the station with me.

"Of course." I'd met her at dinner and breakfast, but I hadn't had a chance to speak to her before now.

"Won't take me but a minute," she said.

Five minutes later, I had started to walk down our hallway to find out if she were coming when she appeared out of the last door on my side. "Here I am. Ready?"

"Yes." I refrained from saying anything cutting. We walked out into the sunshine and started down the drive.

When we turned onto the lane, Helen said, "You've been asking a lot of questions about Sarah Wycott."

"I'm stepping into a murdered woman's shoes. I don't want to make a wrong move."

"I don't think that's likely." Her pale eyes studied my face.

"If we knew why she was killed, I'd agree. But we don't. And until it's cleared up, I won't feel safe, and frankly, neither should you."

"You subscribe to the random nutter in the village theory?"

"No. I've read too many mysteries to buy the random stranger solution. Of course, in real life, that may be the solution more often than we realize." I watched her as closely as she watched me.

"No one has looked at the boyfriend."

"No one seems to think there was one."

"No one asked me." Helen lowered her voice, although the lane was empty. "I had told them there was a family emergency, so I was at my father's home in London the night her body was found. No one asked me anything. But I knew she had a boyfriend. He's stationed at the army camp in the main part of the house."

"Is it someone she just met?" I asked.

"Oh, no. He's from her hometown. They were sweethearts before she came here. Then he signed up and found himself next door."

"That was lucky."

"Until she was killed. By a brutal strangulation. Don't they teach that in the army?" She looked at me with raised eyebrows.

"Yes, they do. And you haven't mentioned this to the police?"

"No, and I don't intend to."

"Why?" No wonder the police couldn't get anywhere with this murder investigation.

"Can you imagine telling the police something they would use to hang someone? It's barbaric."

"Surely you're not the only one who knows about this young man." I hoped she wasn't. A lovers' quarrel would solve this murder quickly.

"I think I am. None of us were supposed to know, but Sarah kept sneaking out at night. I finally followed her. She'd go up to the perimeter fence and he would meet her there. They'd talk very quickly. They'd also hold hands through the fence. At least once they met up inside the house."

"Is it easy to get into the main part of the house?" I asked.

"Of course. Beside the staircase to the dining room, there's a small passage off the kitchen that leads to an even smaller hallway with a door at the end. That leads to a ground-floor drawing room. Sort of a place to take visitors the staff weren't certain would be admitted, but didn't want to insult. Sort of a waiting room while the family decided whether to greet the visitor. Now the room is an office, but I think no one is in it at night."

I smiled at Helen. "A good place to meet someone without alerting anyone else." Then I lost my smile. "How do you know so much about the house?"

"The parties they gave here, last spring and summer as well as during the past few years, were legendary. They made the newspapers and people were talking about them. I was curious about the main house. I snuck in one night and wandered around." Helen shrugged. "No one caught me. But there's nothing to see there. The furniture and paintings are all gone. Now it's nothing except a bunch of classrooms."

We walked almost to the village of Bloomington before I asked, "What's Sarah's boyfriend's name?"

"I don't know." Helen looked straight ahead.

"Seriously?"

"I never asked her."

"And she never said? That doesn't sound as if she were a woman in love."

There was a pause, broken only by our footsteps. Then Helen said, "She called him Charlie. That's all I know." Another pause and then, "I'll tell you something else. Someone else has been slipping out to meet someone."

"Who?"

"I don't know. I'd hear footsteps or see a shadow, but when I'd get to a place to see who it was, I would always miss them. They moved fast."

"You're sure it wasn't your imagination?"

"Positive. Someone on our floor of Bloomington Grove is an expert at moving around without being seen."

All this information was a place to start. "Where are you going in London?" I asked.

"To visit my family. I'm from south of the river."

"I live north of the center." In a flat where I hadn't changed my name yet from when it was Mrs. Denis, in case either Adam or I needed a little anonymity. "Do you have a big family?"

"No. Just my da, my sisters, and a couple of cousins, and a family business to run."

"What kind of business?" I asked.

"Shall I meet you at the train station at a certain time?" Helen asked, ignoring my question.

"Do you plan to catch a specific train?"

"Tomorrow between eleven and noon. How about you?"

"I don't know how long I'll be there. Depends on if my husband is home for the weekend."

"He's in the army?"

"Yes."

Helen looked at me. "This phony war must be getting on his nerves. And yours, too."

"You'll get no complaints about it from me."

"Because it gives the diplomats time to sort out a

solution?"

"Because people aren't getting killed and bombs aren't dropping," I told her.

She nodded. "That too."

The train, when it arrived, was packed with soldiers headed to London or points south. Helen and I stood at one end of a carriage corridor the entire time, balancing against turns and shifts as best we could. I was glad the trip was only a bit over an hour until we reached Euston Station.

We parted company at the Underground station and I headed to my flat. Mail had piled up under my mail slot. I flipped through it, finding a letter from Adam. That I opened immediately.

He missed me. He wouldn't be home for at least a few weeks.

I would answer him when I returned to the flat, but first I needed to go see Sir Malcolm.

Central London, where Sir Malcolm's office was in a converted block of service flats, had sandbags piled around the entrances of every government building. His building also had an armed soldier stationed at the entrance, even on a Saturday. Anyone paying attention would know this nondescript block held offices housing some of the most powerful men in our government.

I entered and requested to see the big man himself. After phoning upstairs, the guard on the door summoned a soldier to escort me to his office.

Sir Malcolm was in his usual position at his desk. His back

was to the windows overlooking the bare top branches of trees and nearby roofs. He looked up and glared. “Where is your gas mask?”

I opened my large bag and removed the case for the gas mask.

“Clever. I like it.”

“Good.” I sat in the chair facing him across the wide expanse of his desk. “I have need of some background material I’m sure you can ask someone to find out for me.”

“You can’t find out for yourself?” He sounded amused.

“No, I can’t. In one case, the information is in the part of Devon where Sarah Wycott was from, and in the other, I need to know about someone who went to Cambridge but would have finished up two years ago, I think.”

“You think?”

He was being difficult that day. “I can’t be certain about the dates. I’d already left Cambridge. But I am certain about the need for this information. I’ve found two possibilities for Sarah Wycott’s murder that have nothing to do with her work for the war effort, but I can’t get any further with them without your help.”

“We don’t have the resources to send all over England on a simple domestic murder.”

I stared at him in disbelief. “You now believe this was a simple domestic murder? You’ve sent me in to investigate people for a crime Scotland Yard should be solving. Wonderful.” What a waste of my time.

He glared back at me. “I don’t believe it was a simple

domestic killing. You do."

I shrugged, bewildered. "I don't know what it was. And I won't know without the information I need you to find out for me while I look closer to home for a traitor."

"We don't have time to do your job. No one does."

Chapter Six

I stared hard at Sir Malcolm. “I don’t need you to hunt for motives and alibis at BP. I have that covered. What I need from you are facts from other locations that I can’t track down because I need to stay there. And without them, I can’t succeed where you need me to.”

After a pause, he nodded. “Give me what information you want, and if anyone is available, I’ll have them check it out. You need to remember we are at war. You are at Bletchley making certain Miss Wycott’s death had nothing to do with her work. Or who is responsible if a traitor is lurking among you. That is your primary task.” He gazed at me from under heavy brows, looking as if the weight of the world was on his shoulders.

“Then let’s call finding out what I need to know clearing the underbrush. If one of them turns out to be the killer, you’ll know her murder had nothing to do with BP.” I was beginning to think of the location by its initials, as the workers there called it.

He dipped a pen in the inkwell. “Go ahead.”

I spelled out what I wanted to know about Charlie, who was from Sarah's hometown and who was now in the army based at the camp at Bloomington Grove, and the girl, Celia Flowers, from my Cambridge college who had once been Sarah's roommate and Peter's friend or sweetheart.

I left as quickly as I could, not wanting to spend any more time with the spymaster than I had to.

Once out of the building, I hiked to Oxford Street to shop at a yarn store. Apparently, everyone else had been there before me. There were few skeins of navy blue and khaki yarn, and no knitting needles of any size.

I asked the young woman behind the counter where I could buy knitting needles.

"Another new knitter. I didn't know there were that many people in London who didn't knit," she told me.

"We're all trying to do our bit," I said. Actually, I didn't expect this new occupation of mine to amount to anything, but I thought it would help me fit in at Bloomington Grove.

"I heard the yarn shop halfway down Regent Street had a delivery of needles yesterday. You could try there."

"Thank you." I hurried on my way.

As it turned out, they had two pair left. Both were quite large, the middle-aged woman behind the counter told me, and she suggested this might not be a bad thing for a beginner. "Makes it easier to see the mistakes and fix them," she told me.

They didn't have any khaki wool, so I bought the knitting needles and a simple pattern for a scarf and trudged back to the first shop. There I purchased another pattern, also for a scarf, and skeins of khaki wool.

If my scarves were too awful, I'd donate them rather than give them to Adam.

I hadn't gone far when I saw Gwen coming in my direction on the pavement. Her delicately boned face and pale blondness made her instantly recognizable. She didn't see me, though, and before I reached her, she darted into a shop.

As I walked to the doorway she had entered, I saw it led to a music shop. Gwen was talking to an older man behind the counter, who pulled out something packaged in a large envelope. She gave him some coins and walked out of the store with a cheery farewell.

"Gwen."

She looked up in surprise. "Livvy. I didn't realize you'd be in this part of town."

"Buying yarn. You?"

"Sheet music. My professor has a new piece for me to work on."

I hoped that was what it was and not something to pass on to the Axis powers. "What do you play?"

"Piano. I was studying music at the Royal College of Music when I got called to work at BP because I speak German. I studied in Berlin for three years when I was barely in my teens. My professor is horrified that anything could interfere with my education and is making me continue to study with him."

"He sounds a real taskmaster."

"He is. I've been a soloist with the London Junior Orchestra and accompanied the college choir, so he doesn't see the war as an excuse to stop practicing and 'ruin my career.'" Gwen gave me a rueful smile with the last.

"How did you end up at BP, and so quickly?"

"My professor has a friend rather highly placed in the government who warned him that his prize pupils would soon become motor mechanics and soldiers. When he asked what could be done for me, and told him that I spoke German, his friend suggested I apply to the Foreign Office. And there I am."

"How can you practice when you're at BP?"

"The Earl and Countess of Haymarket have a baby grand on the second floor of our wing. I can't imagine how they moved it up there, but they did before we moved in. The earl and countess heard me play before the war, and when the countess received a message from my professor, she told me to come upstairs any time to practice. And then I come back here every weekend for instruction."

"Why didn't you ride in on the train with Helen and me?"

"I wasn't ready when you left." She made it sound as if it were the most obvious thing in the world.

"You're dedicated." I was impressed.

"The war won't last forever, and when it's over, I want to be ready to continue to build my reputation as a concert pianist."

I walked with her to the Victorian, red-brick college

building in South Kensington, hearing about concertos and fugues and other things I didn't understand. The important thing was Gwen understood. She was too busy being a musician as well as a BP linguist to be a spy.

Plus, she was too delicate, too fragile-looking, to attack anyone. And she was dedicated, and apparently happy, being a pianist. I doubted when I found the traitor that they would be a content, satisfied person.

On the steps to the college, I asked her to show me the sheet music. She looked at me strangely.

"I've never seen sheet music close up," I told her, quite truthfully. Plenty of phonograph records, but no sheet music.

She pulled the pages out and the now-empty envelope whipped her hand in the breeze.

I took them and studied them. "You can read this? It looks the same as code to me."

"Learning to read music, and learning German, gave me all the skills I need for my present job." She held my gaze, and I understood. This was what made her such a good candidate for working in Hut Six.

I walked back to my flat, stopping for lunch at a Lyon's. The soup was thick and filling, but it lacked the flavor of their prewar dishes. The tea was weak and tasteless, but at least it was hot.

Once home, I answered Adam's letter, telling him how much I missed him and that I'd gone away for a few days, or weeks, for Sir M. Then I called Esther Benton Powell, my best friend from my school days and now the mother of two babies.

"Make that three," she told me when I asked about her children. "James is now working hard at his hush-hush government position and worrying constantly about me and the children. He's fussier than a toddler."

"How are Johnny and Becca?"

"One refuses to eat, and the other eats every three hours."

"Has your grandmother returned to help?" Mrs. Neugard loved Esther to distraction, but she was highly opinionated, and those opinions often weren't shared by Esther.

"Oh, no, I've been fortunate there. My grandmother is staying with my aunt and her family in the far edges of London where she'll be safe, while I am staying here with a refugee nursemaid and a refugee cook plus housekeeper."

"Recent refugees?" Esther had employed a series of refugees over the last few years to get them permission to leave German- held territory and enter Britain. Once they were trained for British expectations, Esther gave them a reference and let them find another position so she could take in another refugee.

"You've drooled over Cook's dinners before."

"I love her cooking." I wondered if she was able to keep up her standards while the war slowly changed everything. I hoped so.

"The nursemaid, Chanah, arrived in late August. Her children, teenagers really, already arrived on a Kindertransport in June. The younger one has a place at a boarding school and the older is living with us, waiting to get a little older so he can join the army. In the meantime, he's making himself useful doing the heavy cleaning and helping the neighbors with various tasks."

"Sounds ideal. A brilliant arrangement," I told her. "I hope you're keeping well while trying to maintain an efficiently run household."

"Efficient. Ha. But I am staying well. And Livvy, my father wonders when you'll return to work. He needs you at the paper."

"I wonder, too." Esther's father, Sir Henry Benton, was publisher of the *Daily Premier* and my boss. I wasn't surprised Sir Henry was impatient with Sir Malcolm "borrowing" my services again without any thought for his inconvenience. Neither he nor I cared for the arrangement, but Sir Malcolm held all the cards while there was a war on. "I'm trying my hardest to get back to my normal life."

"Oh, Livvy," Esther said, "what is normal anymore?"

She was right. With the war, everything seemed to constantly change.

Before the war, when my first husband was murdered, leaving me penniless, it was Esther who convinced her father to hire me for the newspaper. Then they decided to use my knowledge of German and my impeccable British breeding to help her late mother's Jewish relatives, and others, escape Nazi-controlled countries.

That work had ended in September with the start of the war. I knew Sir Henry had begun to make plans for me to make one more trip for the newspaper, or someone else, to Berlin. His real purpose had never been spelled out for me before the war cancelled our plans.

Chapter Seven

After posting my letter to Adam, I headed back to Euston and caught the next train going to Bletchley and points beyond. There was no sign of Helen or Gwen in the train station or on the crowded train.

I rode the whole way standing up and then faced the long walk back to Bloomington Grove alone. I was very glad it wasn't raining, although the skies were already growing dark with low- hanging clouds.

I trudged along narrow, potholed lanes, carrying my heavy bag with my gas mask and my small carryall with my new knitting supplies. No one was out in the gloomy evening weather. No one passed me either by auto or bicycle. Birds didn't sing, farm animals must have been inside barns, and I assumed dogs were wisely curled up by the fire.

Once I reached Little Rowanwood, I saw what I thought was a familiar figure leave the phone box by the green and walk toward the Wren and Dragon. The man looked very much the same as Simon. Curious, I followed him to the pub.

When I walked inside and my eyes adjusted to the light,

I found Simon, George, and John in one corner of the room at a table while the few locals there stayed a good distance away. I walked over and said, "May I join you? I've been on my feet all day."

They agreed, John leaving to get me a half of ale, and Simon shifting over on the bench so I could sit. "Where have you been?"

I gave an abbreviated version of my activities, avoiding any mention of Sir Malcolm. I pulled off my gloves and talked with my hands so I could accidentally bump Simon's arm. His jacket sleeve was frigid to the touch.

I was right about the identity of the man I'd seen outside.

"Knitting seems to be everyone's favorite activity at Bloomington Grove," I said.

"It's become the national pastime," George said.

"So I thought I'd join them and learn to knit."

John returned with my half. After I thanked him, I said, "I thought you were married. Is your family nearby?"

"Near Cambridge. I stay here during the week, and since this weekend I have to work, I won't get home at all."

"Is the train to Cambridge as crowded as the one to London?"

"I wouldn't think so, but it doesn't run as often or have as many carriages, and anytime I've ridden it's been nearly full. It only runs from Cambridge to Oxford and back, stopping here, at least that I've noticed. I hope they don't stop running that train. I need it to get home." John went on to tell me about his family, a wife and two young boys.

Simon and George teased him good-naturedly about being married, and I sprang equally jovially to his defense. "Wait," I said, "George, I thought you have a serious girlfriend."

"Yes, to the everlasting shame of my father and her mother."

"Why?"

"My father is a vicar. Poor, but of high moral character. He doesn't think her family is sufficiently devout. Her mother is the dowager mother of a baronet and very certain of her standing in the village. She's certain that my social rank is not elevated enough to wed her daughter. She gets the post first and never passes my letters on to my true love." He sighed, sounding very sad.

"Are you engaged?" John asked.

"Not officially. Her mother still thinks my one and only can do better. Anthea, that's her name, thinks I'm wonderful and she could never do better. I hope no one ever tells her differently." He sounded too mournful to be serious.

We all laughed, including George.

"Have you thought of telling your parents that you're going to get married and they'll just have to get used to it?" Simon asked.

"Anthea and I have discussed it, but she doesn't want to upset her mother, and I won't push the idea of marriage until Anthea is ready to battle her mother."

"You don't look forward to battling your future mother-in-law to marry your girl?" John asked.

George shuddered. "Would you? I prefer my life quiet and peaceful."

If George wasn't interested in fighting for his right to marry his true love, he certainly wouldn't be a spy for any political movement.

I soon finished my half and said, "Time to walk back before it gets too late."

"It's already dark out," Simon said. "I'll walk you back."

"Thank you, but—"

"Don't want you ending up the same way as the woman who last had your position." He gave me a big smile.

I shivered. "That's true. Thank you." Unfortunately, there was no way I could ask John about the reason Sarah was late returning to Bloomington Grove the previous Monday. That would have to wait until another day.

I put my gloves back on and we went into the dark found in the early evening at that time of year, especially during cloudy weather. "This is nice of you, Simon."

"My mother raised me to be a gentleman."

"I hope you're not repaid by a rainy return trip."

"So do I." He spoke in such a wail we both laughed. "Your husband didn't make it home for the weekend, I take it," he added.

"If he had, I wouldn't be here." Was he being chatty, or was he fishing for information he shouldn't ask for? Troop movements were just as big a secret as anything we were working on at BP.

He must have picked up my thoughts from my tone of

voice. “Sorry. I was just trying to make conversation.”

I smiled at him. “As I would be if I asked who you were phoning from the call box on the green as I walked up to it.”

“Ah, I wondered if you saw me. You came in soon after I entered the pub.” He shrugged. “I thought I ought to phone my parents. Tell them I’m settling into my new job and all is well.”

“That’s nice. If I called my father, all he’d talk about would be my husband. He’s always been disappointed that I wasn’t a boy. Or a docile girl.”

“I think you’d be very boring if you were docile.” I could hear Simon’s grin in his voice more than see his smile in the dark. And it seemed to be settling into full darkness, although it wouldn’t be dinnertime for a while yet.

“I would be a terrible wet rag, but that way I imagine I’d have been easier for my father to raise.” Silence lay over our path as if it were a blanket. “It’s eerie out here at night. I wonder if Sarah called out for help, and no one heard her.”

He made a whimpering sound. “What a terrible thought.”

“Had you ever met her? I think she was at Cambridge. After my time, of course,” I told him.

“I don’t think so.” There was a pause. “Are most of your housemates here this weekend?”

“Most of them. You heard Rosalie say she was going home, and Helen rode into London with me this morning, and Gwen had classes, but I think everyone else is here. How about your—what do I call them—pubmates?”

He laughed. "Don't say that to my aunt and uncle, but that's a good name for them. Yes, we're all here this weekend, working hard."

"That's easy enough for you, but I imagine it's hard on John and anyone else who has a wife waiting for him elsewhere."

I could tell he had shoved his hands into his coat pockets. Was he cold or uncomfortable about the subject matter? "I suspect this war is going to destroy a lot of marriages before it's over, and not just by death."

I glanced over at him. "We're a cheery pair tonight, aren't we?"

"Gosh, yes. And I just felt a raindrop. Are you close enough to your door, now?"

"Yes. Thank you. Hurry back so you don't get too wet."

"Right." Simon began to trot back down the drive, leaving me with the last one hundred feet up the drive to the servants' entrance on my own.

I hurried to the door and pressed the bell, hoping someone would let me in. Had Sarah Wycott stood here waiting on that fateful night? I was starting to frighten myself as I looked around in the dark for any sign of danger.

Then I began to wonder. She hadn't walked all the way there from BP that night. She used some form of transportation provided by BP. Sir Malcolm told me that. I'd only ridden on the bus, which wouldn't have run that late. She was supposed to have been working with John. Now I wondered how he had returned to the pub.

It would have been cold and dark, not good conditions for a hike of a mile or two, as I had just demonstrated.

My thoughts were stopped by the sound of the door opening and a little glow of light coming from the entranceway. I nearly jumped into the space, glad to get inside.

"Good timing, Mrs. Redmond," Betty said. "We're about to sit down to dinner."

"Great. I've worked up an appetite." Then, taking a chance, I put out a hand to stop her. "Betty, the night Sarah Wycott died, did anyone let her in when she first arrived home? Or by any chance, did the bell ring and there was no one there?"

"She rang the bell and I let her in. Then I went back to finish cleaning up after dinner. Elsie had already retired for the night, and I was ready to go upstairs. The earl wasn't well, and the countess had us jumping all day."

"Did you tell the police you had seen her not long before she disappeared?"

"No one asked. And I never saw the police."

My eyes widened. "Have you told anyone this?"

"No. Why should I? Not my business."

"Did you see her after that?"

"No."

"Did she eat anything? Have any tea?"

"No. Not a thing. And now I need to go set another place at the table if you plan to eat with us," Betty said, giving me a hard stare.

I removed my hand from her arm, but I stood in the entryway for a moment thinking. Sarah had made it home. Why had she gone back out? And when?

Chapter Eight

I headed into the loo before I dropped my things in my room. Then I hurried to the servants' hall, where everyone had assembled for dinner.

"Where have you been all day?" Maryellen greeted me.

"London. I bought yarn and wool and patterns. Now all I have to do is learn how to knit," I said, sitting down.

"Did Helen come back with you?" Marianne asked.

"No. We split up as soon as we reached Euston Station."

"Her family must have something on," Maryellen said with certainty.

"Just six of us tonight," Fiona said. "We should have fun all trying to teach Livvy how to knit at the same time."

I laughed at that. "One or two at a time should do well, and when you give up on my ever learning how to do this, you can hand me off to someone else."

"Not me," Gwen said. "I'm going to read."

I wondered when she had returned. "How did your music lesson go?"

"Well. The countess invited me to practice tomorrow

afternoon on their piano."

I looked at Gwen's hands. They were delicate with thin fingers. However, they had to be strong to type on the TypeX and play the piano. Were they strong enough, and was she tall enough, to have strangled Sarah Wycott? Sarah was at least my height.

I guessed Gwen was the only one I could rule out due to size.

Betty started to put bowls of vegetable stew on the table and Elsie brought over a plate of thick-sliced bread. The smell was heavenly, and I was ready to start eating before Aileen stopped me by insisting on leading us in saying grace.

The food was hot and well spiced, and we were silent as we gobbled up our dinners. Then we made quick work of cleaning up to help Betty as Elsie trudged slowly up the stairs to her room.

There was an exodus, followed by all of us except Gwen returning to the large servants' hall with our knitting. Maryellen turned on the radio. We all sat and then everyone stared at me.

"Have I done something wrong?"

"No. We're just waiting to see what you bought and what you plan to do," Maryellen said.

All four women began knitting as they watched me pull the brand-new needles, a scarf pattern, and a skein of khaki-colored wool out of the bag. Then I looked at them. "What do I do first?"

Maryellen burst out laughing. "You are an innocent."

Aileen set down her knitting. "Here. First we need to straighten out your yarn." She had me hold out my hands to keep the yarn from tangling while she wrapped it into a ball. "Fiona, you have a mistake or two in that last row. Do you want help?"

"No. I'm proud of my work. And it is wearable. Someone will be glad to wear this in the cold." She sounded defensive and angry.

"It'll hold together," Marianne said, "and keep someone warm. My mother would never have allowed something similar to that to leave the house, but you don't have to show it to my mother. Just try your best. It's appreciated by our soldiers."

"You knit fast," Maryellen said in amazement. "Maybe if you slowed down just a little, it might help."

"Worry about your own knitting," Fiona snapped. "If it bothers you so much, I'll go knit in my room. Perhaps that would be better."

The other women assured her she was welcome and they wouldn't say another word, but Fiona rose silently, picked up her work, and left the room.

Into the silence, Maryellen said, "I hope you're not going to be as sensitive about your mistakes. We all make them, especially at first."

"I'm used to being criticized," I told them, thinking of my father. "Has no one ever told Fiona she made a mistake before?"

"It's just her and her father, but they run a pub. You'd

think customers would be giving her a hard time daily," Marianne said.

"But that's not the same as the rough side of a relative's tongue," Maryellen said. "Maybe her father is lenient."

"Having a large family, we have our mistakes pointed out to us daily," Marianne said. "What about you, Aileen?"

"My family is small enough, but I'd think someone who spends a lot of time in a pub the way Fiona does wouldn't be so sensitive." Aileen said this last with a sniff. Then she added, "Here you go, Livvy."

"Right," I said, taking the ball of yarn in one hand and the needles in the other. "What's next?"

They showed me, step by step. And then had to show me again as I made a mess of the yarn.

"I wonder if my mother had all these problems knitting during the Great War," I muttered.

"You don't know?" Maryellen asked.

"She died right after the war."

"Was your father on the Western Front?" Aileen asked.

"Yes. He doesn't say much about that time, though," I told her.

"My father doesn't either. He has said a lot of Scotsmen died in France. That's why I'm determined to help the war effort. In their honor," Aileen said. "I see my work here as my duty to my country. We all have that duty. Don't you agree, Livvy?"

"Yes." I wouldn't be here if I didn't, but I wasn't going to point that out to her. I'd only known her a couple of days, but her words sounded the way I suspected my upright colleague thought. "How about your father?" I asked the Allen sisters.

"He was gassed. He died a few years ago, and we think that's why he died so young," Marianne said. She looked around. "Guess we're lucky we're here at all, since so many men never had a chance to be fathers." Then she added, "Livvy, you've got a death grip on those needles."

* * *

Sunday morning, I awoke with aches in all sorts of muscles from balancing in a moving train for trips to London and back, walking down country lanes from the station to Bloomington Grove, not to mention walking all over London, and holding my fingers and shoulders in odd positions while trying to knit.

I doubted I'd ever learn.

I washed and dressed without seeing any of my housemates and went out to the kitchen and servants' hall to find tea, coffee, or food. There was tea, and Betty offered to make me toast if I could wait a while as Elsie worked on Sunday dinner for the earl and countess. They were having a roast with all the trimmings.

"It smells good," I said. The aroma of prewar dinners at fancy restaurants filled my senses.

"And all you get is a smell," Elsie said as she gave me a smile.

I grinned at her. "Well, there is a war on." Although the earl and countess wouldn't have noticed any difference except for occupying only part of their house.

Then I began to wonder. “Is this the kitchen for the whole house?”

“Of course. It wouldn’t be this large for just the servants,” Elsie told me.

“How did you get the food from here into the dining room in the main house without it getting cold?”

“Silly child. Show her, Betty.”

Betty turned and walked off through the kitchen. I followed her into a short hallway where she opened a door. On the other side was a flight of stairs going upward. “That leads up to the butler’s area and beyond that, the main dining room. The footmen used to carry the trays and dishes of food up to serve the family and guests, and then bring the used dishes back down to the scullery.”

What I saw was another way into the main part of the house. “Are you the only one with a key to this door these days?”

“I certainly wouldn’t let those army boys have it. Her ladyship has a key, too.”

Betty closed up and I returned to drink my cup of tea quickly and look out the window. It was sunny and there was no wind to stir the trees. “I’m going out for a minute to enjoy this nice weather.”

“Leave the door on the latch,” Betty called out from the kitchen. “Save me having to let you in.”

I got my hat and coat from my room and went outside. It was cool, but the bright sunshine made it pleasant. The lack of wind made it glorious.

My plan was to look for any clues of someone breaking in from outside to spirit Sarah Wycott away. I climbed through the small bushes, overgrown and scraggly with lack of trimming since the military had probably called up all the young gardeners already. The branches whipped me with late autumn's leftover leaves wet from last night's rain. There were no signs on the outside of my window that anyone had been there.

I started to look outside other windows. There was no sign of anyone trying to force the windows open. No splintered window frames or broken branches on the bushes. When I reached the end of the wing, just as I stepped onto the lawn, a flash of sunlight under a bush caught my eye.

I picked up a small metal object and wiped the dirt off of it with my glove before brushing it against my coat sleeve. It was a bracelet made of a delicate chain of silver links. Hanging from it was a flat disc. In tiny letters were engraved the words, *Newnham College 1936.*

Was this the bracelet someone mentioned missing from Sarah Wycott's body? How did it get to this spot? It didn't look as if it were a place Sarah or anyone else would go willingly. And how could the daughter of a fisherman afford such an expensive bracelet?

I went back inside to the servants' hall. "Have you ever seen this bracelet before?"

Betty glanced at it as she brought me toast and jam, then came to a halt. "That's Miss Wycott's. She always wore it. It was missing when they found her body. And you found it?

Where?"

"In the bushes near the far window on that side," I said, gesturing.

"Now how did it get there?" she asked as if to herself. "Enjoy your toast," she added. "I'll bring you more tea."

I examined the chain as I ate my toast. One of the links had separated. No doubt how the bracelet came to be lost. But why at the far end of the wing from the entrance?

I'd almost finished my tea and toast and was wondering how I'd pass a day in the country with aching limbs and no idea how to catch a killer when a woman in uniform appeared as if by magic from the kitchen. "Are any of the women who live on this floor here at the moment?"

"I am. I don't know who else is."

Betty answered, "Aileen and Gwen are in church. The twins and Fiona are out on their bicycles. No one else is here."

"They're sending a car around. Be here in a couple of minutes. You're to go to work."

I nodded. "How did you get in here?"

"It's a secret." She smiled and walked back the way she came.

I jumped up and followed her down a short hall, turned a corner into a stub of a hall and joined her as she left through a door into an office.

"We're in the main house now?" I asked, looking around at the wallpaper and the fancy plastered ceiling.

"Yes, and you're not supposed to be in here." She picked up the telephone receiver and spoke a few words into it.

"Don't worry. Your secret's safe with me." I took a hard look at the knob and the lock as I went back into the servants' wing. The lock was an old-fashioned type. I guessed any key for the main house would fit. But who could get their hands on one?

Betty and Elsie, probably. Could they be convinced to lend their keys out?

Chapter Nine

I quickly finished my tea and retrieved my coat, hat, bag, and gloves from my room. At the same time, I hid the bracelet in the pocket of my dressing gown hanging in the wardrobe. With a cheery wave to Betty and Elsie and bundled up against the cold, I headed outside and down the drive.

It was sunny, and the cool, still air made it a pleasure to be outdoors that day. I know my cheeks and nose had a rosy glow by the time I was halfway down the drive. Fortunately, that was where I met the estate wagon coming up. A girl of about twenty in a well-cut uniform of the First Aid Nursing Yeomanry—better known as FANY—rolled down her window and said, “Are you the only one?”

“So far as I know.”

“Get in.” Once I hurried into the passenger seat, she said, “You’re my only stop. This will be a quick trip. Where are you from?”

“London.”

“Oh, I love London. Father has a house in Mayfair. I spend as much time there as Mother will allow. She doesn’t trust me. Thinks I'm boy-mad or something."

I decided to use my time wisely. "I replaced the girl who was murdered. Do you know how she got to Bloomington Grove after work the night she died? She worked late."

"I drove her there in this wagon. Up almost to the door. She got back there alive and well. I was shocked when I heard the next morning that she was missing. And then found dead. Horrible."

"Was she your only passenger?"

"No. I also drove two men who left at the same time. To the pub in Little Rowanwood. Why all the questions?"

"As I said, I replaced her. I don't want to end up the same way, which means I need to find out how she died so I don't make the same mistake."

"Don't go wandering about at night by yourself. This isn't London," she told me. "The countryside is dangerous."

From there we went on to talk about the now-silent church bells. It turned out to be my shortest and most enjoyable trip to Bletchley Park so far.

I showed my pass and entered the gate to walk through a surprisingly empty facility. Would it be much busier on the weekends once the war started in earnest? I suspected so.

Once I entered Hut Six, I knew there would be no point in taking off my coat, hat, or gloves. There was a small heater smoking up the room where the men were working on the messages that they passed on to my little group. While the heater gave off a great deal of exhaust, it failed to give off any heat.

It seemed as if it was a very long time until spring. Would I solve Sarah Wycott's murder before then? I really hoped so.

I stood in the doorway to the section where the men were working and said, "Someone called me in this morning."

"Ah, yes, Livvy. That would be us," Peter said. "We want to try some things out this morning while we won't get in everyone's way. We need you, as usual, to tell us if what comes out of your machine is German."

"Of course." I uncovered my TypeX, made certain the tape was ready to go, and waited.

Peter and John came in within five minutes with a bunch of pieces of text for me to try out. The first few made no sense.

"Would it be in violation of the Official Secrets Act to tell me where these came from?"

"If you understand it's not to be discussed elsewhere," John said. He and Peter seemed to be getting along this morning, the fight the other night apparently forgotten.

"Yes."

"These are messages from one German military facility to another sent over the air—"

"Shortwave?" I asked.

"Yes, sent in Morse code, and intercepted at one of our listening posts here in Great Britain. The messages are encrypted using an Enigma machine before they are sent by shortwave, and we are trying to decrypt them," John told me.

"There are a lot of people at these listening posts copying down everything they pick up on these radio frequencies,"

Peter added, "and what they copy down is sent on to us by courier."

"That sounds simple enough. It's the decrypting, I take it, that is the hard part." I looked from one man to the other.

"Yes," John said, "but we think if they send out the same message frequently enough, it will show up as the same number of letters whether it is encrypted with one setting or another. What we're looking at today is the beginning of a bunch of messages sent at the same time. If there is something they repeat at the beginning, some sort of address, it may be our way in to decrypt the rest of the message."

Their efforts with the first batch of messages didn't pay off. Neither did the second. One of the messages in the third batch, however, made perfect sense when decrypted with a change in the settings on my machine.

"This one works," I called out.

Peter and George came running.

George looked at the message and said, "What?"

"It's what you want. It's in German."

"Then tell me what it says. In English."

I looked at him in amazement. "You work here, and you can't read German?"

"Not a word." George shrugged. "Most people here can't."

"And I know very little German," Peter told us. George handed me the paper to translate before Peter hurried it back into the room across the hall.

We waited in eager silence. Peter was back a minute later with a longer message for me to type in. Then they watched over my shoulder as I typed the words onto the tape.

I looked up about halfway through and began to laugh.

"What is it?" Peter leaned over, peering hard at the words.

"A German nursery rhyme," I said, reciting it for him. "Someone is transmitting childish nonsense. I wonder what type of response they'll get from whoever is receiving this?"

"That's a thought," John said as he walked in and then walked back into their room.

By the time I finished typing the message, including the signoff, John was back with more messages. He handed me the copies with the same setting written on each and took my typing away to study it.

I typed away, the results being silly riddles and rhymes. The whole network seemed to be sending worthless messages, but all on the same settings on my TypeX. When Peter came in to pick up some more of my typing, I asked him, "Is this from a training class?"

"Must be some sort of practice. Sunday mornings would be a good time to train recruits on sending Enigma messages, since official message traffic would be light. Makes sense, since we're trying things out for the cottage on a Sunday morning. Training for us."

"The cottage?" Would I ever understand this place? Or was that the idea, that everyone would only learn their own little corner of this facility?

"That's where the smartest people in Britain are trying to break the German Enigma codes. That's where the greatest mathematicians devise models and machines and formulas to try to crack the codes. We just use their work to try to break into the settings for a few of the codes," George told me.

"What do you need me for?" I asked. "Surely you can use a typewriter. This would work even if you only used two fingers."

"Livvy," George said with a grin, "I don't know a word of German. How would I know if what we came up with worked? John and Peter know very little of the language. That's why you ladies are working here in this room. To set us straight as to whether we have settings that give us German or gibberish."

My stomach sent out a message to my brain, and I looked at my watch. It was nearly one in the afternoon. "Does the dining room serve on Sunday?"

"Soup and sandwiches, usually. Do you want to go over there now?" Peter asked.

"Do you mind?"

"It sounds as if we both have the same good idea. Let me see if John thinks we're at a stopping point." Peter walked off, returning two minutes later. "We're not going to get much more out of the training network today. Our receiving stations say they're picking up very little traffic now and we've been through all the messages we've received. Let's get some lunch."

I put on the gloves I'd shed while typing, and since I had kept on my coat and hat, I was ready to walk over to the main house.

"You've taken off the settings from your machine?" John asked as he walked in bundled up against the cold.

"Yes. Everything's put away." I tended to keep a neat desk at the *Daily Premier* and my work habits carried over to Bletchley Park.

"Very good. Can't be too careful."

"But it was only a training session." I couldn't see the importance to the war effort of nursery rhymes and schoolboy riddles.

"Doesn't matter. Breaking into one key, even a training key, leads to cribs and helps us break into others. You realize this phony war won't last forever, don't you?" George said as he leaned on the doorway. "And then we'll need everything we've learned."

I nodded, not wanting to think about what the end of the phony war would mean to Adam or where he'd be posted. "What are cribs?" I asked, turning my mind in less worrying directions.

"Cribs are sections of messages, the longer the better, that use the exact same wording no matter what the message or the code," George answered.

"All this may seem as if it were practice for them, but it's also training for us. When the fighting heats up, we'll need to decrypt German military messages as fast as possible. That means breaking into a bunch of military codes daily and reading their messages immediately. The fate of Britain may rest on our work," John said.

"The faster we break into their Enigma codes now," Peter added, "and the better we develop cribs, the bigger our advantage when the shooting begins."

As long as a traitor didn't give away how much BP had learned about the Enigma codes so far.

I looked at Peter and said, "Is that what I've been working on? Finding lines of nursery rhymes that will be repeated in battle orders?" That didn't seem likely to me.

Chapter Ten

Peter and John stared at each other, and then John said, "Oh, you should probably have been told this. You'll have to look for them every day while we're working here. A crib is a phrase, the longer the better, that will appear over and over in messages. 'Nothing to report' is a good example. 'Nothing' probably appears in these nursery rhymes and that would be useful."

"The messages are sent out five letters at a time, plus special codes for stop, as if it were a telegram," Peter told me. "And the Germans don't use just one cypher. We know the army, the air force, and the navy all have their own, using different ones for different countries and different divisions within their service branch, plus a diplomatic cypher, a training cypher—the list goes on."

"And you're looking for the same wording in different cyphers?"

"Yes. That's how we develop cribs."

"A sort of shortcut," I said, musing.

"Exactly. And the more shortcuts, the better," George

said.

"Does this have anything to do with why Sarah was here late on the night she died?" I asked as I looked at all three men.

They glanced at each other. "Yes and no," John finally answered. "I was trying something that no one else thought would work. A mathematical model to break into one of the codes. It turned out not to work, but I thought it was worth attempting."

He frowned. "And so did Sarah. She was interested in the mathematical side of this. Monday night was the last night we were going to try this system, and it failed the way it had every other night. If I just hadn't tried my system one last time."

John squeezed his eyes shut and sighed. "I blame myself for her death."

"Don't," George said. "You didn't kill her. And if it hadn't been Sarah on that night, it would have been someone else on another night."

"She was walking home alone on a dark road because of me and my idiotic theory," John said.

"It might have worked. You didn't know until you tried," Peter said.

"She reached Bloomington Grove safely. I found someone who let her in on Monday night. Apparently, she didn't stay inside long, but she did get inside before she must have gone back out."

"Really?" John's face took on a look of hope. "It wasn't

my fault, Sarah being outside and in danger?"

"No." I watched John sag with relief.

"Now, with all that to think about," John said, "and never talk about again, let's go to lunch."

"I'm ready," George said, backing into the hallway.

We walked over to the main building and into the dining room. I got tea, vegetable soup, and a small fish-paste sandwich. The food was more hot than tasty, but I couldn't complain. There was a war on, and the main building was relatively warm inside.

After the first rush of eating, I asked the men, "What is there to do around here on the weekends?"

"In this weather, not much," Peter told me. "Although today is nicer than most."

"In the autumn, we could go on bike rides and picnics and there were games of rounders after lunch by the pond. Now that winter has set in, the only places to find any entertainment are London or Cambridge. Concerts, plays, dance halls," George said. "Not around here."

"And our chances for getting away from Bletchley are going to go down quickly," John said. "Even if our families live in Cambridge or London."

I looked from one man to the other. "What aren't you telling me?"

Peter looked to John, who shrugged. Peter then leaned forward and, in a voice barely above a whisper, said, "There's a rumor we'll soon go onto three shifts to keep this place going 'round the clock. Then we'll have little chance to get anywhere since we won't have more than sixteen hours off for weeks at a time."

"I'm tired just hearing that." The schedule sounded exhausting, particularly when I had a second task to fulfill.

George looked glum. "It ruins any hope of getting away from here. And we all have people we want to visit, even us single men."

"Anthea?" I asked him.

He nodded.

"When will it start?"

"No idea," John said. "It's just a rumor right now. It depends on how quickly the people in charge can find enough graduates with the right credentials to staff three shifts."

"And enough money to pay their salaries," Peter added.

"Before Christmas?" I wanted to be home for Christmas. I hoped to be finished with my investigation before then so I could get on with my life.

Particularly if Adam got Christmas leave.

"Depends on Hitler, don't you think?" John said.

A depressing thought indeed.

* * *

Over the next two days, I learned how boring life in the countryside could be and how frustrating knitting was. I understood Fiona's reluctance to correct her knitting at the insistence of our housemates. They could be overbearing, even when they were trying to be helpful. My scarf seemed to shrink rather than grow under their watchful gaze.

On Tuesday morning, I was working on the cards given to

me containing intercepts when John came over and said, "The admiral wants to see you in his office in the main house. Immediately."

The room fell silent and everyone looked at me from the corners of their eyes. The tension level rose until it should have heated the chilly room.

"All right," I said, pasting a fake cheery smile on my face. I put on my hat and gloves, my coat still on from that morning, and left the room. Something had gone wrong. I was certain of it.

I must have fallen afoul of the security regulations while asking questions about Sarah Wycott. But how? Were they throwing me out of here? Was it worse than that? Was I going to prison? I didn't think I'd violated the Official Secrets Act. At least, not wittingly.

By the time I reached the main house I was trembling. I asked my way from two expressionless people, neither of whom seemed fazed by my request. I presented myself to the admiral's secretary, who rose and escorted me into the office.

The admiral was an average-sized man with white hair and sharp dark eyes who was seated at his desk looking over some papers. The secretary said my name and walked out, shutting the door behind her.

Once the door was closed, I discovered another person in the room. Sir Malcolm Freemantle.

"You don't look pleased to see me," Sir Malcolm said.

"I'm surprised." My legs were shaking. I was certain I was

in serious trouble. I walked over and sat in the chair in front of the admiral's desk. "What do you want?"

"It's what *you* wanted." Sir Malcolm perched on the corner of the admiral's large desk and loomed over me. "I have information on the two suspects."

"One of them isn't a suspect. She's a motive."

"Do you want the information or not?" Sir Malcolm gave me a hard stare.

"Yes." I dropped my gaze.

"Charlie Adler was Sarah Wycott's sweetheart. He is a private, currently stationed at the army training facility at Bloomington Grove. Sarah Wycott's roommate at university, Celia Flowers, had a brief romantic attachment to Peter Watson of BP. Now Celia Henry, she is married and living in Lancaster. Here's her address." Sir Malcolm gave me a slip of paper with the information.

"Have you spoken to either of them about Sarah's murder?"

"No. That's your job." Sir Malcolm's tone held a note of finality.

"Can you make arrangements for me to speak to Adler, alone, some evening this week?"

"Can I? Yes."

"Good. Will you?" I pressed.

He paused long enough that I thought he'd refuse. "Yes. Expect a summons late some night."

I turned to the admiral. "May I have the coming weekend off to travel to Lancaster?"

"Has anyone in your section mentioned anything about needing you this weekend?"

"No, sir."

"Then, if anyone orders you to work, tell them to see me." The skin around his eyes crinkled in a smile. I suspected he enjoyed surprising his underlings on occasion.

"Do you have anything to report?" Sir Malcolm asked.

"The murder took place along a stretch of lane that is seldom traveled, not overlooked by any buildings, and at a bend in the road, assuring the best chance for the murderer to get away with his crime without being seen. That makes me think someone familiar with the immediate area is the killer. And the ease by which this person convinced Sarah to go with them to this remote spot makes me think the killer could have been a friend of hers and not anyone who appeared threatening or was a stranger."

"The soldier fits the description. I'm not certain Peter Watson does," Sir Malcolm said.

"I don't think it's either one of them, but I won't know until I investigate further. Also, I found the person who let Sarah into our section of the house after work the night she was killed."

Sir Malcolm's bushy eyebrows rose. "Who?"

"Betty, the maid for the earl and countess who live upstairs from us."

"When did the girl arrive?"

"After dinner was served, eaten, and just about cleared up. Certainly after seven. I asked all of my housemates yesterday and haven't found anyone who saw her after that. Were all of her things in her room when the police searched it?"

"They have a report of everything they found. Whether it was 'all' of her effects, we don't know." Sir Malcolm handed me the badly typed list.

Her purse, her knitting, and her books were all there. Her coat and hat were missing, presumably with the fully dressed body when she was found. Her gas mask was also missing. I looked up. "Was her gas mask found with the body?"

Sir Malcolm dug through his folder. "Yes."

"Then for some reason she planned to leave, if only for a few minutes. If she'd dashed out on the spur of the moment, she probably wouldn't have bothered with her gas mask, since she would have expected to run back inside almost immediately."

"Did anyone ring the bell at the front door after Miss Wycott?" the admiral asked.

"Not that I've learned so far, but so far, no one at Bloomington Grove has admitted hearing it. She must have left almost immediately after she arrived, because she didn't have any dinner or even a cup of tea. And the food at Bloomington Grove is good."

"Trust the earl and countess to make certain their supplies are all first-rate." Sir Malcolm seemed to find this amusing. I wondered how well he knew our landlords. None of us on the ground floor had even seen them, except Gwen.

"Anything else?" Sir Malcolm asked after I paused.

"One more thing. Sunday, I found the bracelet Sarah Wycott usually wore that wasn't found when her body was discovered. It was one of the reasons the police suspected a robbery gone badly wrong. I found it lying in the bushes at the far end of the wing from our entrance, nowhere near where the body was found. And none of the windows appear to have been tampered with."

"What do you make of this?"

"I don't know, sir. The bracelet looks expensive. It's made of silver. One of the links had come open, possibly by being snagged on a bush by the house, but I have no idea why she'd have been in those bushes."

"Hiding?" Sir Malcolm asked.

"It's possible, but those bushes are too short for hiding behind. The windows for our rooms look out over them."

He nodded. "Ask Adler if he knows how she ended up with that expensive bracelet, and why she was in those bushes."

"I intend to, sir."

"You need to get back to work. The work you're here to do while you are hunting down a killer is important. Don't waste time."

Inwardly, I groaned. Sir Malcolm was making another pronouncement. I rose, nodded to both men, and walked quickly out. I shut the door quietly and had reached the side hall when I found myself face to face with Simon Townsend. We nodded and then he turned into the admiral's secretary's room.

I tugged my coat tighter around me as I headed for the front door of the main house, expecting the air to be much colder outside, but I didn't notice the temperature. I was too busy wondering why Simon had been called in to talk to the admiral and Sir Malcolm. Was he also investigating Sarah Wycott's death? Or was he inquiring into someone else's behavior? Was I his target?

* * *

Rosalie and I took the second lunch shift, so I returned to the main house to eat in the dining hall after Gwen and Aileen had returned. We had our meals in front of us, a rather earthy mushroom and vegetable stew, when I asked her, "Are you heading to Lancaster this weekend?"

"I'm planning to. Why?"

"I'm heading there this weekend to see a college mate of mine. She lives in a village outside Lancaster called St. Mary's Wall. Do you know it?"

She grinned. "It's three miles from my house. If she's not expecting you, come stay at our place for the weekend."

"Are you certain your husband won't mind?"

"He loves company, particularly intelligent, attractive young women."

"Then I'll be a disappointment." I was feeling a little frumpy and rather stupid and hurt after dealing with Sir Malcolm and wondering if he had ordered Simon in to investigate me.

Rosalie laughed. "Don't be so modest. He'll love you."

I couldn't help smiling at her laughter. "Then I accept

with pleasure."

"What's your friend's name?"

"Celia Henry."

"I know the Henrys. A family of solicitors." Rosalie frowned as she thought. "But I don't know Celia."

"I've forgotten her husband's name." Actually, I forgot to ask. "She's a newlywed."

"Must be Arthur's wife. He's only been married, oh, I know it's been less than two years."

"That's it. Arthur," I guessed. I should have asked, because Sir Malcolm wouldn't tell me anything I didn't ask for. He knew how I tended to run away with ideas. The fact that these ideas were often helpful didn't make any difference to him.

We made plans to get tickets after work that day for a train Friday night and when we knew what time we'd get into Lancaster, Rosalie would arrange for someone to meet us at the station.

That would give me a chance to question Rosalie for any possible information she might have about Sarah's death as well as learn something about Peter Watson during this weekend.

As we ate our pudding, I said, "I'll be glad to get away from Bloomington Grove this weekend. I found out from Betty that Sarah Wycott came back from work and was actually inside our wing before she was murdered last week. Somehow, somebody tricked her into going outside and then killed her. But who came to the door after Sarah returned?"

Rosalie shrugged. "I didn't see her, and I didn't let anyone else in. I was tired from traveling back from Lancaster and then working all the next day. I lay down right after dinner. I slept through anyone ringing the bell, the murder, everything. The next night, I had the sniffles and went to bed right after dinner again. I stayed there until Gwen woke me up because the police wanted to talk to all of us."

She smiled ruefully. "I threw on an old robe and came out yawning to fall into a chair. It wasn't until Maryellen said, 'Would you wake up, Rosalie? Sarah's been murdered,' that I woke up with a start."

Chapter Eleven

After work, as we waited to go out the gate, Rosalie and I told Marianne that we were going to the train station and would come back by foot and to please have Betty save our dinners for us. She agreed, waving to us from the bus before the other women drove off to Bloomington Grove.

Since we were moving toward the shortest day of the year, it was already fully dark when we left BP to walk to the station. With the blackout, it was completely dark, forcing us to watch our footing both to the ticket booth and then as we started our return journey past BP through the countryside back toward our living quarters.

I could make out the tops of the bare trees against the night sky over BP and the outline of buildings, amazed at how bright the stars were compared to in London before the blackout began. Still, I knew we'd have to guess where the edges of the lanes were and avoid the holes in the road by luck and memory.

We had just reached the entrance to BP when a figure stepped out of the darkness into our path.

I jumped a foot.

"There's a couple of us who need a ride back to Little Rowanwood. Do you want to ride along?" Simon Townsend's voice asked.

"Yes," Rosalie said. "Is there room?"

"We'll make room."

"I didn't realize people were working late tonight," I said, still unsure about Simon's purpose there since I'd seen him go into the admiral's office after me. My heartbeat was now slowing down to normal. "Was it helpful?"

"It's all helpful," he told me.

Realizing I sounded as if I were prying, I changed the topic. "It's really cold out tonight. Windy. Thank you for offering to let us join you."

"And you're afraid of the killer loose in the parish," Simon said. I thought I noted a bit of sarcasm in his tone.

"I am. I think it's creepy that someone killed Sarah Wycott after she headed back to our living quarters at this time of day. And the police can't figure out who did it." I tried to sound worried without sounding hysterical. I'm not sure I succeeded.

"We'll get you back safely," Simon said.

We waited for a few minutes, stomping our feet and hugging ourselves, until an estate car showed up. We climbed in and while Simon told the driver we were waiting on two more, I noticed she was the same FANY driver I'd had on Sunday.

Soon George and Peter showed up and we took off for

the village of Little Rowanwood. We chatted about the weather on the short ride to the Wren and Dragon, where all three men climbed out. We shouted farewell as the driver took off for our usual stop.

Once we were dropped off, Rosalie started a quick pace along the dark lane and then up the slope of the drive, too fast to carry on a conversation in the cold and wind, and I hurried to keep up. Helen answered the door to our ring and said, "Come in quickly out of that wind. Brr." She slammed the door behind us.

Maryellen called out from the kitchen, "I'll put your dinners on the table. Go hang up your coats and get in here." Behind her, I could hear a piece of ecclesiastical music playing on the radio.

Our quarters were feeling cozy that night with the knowledge that the unseasonably cold weather was kept out behind closed doors and blackout curtains. I went in my room long enough to throw my coat on my bed and hurried back to sit down to my dinner. I tried to wait for Rosalie, but after a minute or two, I gave up and began to eat.

I was halfway done when Rosalie sat down across from me at one end of the table, the knitters clustered at the other end. "I hope you don't mind that I started already."

"Not at all. You want to eat while dinner's still warm."

"Without a word of thanksgiving," Aileen said, never missing a stitch while she criticized me.

"I said it silently," I replied.

After I finished eating and then washed up in the scullery,

I retrieved my knitting from my room and hung up my coat. When I returned to the servants' hall, Rosalie complimented me on my scarf and left to get her book. Marianne and Maryellen sat me between them and proceeded to have me watch their hands and then copy their movements.

My knitting wasn't getting any smoother.

Fiona shook her head as she rose to tune in the radio to a play. It was a mystery, suitably haunting for the windy night outside.

We hadn't been working very long when an army sergeant appeared in the kitchen. "Mrs. Redmond?"

"That's me."

"Come with me, please."

"Ssh," Aileen said.

I hoped it was to see Charlie Adler and not to learn something had happened to Adam. We weren't having a shooting war yet, but there were always casualties during training. I rose, set down my knitting, and followed him, no one saying a word as they watched us leave. The only sounds were the voices and the background sounds ringing out from the radio and my knees knocking together in fear.

Please don't call me in about Adam. Please.

We turned the corner from the kitchen and continued on to another short hall on this floor. He opened the door into the office in the main house that I'd seen on Sunday. An army officer stood by the desk, waiting for me to come in.

"Mrs. Redmond?"

"Yes?"

He introduced himself. "I understand you need to see one of our soldiers."

"Yes." *Thank goodness nothing bad has happened to Adam.* I stiffened my knees before I collapsed in relief.

"Private Charles Adler."

"That's correct."

"What is he accused of?"

"Nothing. He was friends with a murder victim. We're speaking to all of her friends, trying to get a picture of her life. The more we learn, the more we can eliminate false leads." I hoped he bought my story.

"I'm going to stay."

I doubted Adler would be as forthcoming with an officer standing there. "Do you believe he's guilty?"

"Why should I?"

"Why else would you feel the need to listen in on a purely routine inquiry?"

The officer's mouth opened and closed twice. "No, I don't think he's done anything wrong. He's one of our better recruits. But I don't want you twisting his words or actions around."

"There's no danger of that," I told him. "Are you going to send for Adler or are we going to him?"

"Sergeant," he said, turning slightly, "bring Private Adler here."

We faced each other in silence across the office for a few minutes. The flocked wallpaper in a deep rose and light pink seemed an amusing choice for a military facility, but then, these were borrowed quarters and there was a war on.

Charlie Adler, when he arrived, turned out to be a tall, broad-shouldered blond man in his early twenties. He had a wide face and a tendency to try to shrink his body whenever he glanced in the direction of the officer.

I asked Adler to take a chair and sat across from him. The officer, a major, was about to object until I shot a threatening look at him. He must have decided it wasn't worth the effort and sat on one of the nearby desks.

"Now, Private Adler—may I call you Charlie?—I understand you were friends with Sarah Wycott."

He nodded, his mouth clamped shut. His gaze seemed to travel through the wallpaper and into the past.

"You've heard what happened to her?"

"She died."

"She was murdered." There was no way to soften my news.

"What?" He half-sprang from his chair.

"Sit down, Charlie. I want you to help me figure out who killed her."

"Well, I didn't."

"I didn't think you did." I waited until he subsided into the wooden desk chair. "I want you to help me. You were her friend, weren't you?"

"Yes. I want to help."

"Good." I tried to sound encouraging. "But to help, you need to be completely honest."

He nodded.

I faced the officer. "Major, I want Adler to be truthful and I don't want him to face any consequences from you for anything he might tell me. If you can't guarantee that, then I want you to find me another officer who can."

He turned bright red.

"I'm serious, Major."

He looked away, considered his options, and then turned back to me and nodded.

"I want to hear you give me your word."

"Oh, for—all right, I give you my word as an officer that I will not seek any disciplinary actions against Adler for anything he may say here. And on your head be it."

"Thank you." His annoyance told me he'd stick to our agreement. "Now, Charlie, how long had you known Sarah?"

"Ages. We were in school together. Then after I left school to go to work at the boat factory, both building and repairing them and earning a good wage, and Sarah stayed in school, I'd see her at chapel or in the village. Then she went away to university, and I only saw her on holidays, but we still made a point of seeing each other whenever we could."

"Tell me about her. About her childhood. What was she like?"

"She was the best, smartest student in our school. She was a leader in her Girl Guides group. Everyone in our town loved her. She was nice and kind and loyal."

"Were you sweethearts?"

A big, wistful grin spread across his face. "Yes, ma'am."

"How did her father feel about that?"

"He thought we were too young, but he didn't stand in our way. He only asked we wait a year or two, and then the war came, and Sarah had to come here."

"Did you know she was here?"

Charlie glanced at the major, who was staring at the blackout curtains. "When she came up here for her interview, I rode up and back on the train with her. I knew where she was working. Then I enlisted."

"And found yourself stationed here."

"Marvelous piece of luck. I had no idea she was staying here in the house until I saw her one morning walking down the drive. I whistled, and she turned around. She signaled me to be there at six that night. There was nothing on at that time here on the base, so I slipped away and met her."

He could easily have convinced her to walk down the lane with him that night and kill her, but I didn't believe he had. Either that, or he was the best actor I had ever seen.

"Did you continue to meet with her?"

"Of course."

"Where?"

"Here and there." He shrugged.

"Did you meet her the night she died?"

"No."

"Were you supposed to?"

Charlie glanced at the major, who was still looking at the blackout curtains, pretending he wasn't listening. "Yes."

"At what time?"

"I'd rather not say, ma'am."

"I'd rather you did. It's important. Major, could you get me a glass of water, please?"

The officer glowered at Charlie. "Answer her questions, Private." Then he rose and strode out of the room.

I gave him the ten seconds it took his footsteps to retreat across the house before I said, "Quick. What time?"

"Eight-thirty. There's a half-hour from eight-thirty until nine when this office is empty. I would come in here, unlock the door to the other side, and wait. That night she didn't show up. I figured she was busy at work and couldn't make it, so I locked the door and left."

"When did you see her the last time?"

"You mean before Monday night?"

"Yes."

The major walked in and set the glass of water on the desk next to me.

"The night before."

"How did she seem?"

"Distracted. I asked if there was anything I could do, but she just shook her head. I figured it had to do with work. I knew she couldn't talk about that, so I just dropped it."

"How long did you talk?" I glanced at the major, who had taken up his post staring at the curtains again.

"Just a few minutes. Then she said she had to get back."

"Did you make a date to meet the next night?"

He grinned. "Yes. She said she'd have everything all sorted by then. That she wanted to see me without this hanging over her head."

I leaned forward slightly, feeling that we were making progress. "Were those her exact words, Charlie?"

"Yes. 'Without this hanging over my head.'"

"Did she give you any clue as to what she was referring to?"

"No. I just assumed it had to do with her work."

"What else did she say? What else did you talk about?"

"I told her I received a letter from my ma. My sister's baby had been sick, but appeared to be doing better. She didn't seem to pay much attention, and that was unusual. She and my sister are—were—close."

There had to be a clue. Something that would tell us why she was distracted. "What else did she say? What else did you say?"

He looked at me, the pain of his loss showing in his eyes. "It's important, isn't it?"

"Yes, Charlie, it is."

"She asked me if I thought what we were doing, standing up for Britain, is important. I told her of course it is. She just sort of nodded to herself. Then she said, 'The Germans can be stopped. We can't let them win. I've seen something, Charlie, but I don't know what it means. I must do something, but I don't know how to stop it or if I should stop it. I could be wrong. I probably am wrong, in which case I don't need to do anything. This whole thing makes no sense.'"

Chapter Twelve

The major came off the corner of the desk where he was sitting. “She saw something? What did she see?”

“I don’t know,” Charlie said, sounding miserable. “She didn’t say.”

“If there’s a German spy lurking around here, watching our base, our training, we need to stop them. Catch them. You should have reported this, soldier.”

“Report what? The problem could be where she was working. That’s a very hush-hush place, too,” I said, “and there’s no reason to believe the problem is a spy. It might be someone hoarding or black-market dealings, or theft.”

“Nonsense. This is an ideal target for a spy. Has to be here.”

“No, it doesn’t. There is more around here than just this facility,” I told him. “Sarah was well indoctrinated with the need to report anything suspicious. Since she didn’t, we can be certain she wasn’t clear as to what she’d seen.”

“Something inexplicable?” Charlie said.

I nodded. “Inexplicable, but not on the surface dangerous.”

"I have to report this," the major said.

"I'm sure you do. Remember, Private Adler is not to get into any trouble. He's been a great help. I'm sure Sarah would be proud of you," I added, speaking to Charlie. "I have one more question. Where did Sarah get the silver bracelet with the disc on it engraved with 'Newnham College' and the year she finished?"

"I gave it to her as a graduation present. Saved for over a year to buy it. She loved it. Said she'd never take it off. We couldn't get engaged yet, so it was a token...Why?"

"I found it last weekend."

"Is it a clue?" he asked, leaning forward hopefully.

"Yes. I'll see it gets returned to you in due course. It may be needed for evidence at a trial first."

"Yes, ma'am."

"You're dismissed, Private," the officer said.

Charlie rose and began to walk out of the room. He turned back and said, "Find the bloke who killed her. Sarah was a good girl, ma'am. She deserves for her killer to hang."

"The killer may well also be a traitor. You can be certain he'll hang." Or she, I added to myself. There were a lot of women here who knew too much. Women who could be a great help to the Nazis.

The question was, how would anyone, male or female, learn the most important secrets of Bletchley Park and then transmit them to the Germans?

* * *

The next morning, which was Wednesday, after I'd been

at work for an hour or more, I left and went to the main house. I hoped the admiral would allow me to call Sir Malcolm with my findings from the telephone in his office. He was the only person in BP who knew of my dual role.

And no one else was supposed to know.

His secretary informed me the admiral would be in London that day and the next and I could not use his telephone. She didn't care who I was calling.

Defeated, I returned to work. There was the phone box in Little Rowanwood. I'd get off the bus there tonight and walk the rest of the way, hoping the whole time I wouldn't find Sarah's attacker en route.

The heater in our office gave off more smoke than heat all day, and by the time we left that evening, we were all coughing, our throats scratching and our eyes watering. Our lack of success that day added to our misery.

"We need to stop at the Wren and Dragon. Get something to soothe our throats, and then walk the rest of the way in cold, clear air. It's the only thing to cure an entire day spent breathing in fumes," Rosalie said. "Who's with me?"

"I am," I said.

"No, thank you," Aileen said, sounding prim.

Gwen shook her head. "I want to go practice. That always makes me feel better."

At least I had an excuse to stop in the village so I could call Sir Malcolm. If anyone asked, I'd say I was calling my father.

By the time we got outside the gates, we had an entire busload ready to descend on the Wren and Dragon. The Allen sisters, Fiona, and Helen, subjected to the same smoky conditions in their room, decided to join us. They worked in the Registration Room, where German messages overheard at British listening stations arrived at the front of Hut Six.

Already I felt my lungs clearing as I breathed in the cold night air and coughed.

The men discussed whether the landlord would let them play with the darts set again as we rode along the dark lanes. We arrived before they decided which of them would approach the landlord with their request. We all piled off and waved to Gwen and Aileen, who rode on to Bloomington Grove alone.

As the others walked toward the pub, I headed toward the green and the telephone box. I was almost there when I heard footsteps behind me on some loose rocks. I swung around, ready to fight or scream, only to find Simon walking up behind me.

"Are you heading for the phone box, too?" he asked. In the light from the night sky, his expression appeared innocent.

"I am."

"I'll let you go first, then."

"I've got to make a trunk call, so you go ahead."

"That wouldn't be very gentlemanly of me."

"But I'll talk longer than you," I told him. "To make up for it, you could be a gentleman and buy my half of ale."

"You're sure you don't mind?"

"I'm sure."

I stood a little way off from the phone box along the lane, finding I couldn't make out his side of the conversation from where I stood. I moved around the glass and metal box on the village green side, and still couldn't hear what he said as I blew on my gloved hands.

He was done in two minutes and left the box, holding the door, the glass panes covered with anti-splinter bomb tape, open for me.

I thanked him and slipped in, ringing the operator and asking for a trunk to London. As I waited, I looked around, but I didn't see anyone lurking nearby.

Finally, I reached Sir Malcolm, who was in the office as he always seemed to be. "I talked to Private Adler," I told him.

"Anything of interest?"

I told him, as cryptically as I could.

"And the army thinks they are the target?" Sir Malcolm asked.

"Yes, although I assured them they weren't." I doubted the major believed me. "I'm going to Lancaster Friday night. I should be back sometime Sunday. One of my colleagues lives a few miles from Celia's village."

"The Billingsthorpe woman." Sir Malcolm paused. "Check out that situation while you're at it, although I don't believe there's anything to find. Her husband's mother lives in Germany, married to some count. Her husband was born here, and was raised here by his father after the split. No Nazi leanings that we know of, but it wouldn't hurt for you to check."

Great. Now I had another assignment for the weekend beside checking out Peter Watson. I said good-bye and hung up before I had to feed any more coins into the telephone.

As I came out of the telephone box, I looked, but I didn't see any movement around me. The cold spurred me on to the door of the Wren and Dragon. When I entered, my half was sitting next to Simon's pint on the table in front of him. Obviously, he hadn't lingered as I feared he would.

I should ask Sir Malcolm to check on him.

"Everything all right with your father?" Simon asked.

"Oh, yes. Everything is my fault as usual." I looked around. "No darts tonight?"

"The landlord said no. Something about John's aim."

I shook my head, remembering how close the dart had come to Peter's head. "What if John promised not to play?"

"The answer's still no. He doesn't trust any of us."

I smiled at Simon. "Any reason why he should?"

He grinned back and shook his head.

George came into the pub, smacking his hands together to get his blood pumping, and ordered a pint. Then he came over to join us. "I had a letter to mail before the last post goes out."

"To your girlfriend?" I asked, softening my nosiness with a smile.

"I keep writing, hoping at least some of my letters get through, but I don't hear anything. I've sent this one to a friend to give to Anthea. If this doesn't work, I don't know what I'll do."

"Send her a telegram," I suggested.

"Her mother would just intercept that, too." George looked forlorn.

"Too bad you can't broadcast over the radio to her," Simon said.

"We both have shortwave radios. We used them all the time during term while I was at Cambridge. I wish we weren't at war so we could continue to send messages to each other." A grin creased his face. "We even have our own special little shortcuts in Morse code. Not that her mother knows Morse code, but we use initials of our pet names, things such as that, which wouldn't mean anything to anyone else."

A whole circle of laughing, chattering people took up the main floor area of the pub. "What's going on?" I asked.

"Take a look," Simon said.

I took my half with me. Helen was in the middle of the circle, making a coin disappear in someone's ear only to reappear in someone else's. Then it appeared under someone's pint glass and then in John's pocket.

The locals applauded as enthusiastically as the BP staff.

"How does she do that?" I asked.

"Her whole family are magicians. They perform in variety shows. That's why she goes back to London every weekend," John told me, laughing at the way she found a coin that hadn't been in his empty pocket before.

We only talked for another moment before Maryellen

came over and said the rest of the women were ready to walk back now that Helen was finished with her sleight of hand demonstration. I nodded, drank a little more of my ale, and thanked Simon as I put on my gloves and hurried after my housemates.

I caught up to Helen on the lane. "That was impressive. You must have practiced for years to be able to perform tricks such as those."

She shrugged. "I started as a child. And they're called illusions."

"Did you learn from your parents?"

"Have you ever heard of the Magnificent Prestons?"

"When I was younger, I went to see them in London. At the—Southside?" I'd gone with schoolmates from St. Agnes one weekend. "Was that you?"

"And my family."

"How I envied you and your freedom, doing interesting things. I was in boarding school at the time and hated it."

"What freedom?" she asked. "Rehearsing. Performing. Rehearsing. Performing. And surrounded by family twenty-four hours a day. I've spent my entire life trapped by my family and family duty. You're the one who's been free, while I've only dreamed of it. That's why I love working here, where nobody judges my performance."

I thought of the scrutiny all of our work was given. "You still have to perform every day at work."

"Don't you see, Livvy? There's no audience. Bosses, yes, but no audience. And no family."

Chapter Thirteen

"There go my dreams of a freer life," I told her. "Where did your parents learn all these illusions? From their parents?"

Helen sighed. "It started as a family act, with my grandfather, my uncle, and my father. But when my uncle was killed in the war and my grandfather died of influenza in the epidemic, my father found himself having to support the entire family."

She walked a little further before she continued. "As a result, my siblings, cousins, and I learned at an early age to perform onstage. Otherwise, we would have starved. I've learned to like it now, the feeling of having an audience in the palm of my hand, but it wasn't always that way. And that fear of failure never goes away."

"They loved you tonight." I certainly did, and I thought it showed in my voice.

"It was a free show. What's not to love? It can't fail."

We exchanged smiles in the faint moonlight. I understood fear of failure, but in my case, it was fear that a murderer and traitor would escape.

"I'd have liked to have gone to boarding school," Helen continued, "where there were no relatives, at least for a while."

"Was that where you went last weekend?" I asked. "To put on a show with your family?"

"We had two shows at the Palladium, plus I have to help train my youngest sister. She'll have to take my place when we start having to work weekends here."

"How did you end up here?"

"I signed up to do war work, and I put on the application that I do sleight of hand and illusions. Guess they figured that's what we're doing at BP." Helen slapped her hands together. "Wow, but it's cold out."

Gwen opened the door for us with, "It's about time. Dinner's ready." I could hear the news on the radio in the servants' hall. Hitler hadn't made his move yet. Thank goodness.

We quickly put away our outerwear and made our way to the table. It was a mostly vegetable stew again, similar to yesterday's dinner, with freshly baked bread, and weak tea, and a pudding for a special afters. We all dug in with enthusiasm.

The pattern of the remainder of the week went on the same as the ones before it. Food at the Grove, as we'd come to call it, and at BP was meatless but not bland, and always warm and tasty enough.

When we typed out the messages of the German army

and air force that the radio intercept locations sent us, they translated to nursery rhymes or weather reports. Or unintelligible nonsense if the keys weren't right. Getting the decoding correct was very much a hit-or-miss affair.

We ate, we slept, we worked, and for short periods of time, we knitted as we listened to the radio. Life didn't vary, the cold didn't vary, and if I was going to get any further on my investigation, I needed to talk to everyone about their lives.

One evening I bumped into Aileen as she left the bathing room and I was about to go in. "I think I have the right time," I told her.

"You need to keep to the schedule," she warned me.

"I have my own flat and had to work odd hours for the newspaper," I told her. "Having any sort of schedule is much different from my life before I came here."

"You'll have to adjust."

"What were you doing before you came here?"

"After I graduated, I taught modern languages in Edinburgh for a year before I came here."

"And you gave up a deferred occupation, teaching, to come here? Why?"

"I felt teaching in Edinburgh was shirking my duty to my country." She was about to walk away when I said, "So were you able to live at home while teaching?"

"Yes. My parents still haven't adjusted to my living away from them. They fear I'll be corrupted by the devil. Families that are truly chapel don't want their children to leave home until they marry."

"Did you go to university in Edinburgh?"

"Of course. My father's a mathematics professor there who knows the men who did decrypting in the Great War, which was why he finally allowed me to come here to work." She sounded pleased about that. "He feels it's better I work for people he knows and can trust."

"How did your parents react to the murder?"

"How do you think? Here was another chapel girl working and living where I am, and she was killed." She glanced around before she added, "I had to tell them that she turned out not to be particularly devout. Otherwise, they'd have made me come home."

"Were you here the night she vanished? Betty said she let her in late from work, so she was inside here, and no one saw her leave or anyone else come in. What happened?"

"Obviously, she snuck out. She couldn't have been a very religious girl. No one can get in without someone letting them in. She must have slipped out to see a young man and he killed her."

"How would she have come inside again after meeting this young man? If he hadn't killed her," I added.

"Not anything I've considered, so I don't know." Aileen turned and walked off to her room.

I decided I could rule Aileen out. She didn't have the imagination to be a spy, and she definitely wouldn't be a traitor since it broke the rules and interfered with her duty to her country.

Late one evening, Fiona and I were the only two still in the servants' hall knitting. "What made you agree to come to work here?" I asked her.

"Why did you?" she responded.

"I speak German, and my father is in the Foreign Office. I hope that doing my duty to my country will make him proud of me."

"You sound like there's not much hope of that."

I shrugged. "Probably not. But you said you and your father get along well."

"We do, but I want to do something more exciting than wiping up stale beer. Now I'm near London and living in a manor house. What's not to like?"

"In the servants' quarters," I scoffed.

"But I don't have to clean and polish to stay here or earn my money." Fiona gave me a smile. "I can carry out my work without having to do it with a rag in my hand."

When Friday finally arrived, Rosalie and I brought our suitcases with us to BP that morning, ready to leave after work. Finally, I'd be making progress on the reason I was there.

At nearly four in the afternoon, John called us together and gave us the bad news. "We're going to need to go to three shifts soon, probably at the beginning of the new year. We should have enough personnel by then to handle operating around the clock. Toward that, we'll have two new women starting on Monday in the other rooms and one more in here."

"It'll take more than one extra to cover three shifts," Rosalie said.

"Yes, it will," John agreed. "In the meantime, we're going to split you ladies up into two groups, so that you cover every other weekend, although still with one shift."

"And if we have plans for this weekend?" I asked.

"We'll start Monday. This will be the last free weekend for everyone, so enjoy it." He studied the floor. "Just wanted to give you warning that things will be shaken up come Monday."

I glanced at Rosalie. Her eyes and mouth were tightly shut. I suspected she was sorry she'd chosen this weekend to invite me to stay at her manor, since she was going to have to break the news to her invalid husband.

"What about Christmas?" Gwen asked.

"It's on a Monday this year, so we'll handle it the same way as any other weekend day. Half the personnel will be on their regular duty."

"But..." Aileen began.

"There is a war on, Miss MacLeith. Sooner or later, it will become a shooting war." John sounded equal parts stern and sorrowful. "The more we can do in preparation, the better positioned we'll be when the time comes."

The hut was quiet for the rest of the workday, each of us with our private thoughts concerning the coming bleak holidays. Afterward, I followed a silent Rosalie into the town of Bletchley to the railroad restaurant. We were both quiet as we tried to choke down the worst fish and chips I'd encountered in a long time.

Then we went to the station to await our train.

When it arrived, we could see most of the cars were bulging with passengers, primarily soldiers. First class, which Rosalie had insisted we buy tickets for, was busier than I expected to see, but we were able to get seats. It was a long trip, much longer than just going to London. Rosalie was smart to travel this way. It meant we were able to sit for the entire journey.

The shades were kept down on all the train windows because it was dark outside, so we had to bring our own entertainment with us. I read a newspaper, relieved to avoid knitting for the weekend. Rosalie stared at the same page in a magazine for over an hour.

The farther north we traveled, the colder the train carriage became. By the time we made our way to Lancaster, I was bored, frozen, stiff from sitting, sleepy, and in desperate need of a cup of tea.

We climbed down with our suitcases, had our tickets checked at the barrier, and headed through the small station out to the car park. Rosalie walked straight for a Rolls sedan as a middle-aged chauffeur in livery climbed out of the car and opened the boot before stowing our cases inside.

"Thank you for meeting us, Miles," Rosalie said. "This is Mrs. Redmond, a colleague of mine."

He tipped his hat. I nodded in reply.

"How is his lordship?" she asked as soon as we were seated in back and Miles was in the driver's seat.

"The same, milady. Looking forward to seeing you."

His lordship? Milady?

I couldn't see much of the town since everything was blacked out. I could tell when we began to drive through the countryside and left traffic behind. Now we had the roads to ourselves.

At a fork in the road, Rosalie said, "St. Mary's Wall is down on the right. Don't worry, there's a shorter way to get there from the manor."

We took the left fork and rode for what I guessed was two or three miles, stopping at the front door of a huge, dark structure. We climbed out and walked in the door as a maid came out to take our cases from the boot of the car.

I heard something rolling toward us and then a man in a wheeled chair came through a doorway into the ornate, two-story front hall and said, "Darling! We've waited a late tea for you. How was your journey? Oh, hello," he added when he glimpsed me.

The man was probably at least forty, with a gaunt face and a thin build, as if he were wasting away. He wore a jacket, sweater, and tie above the most beautiful knit blanket I'd ever seen. I was familiar enough with knitting now that I could appreciate the shifting patterns and stitches as well as the colors.

A larger, older man pushed the chair. "Hello, your lordship," I said to the seated man. "I'm Olivia Redmond, a colleague of Rosalie's. She never told us she was *Lady* Billingsthorpe."

I was surprised Sir Malcolm wanted me to check on the loyalty of a pair of aristocrats. I'd had to with Sir Rupert Manning, but that was different. He was a Nazi zealot, and as a baronet, he was not a real aristocrat. Rosalie, and presumably her husband, were loyal Brits.

Unless they were followers of the Duke of Marshburn.

Marshburn was a vocal follower of the Nazis and their belief in racial superiority. He wanted Edward back on the throne along with Wallis Simpson as Queen, and to that end, he was suspected of hiding German spies on his estates and leading a group of aristocratic British fascists. Sir Rupert Manning had been one of his most devoted followers until he'd died two months before the war began.

I really hoped Rosalie and Lord Billingsthorpe weren't friends of Marshburn. I liked them.

Chapter Fourteen

"She didn't think it would make her too popular with her colleagues to have them call her 'milady,'" Rosalie's husband said, looking up at me from his wheeled chair with a cheery smile. He held out his hand, which I shook. "A pleasure to meet you. You must be famished. Come in. Cook said you'd want something light this time of night, so she fixed teacakes and tea sandwiches."

"That sounds exactly what we need," Rosalie said, taking my arm and leading me through a drawing room and then into a huge formal dining room beyond it. I could hear her husband's chair being pushed behind us.

Three places were set around one end of an enormous table, and there was no chair set at the very end. Rosalie took what I guessed was her usual spot and I sat across from her as her husband was wheeled into position.

Above the center of the table was a huge crystal chandelier, electrified now. It gave off enough light I could see the fancy plaster decorations in the lofty ceiling and the beautiful paintings hanging on the walls.

My attention focused on the older man who set the food and the tea service on the table and departed. Rosalie served us tea and offered me the platter of sandwiches first.

I took one, and her husband said, "No, Mrs. Redmond, please take more. There's plenty."

I took a second one. "Thank you, your lordship."

"If you're eating at our table, the least you can do is call me Thorpe. All our friends do."

"Then please, call me Livvy."

"How was your journey, Livvy?"

"It was quite nice. Rosalie had a good idea in traveling first class. We'd have had to ride standing the whole way otherwise."

"Are all the trains that crowded these days?"

"All the ones I've been on." I ate both sandwiches and a cup of tea as quickly as I could without appearing to be ill-mannered. Rosalie, who was eating almost as quickly as I was, pressed another cup of tea on me while Thorpe offered me more of the sandwiches and the tea cakes.

Then Thorpe asked me about my father and my husband and my life before BP. We didn't have any acquaintances in common, since he was several years older than me and neither my father nor Reggie, my first husband, nor Adam, my current husband, had any interest or experience in skiing or polo or shooting parties.

Then I realized Adam would have a great deal of interest in shooting when the war began in earnest, and his target wouldn't be gamebirds.

Thorpe seemed to be the right age to have been in the Great War, so I asked him about his experiences.

He chuckled. "I was called up a few months before the end of the war. By the time I was trained and sent to France, the war was over. I was one of the lucky ones."

I had to agree with that.

Next I asked Thorpe to tell me about the estate and the farming there. Apparently, some ancient ancestor had wisely kept the best land for himself, which Thorpe told me about in an amusing way, and then more recent ancestors founded mills and factories. He told me about working with various government ministers to change his factories over to wartime production and a few humorous flubs in the process.

His face was expressive, mostly laughing and happy, while Rosalie smiled as she listened to stories she'd no doubt heard before.

When we said good night, I found the room they gave me was spacious and comfortable. I slept as if I were a rock.

I came down the next morning at about the time Rosalie said she would be at breakfast. When I headed for the room where dinner had been served the night before, I was gently redirected toward a breakfast room by the older man I'd seen.

"Thank you, er..."

"Cummings, ma'am."

"Thank you, Cummings. His lordship has a wonderful attitude toward strange women showing up with his wife for a weekend at his house."

"He enjoys meeting people. Both their lord- and ladyship are hospitable people. There've been few melancholy souls in this family."

"And I enjoyed meeting him. Will he be down for breakfast?"

"The late hours last night wore him out. I doubt he'll be up before luncheon."

"I look forward to seeing him then. The breakfast room is this way?"

"Yes, ma'am."

He showed me where it was tucked away on the sunny, east side of the house. Rosalie was already there. We had one of those conventional conversations, about how pretty the house was and how I should see the grounds in the daylight, as we helped ourselves from the sideboard and ate a hearty breakfast.

"Since I'm beginning to notice, really notice, knitting, I studied your husband's blanket."

"Lap robe."

"Lap robe. The way the colors and the patterns fade one into another is amazing. I can't imagine having that skill or how very long it would take to dream up that pattern and then stitch it. It's a work of art."

"It is, rather, isn't it?" Rosalie then offered to take me on a tour before walking me over to St. Mary's Wall to meet Celia Flowers Henry. Rosalie said she was friendly with the vicar's wife there and needed to pay her a visit.

"Don't you want to spend the morning with your

husband?" I asked.

"He'll sleep all morning. I'd rather be here for the afternoon when he's awake. And he'll want to see you then, too. A new face. A new interest," she told me.

After breakfast, Rosalie found me a pair of gumboots that fit and we dressed warmly for our walk. I could tell the grounds must be lovely in summer. Even this late in the year, they had a stark beauty to them.

The house was Georgian, classical, and well-proportioned in a warm, light-colored stone. Three stories above ground with wings off the main block, the house sat nestled in the side of the highest ridge with views over the farms and woodlands.

Eventually, we followed along a path to the village in the shade of the manor house and then over another mile across winter-dry fields to St. Mary's Wall. I had Celia's address on a piece of paper I'd carried with me, and while Rosalie talked to the vicar's wife, I followed their directions to the large, elegant stone house on the edge of what they called a village.

As I walked, I realized St. Mary's Wall was good sized and should rightfully be called a town, not a village. Fortunately, it wasn't windy or raining, and so I didn't arrive on Celia's doorstep looking bedraggled.

I rang the bell and a middle-aged woman in a maid's uniform answered the door. I asked to speak to Celia and handed her my card. It was a plain social card, and the woman glanced at it before indicating a chair in the front hall.

About two minutes later, Celia came down the stairs

looking pregnant and happy. Her dark hair, pulled back from her face, and dark eyes stood out against her pale skin. That was what I remembered about her, the contrast of light and dark that she used to accentuate her looks when we were in college. She wore a plain, dark blue dress with a tiny white pattern printed on a thin wool.

"Yes?" she asked as she reached the bottom of the stairs.

I rose. "Celia. I'm Livvy Harper, from college. Hopefully I haven't changed that much."

"Livvy? What are you doing in St. Mary's Wall?"

I needed to step carefully. "I'm doing some war work with Rosalie Billingsthorpe, and she invited me home for the weekend. Since I discovered you lived nearby, I thought I'd stop by and visit you." I nodded at her midsection. "Apparently, you have lots of news."

"Yes. I married Arthur a year and a half ago, and now we're expecting our first."

"Did you meet him in Cambridge? I finished before you, and have no idea what went on after I left." I hoped I could use this to get to Peter Watson.

"Sort of. He was a friend of a friend of my brother's, and we met when he and a group of friends came to Cambridge for some law lectures."

"I guess Peter Watson was out of the picture by then. I remember you two were close."

Her eyes narrowed. "He was. I wasn't."

"He was the clingy type? I didn't pick up on that."

"No. He was demanding. Pushy. He was seen with

another woman, a townie, but I couldn't be seen with any other men or he went into a rage. Well, not what you'd call a rage. He was cold, icy, and suddenly he'd be physical."

"Golly. That must have been scary." I felt my eyes widen. Apparently, his behavior the previous weekend wasn't unusual. How long could he survive under the pressure of working at BP?

"My roommate, Sarah Wycott—remember her?—stopped him on two occasions when he'd grab my arm hard. He left bruises."

"You're lucky he just left bruises and didn't do anything more damaging."

"Sarah looked out for me." She lowered her voice. "Especially after he threatened to kill me."

"Celia, who's this?" a middle-aged, fair-complexioned woman asked as she walked in from the room to the right of the hall. She pinned us with her steely gaze. "Why haven't you invited her into the drawing room? You'd be more comfortable there."

I stopped myself from growling at her to go away after Celia made her astounding revelation. Celia stopped and blinked, apparently surprised by the woman's arrival. "Mama Henry, this is Livvy Harper, a collegemate. She just dropped by to say hello."

"Actually, Livvy Redmond now. I recently married."

"How do you do, Mrs. Redmond? I'm the senior Mrs. Henry." *And don't you forget it* was in her tone.

"Pleased to meet you." Just not at this moment.

Her eyes narrowed and her voice took on an interrogating tone. “What brings you to St. Mary’s Wall?”

“I’m spending the weekend with Lady Billingsthorpe and walked over from there.”

She put on a practiced smile. A little too practiced. “Where do you know her ladyship from? And it’s the Countess of Briarcliffe, not Lady Billingsthorpe.”

I quickly surmised Celia’s mother-in-law knew the status of everyone she knew or who came through her door. This was handy, because I’d had no idea Thorpe was an earl. Being the daughter of a baronet and a houseguest of “her ladyship” meant I was welcome. So welcome Celia and I would never have another moment to ourselves.

Equally quickly, I made my excuses and left. I never felt safe in telling Celia that Sarah had been murdered. Her mother-in-law was overbearing, and I didn’t want to make Celia’s position difficult. Having a friend who was murdered would no doubt make Celia’s position uncomfortable in the eyes of the senior Mrs. Henry.

I had reached the gate when Celia slipped out to say good-bye without her mother-in-law listening. “I suspect you had some reason to come here.”

When I smiled, she said, “I heard from classmates that your first husband was murdered and you found the murderer. And then you found the murderer of some French seamstress in an haute couture house in London.”

“Yes. And now I’m trying to find the killer of Sarah Wycott.”

She gasped.

"Peter Watson is working at the same location that Sarah was. I wanted to know if he was violent. If he had a reason to kill her."

"Yes, he's violent. Or he was toward me. But would he kill Sarah all this time later? I don't think so. He was never that angry for more than a few minutes or so. Certainly not three or four years."

Mrs. Henry was now in the doorway looking at us. I waved to her with a smile and said to Celia, "You'd better go in. And thank you."

"Find her killer. Please. And thank you for telling me." She hurried back down the path, then stopped and waved as if nothing important had been said.

Her words were useful to me. They'd shed light on Peter Watson's character. At least I had something to ask him when I returned to Bletchley.

I walked back to the vicarage and then Rosalie and I walked back to the manor house in time for luncheon. Thorpe was up and dressed and ready to join us in the dining room when we returned. Once again, he was using the magnificent lap robe.

The food was good and I had worked up an appetite during the walk to St. Mary's Wall.

"Is the senior Mrs. Henry a friend of yours?" I asked Rosalie during the soup course. A soup course during luncheon was a luxury I had almost forgotten, and this was a flavorful onion broth.

"Did she say she was?" Rosalie asked.

"She gave me the impression she'd enjoy the status of being a close friend," I told her, hoping I wasn't saying the wrong thing.

Both my hosts laughed. "Rosie, you said she was sharp," Thorpe said.

"You have her measure," Rosalie told me.

"I was afraid I'd spoken out of turn. Especially since she corrected me on your title, Countess of Briarcliffe."

They both laughed. "You've been found out, Countess," the earl said.

"That's something I want to keep separate from my war work." Rosalie's tone was somber. Then she smiled and asked, "How is your school friend doing since she married the younger Mr. Henry?"

I remembered her hurrying out of the house when the older woman's back was turned to ask me what she wanted to know, and then to tell me what I needed to learn. "Celia seems to have figured out how to work around her mother-in-law without triggering any alarms."

"That's good. The one time I met her, she seemed very nice. And very bright," Rosalie said.

As soon as we finished with the soup, the bowls were silently whisked away and the main course brought in. I spent ten minutes eating as I waited for a good time to spring the question I needed to ask for Sir Malcolm.

"Thorpe, you're a neighbor of one of the Duke of Marshburn's estates. How is that working out since war has been declared? Lots of strangers wandering through with binoculars?"

I deliberately made no mention of Marshburn's politics. I wondered what Thorpe would say about their relationship.

Chapter Fifteen

"Oh, you mean the counterespionage johnnies keeping an eye on his estate? Well, they have to. They keep on the public footpaths and haven't bothered the crops, so it's been no problem for us." Thorpe gave me a smile and took another bite.

"No one has taken their patriotic fervor out on the estate workers, have they?" I thought I'd ask while I could.

"Marshburn owns the estate, but he's rarely there. His estate workers' families have been there for centuries, since before Marshburn's maternal grandmother owned it. Those families are known to everyone. No, there's been no torchings or mayhem around here."

"Oh, that's good. I don't want Rosalie having to worry about you and the people around here while she's away."

"You're a good friend to be concerned for me," Rosalie said, "but everyone knows everyone else here. It's not the same as London with all sorts of turnover and people milling about. We all do our work and take care of each other. I doubt most of the people around here would even recognize the duke. He's very much an absentee landlord."

"Were the losses very great around here during the last war?"

"I lost my two older brothers," Rosalie said. "That's what drives me to work at BP. I want this war over quickly, in our favor, so other little girls don't go through what I did."

"I'm sorry. I shouldn't have spoken," I said, feeling dreadful to have brought it up. After more than twenty years, the deaths on the battlefield still left a hole in many families in Britain.

"I don't think there's a family around here who didn't lose someone in the war. And then someone else in the epidemic that followed," Thorpe told me. "It drew the whole district together, so yes, we all try to take care of one another."

"And I imagine everyone knows you. You're such an outgoing, welcoming man," I said, giving him a thankful smile for his hospitality.

"And such a brilliant chess player," he replied. "You don't happen to play, do you?"

"Very badly. Two moves and you'd have me in checkmate."

"Then you don't mind if I have Dr. Hamelstein in for a match this afternoon?" he asked us both.

"Not at all," I said.

"Oh, good. Will he be staying for dinner?" Rosalie asked.

"I don't believe so," Thorpe said. "Hamelstein is both my doctor and an excellent chess player," he said to me. "He escaped Vienna last year and settled here. I'm grateful he did."

Rosalie looked shocked for an instant. "It was only last year, wasn't it? So much has happened since then." She turned to me. "Dr. Hamelstein has treated Thorpe since his accident. When the Nazis rolled into Austria, we sponsored the doctor and his entire extended family, finding jobs where needed on the estate."

Like Esther and Sir Henry. "Good for you."

"I'm afraid it's only been a year and a half," Thorpe said. "Back to the subject and your concern, Livvy. It's such a small holding for Marshburn that no one is going to bother with it or his workers, which means no danger for anyone else."

"We'd recognize him, of course," Rosalie said, "but that's from seeing him in London from long before the war."

"I imagine he's keeping a low profile these days. And when the war heats up, he'll be even less popular," Thorpe said.

I noticed he said *when*, not *if*. I suppose that showed he was a realist.

"Still, I'm sure the government needs to keep an eye on his land in case he gets some wild idea, such as putting in an airfield for German bombers, or something equally foolish," Thorpe added.

"Oh, golly, he wouldn't do something such as that, would he?" It sounded as if it would be a nightmare for anyone living nearby.

"I suspect there's no limit to the stupidity of that man,"

Rosalie said. "But I'm sure the government would stop him."

"Rosalie's never been able to stand him. The first time they met, at a London gathering before we were married, he mistook her for a vapid young thing and belittled her brains and education in front of her and everyone." Thorpe laughed. "He may be the only person to have ever misjudged Rosalie's intelligence. When he persisted, she cursed him out in Latin. Quite a long and vigorous curse. Left him speechless, for once. I believe I heard some applause."

"From you," Rosalie said and burst out laughing. "You didn't help things, Thorpe."

"You won an ardent admirer that day, but not in Marshburn."

They shared a laugh and apparently a fond memory.

"He sounds odious," I said. The only time I'd met him, I thought he was in love with his own importance. I was glad Rosalie put him in his place.

"He is, rather," Rosalie said, dabbing at her tears from laughing so hard.

If Sir Malcolm had any thoughts about this pair joining forces with Marshburn, he could forget them.

Rosalie was giving me a guided tour of the artwork on the ground floor when we walked into one grand room and found Thorpe in a corner playing chess with a dark-haired man with a neat beard.

We were introduced, but the thing I noticed was the beautiful sweater vest Thorpe wore over a long-sleeved shirt. The pattern brought navy blue, red, and two shades of beige on a brown background. When I asked Rosalie later on our tour if she had knitted his vest, she changed the topic.

Why would she hide such an obvious talent, if she had knitted his vest?

The rest of the weekend was quiet, but lovely. I was fed well, slept in luxury, and entertained Thorpe with stories about theater productions I'd seen.

He asked me about Adam. I answered as briefly as I could. I was worried about my husband and that was hard to disguise in my words and my tone.

It was then I learned Rosalie had told Thorpe about the changes in her work schedule. He admitted he was concerned about her, too, and said our worries made a bond between us. I agreed, not mentioning the difference between Rosalie's safe position at Bletchley Park and the dangers Adam faced. There was little else I could decently say.

Rosalie and I were driven back to the rail station early Sunday afternoon after a delicious luncheon that reminded me of prewar fare. It was so good that we were late getting into Lancaster and so Miles, the chauffeur, raced us along the streets and then hustled us into the station as he carried our cases.

Rosalie carried a tin box. I hoped it contained something delicious from the Briarcliffe kitchens.

We made it onto the platform just as the train pulled in.

The train was past Manchester before we had to draw the blackout shades. It was then Rosalie opened her tin box and we enjoyed a dinner of sandwiches.

We'd have a long, cold walk in the dark before we reached our Bletchley home. Fortunately, we had first-class tickets and that meant we had seats for the entire journey, so we'd be rested for the trek.

By the time we finally reached Bloomington Grove, it was late. I was famished, chilled to the bone, and my feet hurt. Marianne opened the door for us and said, "Tea's on."

We dropped our cases and our coats in our rooms and went to the servants' hall for tea. I'd have loved something to go with it, but we weren't that lucky. The kitchen was scrubbed and any food was put away.

"Anything exciting happen in the last two days?" I asked as I watched knitting needles flash with quick, even motions around the table.

"Peter and George got into a bit of a bust-up. I thought they were going to come to blows," Marianne said.

"They certainly did a lot of shouting," Maryellen added.

"When was this?" I asked, pouring myself a cup of tea.

"Last night at the Wren and Dragon."

"Good. The landlord would put a quick halt to that nonsense," I said.

"John and Simon and a couple of the other men stopped it before it got out of hand," Marianne said.

"The landlord said he'd bar them both if they didn't settle down," Maryellen said.

"Since they both live there, that would be stupid on their parts," Fiona said.

"I'm sure the landlord could tell the administration to

find them other billets and he'd take people less likely to fight in his pub," Gwen said.

"Then for their sakes, I'm glad it was stopped," I said after a nice warm swallow of tea. "What started it?"

"You," Maryellen said and burst out laughing.

"What?" I felt my cheeks heat. What had I done?

"Peter said you were a nosy old bat and George said he thought you were all right," Fiona said.

"Hardly the positions of two men who were going to fight over me." Whatever else, it was not flattering. And I didn't need anyone pointing out all the questions I was asking about their dead colleague.

"The argument was whether you were sticking your nose where it doesn't belong. Whether you are too interested in other people's business," Maryellen said.

"George said he thought it was nice that you listened when he complained about not getting word to his girlfriend or then not receiving any return mail. Peter said it just showed you were nosy," Fiona said.

"That's just wonderful," I said, sounding as glum as I felt. "I'll be embarrassed the next time I set foot in the Wren and Dragon."

"Don't be," Gwen said. "I'm sure George has forgotten all about the argument by now, and Peter's a hothead who cools off quickly when someone isn't egging him on."

"Who would do that?" I asked.

"Simon."

"Simon?" Why would he do that? For someone so

friendly, he sounded capable of turning around and causing problems between people.

"Marianne and I were there," Maryellen said. "When Peter said you were nosy and George said you weren't a bad sort, Simon said anyone with anything to hide was in danger with you around. 'The same as a ferret,' I think he said."

"Oh, that is flattering." It made me wonder if Simon and I were on the same side. How closely had Sir Malcolm looked at him?

"When Peter said he didn't have anything to hide, Simon said you could always find something. That your sort always does. Then George tried to defend you." Marianne shook her head. "They ended up with their hands around each other's throats."

The way Sarah Wycott was killed. "And Simon?"

"Helped break it up," Fiona said.

"After he helped start it," I said with a shake of my head. "I'm not certain I trust him."

"Trust him to do what?" Fiona asked.

"Oh, anything. Be my friend. Play cards with." Lame, but I had to say something to divert suspicion that Simon was right. I needed to speak to Peter as soon as possible. Tomorrow wouldn't be too early.

"Things should be interesting at work tomorrow," Maryellen said.

"Oh, I don't know," Rosalie said, getting up to wash out her teacup, "we could just get on with our tasks. Isn't that what they hired us for?" She glanced at me with an expression I couldn't read.

* * *

The next morning, I rose extra early to bathe before breakfast and be ready to catch our transport to BP. That day it was the bus that showed up at our usual place rather than an estate car, and then we rode toward the stop in the middle of the village of Little Rowanwood. Peter was among the men to climb aboard and chose a seat by himself. George sat next to John.

As we reached Bletchley Park, I rose and dropped into the seat next to Peter. "I'd like to speak to you today. Lunch?"

"One o'clock?" he asked, looking red-faced and glancing away from me.

"Fine." The bus came to a halt and I rose with the others to climb off.

There were three new women in the hut that day, and a good part of our morning was spent in showing our tasks to the newest German speaker in our group. John then told us we'd do this process again the next day when another woman started in our section.

In the meantime, we had decryption texts to check to see if they were in German and if they were, then to translate into English.

At one o'clock, I told John I was going to lunch and headed over to the dining hall in the former manor house. I found Peter sitting at a table by himself and joined him.

"I suppose you heard about Saturday night," he said once we both had our meals.

"Yes. I'm sorry you think I'm sticking my nose in your business."

"You do ask a lot of personal questions."

"Then you don't want me to tell you about seeing Celia this past weekend."

His fork hit his plate with a clatter. "You saw Celia? Celia Flowers?"

I watched him carefully. "Yes."

His expression went from hope to anger. "Why?"

"She's a neighbor of Rosalie's."

"And you couldn't wait to tell me that." He folded his arms, showing no interest in his lunch.

"Eat. We don't get much time for lunch."

He muttered something under his breath that I was certain I didn't want to hear, and he didn't pick up his fork.

"She told me why she broke up with you."

"Because Sarah kept us apart."

I set my fork down. "No, because you were violent toward her."

"Once."

"Let me clue you in, Peter. Once is all it takes."

All of a sudden, it felt as if the air went out of him. "That was all I ever knew growing up." He started to slowly eat his lunch.

"I'm sorry. That had to be rough on you. But you don't have to act that way. Most people don't, you know."

He swallowed a bite. "As I've been told since then." He smiled ruefully. "Several times."

"Is there anything you want me to tell you?"

We both ate in silence for a moment, our food already cool. Then he said, "I don't suppose she's fat and shrewish and I've had a lucky escape?"

I had to smile at that. "Not even close."

"I didn't think so." After another bite, he asked, "Is she happy?"

"Yes."

He nodded as he considered my answer. We continued to eat in silence.

"Peter, did you blame Sarah enough to harm her?"

"Did I blame her? Yes. But not entirely. I've grown up a bit since then, and now I realize how much I was at fault for Celia breaking up with me. I wish Sarah had allowed me to apologize, to hear from Celia herself that we were through because of my actions, because I could never take back what I did. But Sarah took away my chance for the one thing I could have done."

He set down his fork again. "I suppose it's too late to apologize now."

I nodded as I finished my lunch. Once I swallowed, I said, "She expressed no interest in hearing from you or about you or receiving an apology. You are a sad memory to her, and that isn't going to change."

He leaned toward me and said in a low voice, "I didn't kill Sarah. No matter what you may think, I didn't see her that night nor harm her in any way."

"Where were you the night she disappeared?" I kept my

voice equally quiet.

“In Little Rowanwood. I went for a walk after dinner at the Wren and Dragon and then came back and had a pint or two and talked to George.”

“How long did you walk?”

“Not long. Twenty minutes maybe. A couple of times around the green and over to the church. It was cold and dark out, and I really didn’t want to freeze. I have witnesses for where I was the rest of the time.” Peter frowned. “One odd thing, though.”

“What was that?”

“The next night, the night after Sarah disappeared, the night when they found her body, Simon was in the pub. I know everyone has a double somewhere, but this was definitely Simon. And then Thursday he arrived as if he just came into town. But he’d already been here. I don’t understand.”

Chapter Sixteen

I didn't understand, either. "I met Simon in the train station here the day I arrived, Thursday, carrying suitcases just as I was."

"Why would he be in the Wren and Dragon one night, and then arrive for work at BP carrying his cases almost two days later?" Peter asked.

I raised my eyebrows. I needed to know the answer to his question, but I couldn't admit it or my reason for being there. "He can travel through time?"

Peter smiled, the first relaxed smile I'd seen from him that day. "A nice idea, but what I want to know is when Simon really arrived in Bletchley. And where he's staying."

"He told me with his aunt and uncle. His uncle is a vicar around here somewhere." And then I began to wonder if that was true.

"He spends a lot of time in the Wren and Dragon for being the nephew of a vicar." I could see a gleam of humor in Peter's eyes as he spoke.

"Does he eat his meals there?"

Peter shrugged. "Sometimes."

That could mean he preferred the food at the pub and the company of others his age, or it could be his aunt and uncle, if that's what they were, weren't kindly disposed toward him. "Do you know the name of his uncle's church?"

"No." Peter then looked closely at me. "You're going to check him out? The government looked into the background of everyone here. They talked to people who know us, to our professors, or friends, or families, or to our colleges. There's no reason for you to be suspicious of him."

"Then what was he doing in the Wren and Dragon two days before he arrived by train from London? You were the one who found that odd," I reminded him.

"Maybe he was visiting his aunt and uncle ahead of starting here." Peter shrugged. "Not my concern. Or yours."

"No, but we have a couple of devout churchgoers at the manor house, and I wonder if that's the church they go to. It would be interesting to hear Simon's uncle preach." Well, maybe not *interesting,* but not too painful. I'd sat through many poor sermons in my life. The Church of England didn't appoint people based on their preaching ability.

"Thanks, but I'll skip that experience," Peter said with a smile and a shake of his head. "Ready to return to work?"

"Absolutely. Friends?" I held out my hand.

"Friends." He shook my hand.

* * *

Near the end of the day, I slipped out as if heading for the facilities, but instead I hurried to the main house and the admiral's office. His secretary wasn't at her desk, so I walked to his closed door and knocked.

"Come."

I walked in to find the admiral was alone, bent over papers at his desk. He looked up in surprise to see me.

I shut the door and said, "I'd appreciate using your phone to report to Sir Malcolm."

He nodded. "Do you want me to leave?"

"No, sir. You already know my role in this from him."

"Use the secure line." He gestured toward the phone sitting at the far right-hand corner of the desk and went back to his reading.

I dialed the familiar number, a trunk system having been built when the government first came to BP so the call was a local one and scrambled. I reached Sir Malcolm almost immediately. "I see you had the sense to call me on a secure line this time," he greeted me.

Equally without preamble, I began with, "Peter Watson has a bad temper and a foul upbringing, but there are witnesses who can confirm he couldn't have killed Sarah Wycott. He lacked the time and his temper only runs hot for a few minutes. Charlie Adler had no reason to kill her, and witnesses who will show he was on the base at the time she must have been attacked."

"So, you believe we're looking for a traitor."

"One more person I need to check out first. Simon Townsend."

"No. Can't be him." Over the telephone line, it sounded

as if Sir Malcolm bit off his words.

"Why not? We know he was in Little Rowanwood the night after she was killed. Two days before he was supposed to have arrived."

"Fool. He shouldn't have let himself be seen before he was supposed to arrive." Sir Malcolm's voice growled down the line to me.

Now I understood Simon being called into the admiral's office immediately after me. "He's also attempting to find Sarah's killer. Why didn't you tell me? It would be easier if we were working together."

"I'd rather you came to your conclusions separately. We need to be certain about this if we're dealing with a traitor in the midst of the most secret facility in Britain." Sir Malcolm made another of his deep-voiced pronouncements. "We can't afford any mistakes."

"We always need to be certain about calling someone a traitor or a killer," I told him. I sounded officious to my ears, so I could imagine what Sir Malcolm made of my statement.

"This time, we not only have to be certain we have the traitor, we need to be sure we have everyone involved in their network. The secret of Bletchley Park is too important to let any word of it reach Germany or her allies."

"Are you really worried about someone giving away what we are working on here to the Nazis? It wouldn't be easy to send messages the whole way to Germany and not be seen or overheard." I didn't see how smuggling out information to the enemy during a war could be possible.

"The work you are doing is the difference between Britain surviving this war or becoming an outpost of the Third Reich. Never forget that. And there are always ways to send messages, even in a time of war." No one could make a declaration quite the same as Sir Malcolm.

"Have you found any messages going out from this area?"

"No, but we don't know what we're looking for. That's what I need you to find out. What kind of message is our traitor sending? How are they being passed along and in what form are they being sent?"

He was certain there was a traitor, but so far, I'd not seen any indication of one. "I'd imagine they're in some kind of code. We have numerous experts in codes here at BP. It could be anybody."

"Only someone who was available to kill Sarah Wycott," he reminded me.

"What had she learned?" I asked of myself more than Sir Malcolm.

"You may not know now, but nevertheless, that question should lead you into the investigation and toward the solution. Good luck." I heard a click as Sir Malcolm hung up on me.

I hadn't asked if Simon knew about me. There was only one way to find out.

Returning to Hut Six, I had barely begun work again when it was time to leave and catch the bus to Bloomington Grove. We closed up shop and walked out toward the gates in a group. I realized John hadn't given us our new schedule yet, which meant the administration hadn't decided what hours we should cover for our translation duties.

Simon climbed onto the bus ahead of me. I walked over and sat next to him. "I was speaking to a mutual friend about you."

He peered into my face and read my expression correctly. "Ten o'clock tonight. Bottom of your drive," he said quietly.

I smiled and said "Yes," despite the fear crawling up my insides that I would disappear the same as Sarah. It was hard to concentrate on anything as I walked from our stop to the servants' wing at Bloomington Grove. Dinner tasted dry and unappealing. Afterward, I found knitting on my scarf harder than ever.

"No," Maryellen said for the fourth or fifth time. "Over this way. Under this way. If you get it backward, you get knots the same way Fiona makes them in her scarves."

"No, Fiona keeps dropping stitches. Doesn't she?" Marianne said.

"She's getting knots, too," Maryellen replied, taking my knitting from my hands and unraveling it back to the error. "There, try it again," she said as she handed my project back to me. "Fiona, are you sure you don't want me helping you, too?"

"No, I'm almost done with my scarf and I intend to take it over to the WI tomorrow, errors or no errors. They give it character," Fiona said.

Marianne pursed her lips together while Maryellen giggled.

"You're a lot faster than me. I should be ready to turn mine in about the time you have your next one completed." Well, it was a polite response after Maryellen's giggles. "Will you introduce me to the WI ladies?"

"Of course," Fiona replied, her needles clicking away.

"You're almost done as well, Livvy," Marianne said. "You're doing very well for a beginner."

Aileen looked up from the navy blue knit cap she was making as she sat next to Fiona. "You are doing quite well, Livvy. Fiona, hold up your scarf for a moment."

Fiona did as she was asked for a second before lowering it again.

Maryellen set down her nearly finished sock and walked over, taking Fiona's scarf from her hands and holding it up. "Your errors are all over the place. Are you trying to make a pattern?"

Fiona snatched her scarf back. "No. This doesn't come as easily for me as it does for you and your sister." Her tone was angry, but the way she faced the other women, holding her scarf against her chest, made clear that she was hurt.

"I didn't mean to upset you, Fiona. I thought you were trying a new pattern," Maryellen said, almost sounding sincere. The way she pursed her lips to hide her smile ruined the effect.

"Well, I wasn't."

Fiona and Aileen were both glowering at Maryellen as

Rosalie came back into the room and turned on the radio. "I hope you don't mind. There's a symphony broadcast I'd like to hear."

We all assured her we didn't mind, and we continued to knit to the music of a classical orchestra as the tension in the room declined. I'd have preferred jazz, but it was Rosalie's radio. Soon, the experienced knitters clicked in time to the melody. I sounded as if I were an out-of-step drummer.

At ten o'clock, everyone was putting away their yarn.

I hurried back to get my coat and hat. "Please leave the door on the latch. I need to take a short walk to work out the kinks in my neck and back after all that knitting."

"Do you want me to go with you?" Marianne asked.

"No. I'm fine. No one would be daft enough to be out there this late." I put the door on the latch and slipped outside before anyone else could offer to accompany me.

There was enough of a moon to see a figure at the end of the drive before I reached him. I strode forward before it occurred to me that it might not be Simon.

As my steps began to falter, he called out, "Livvy?"

Recognizing his voice, I said, "Simon?"

"Let's make this fast. I'm freezing out here."

When I reached his side, I said, "Sir Malcolm is your boss?"

"Yes."

"Did you know I work for him, too?" I deliberately kept my voice low. Who knew who else was out here?

"I figured it out pretty quickly."

"Faster than I did," I admitted.

There was enough light that I could see a haughty expression on his face.

"Have you figured out who did it?" I asked.

"No. Have you?"

"No. But I seem to have eliminated everyone from a charge of treason. There seems to be another reason for their behavior."

"Including Peter?" Simon kept his voice low as he glanced around us in the dark.

"I think so."

"I agree with you." He blew on his hands. "What's your next step?"

"Trying to figure out how anyone could be passing along information."

"There are dozens of ways. Talking to tradesmen passing through the village where they reside. Newspaper adverts. Short wave radio hidden in someone's attic. Letters. The list goes on and on," Simon said.

"It does seem hopeless when attacked that way," I admitted in a whisper. "What do you suggest?"

"Watch everyone until we see them do something out of the ordinary. Talk to someone they have no business talking to."

"I wouldn't do it that way if I were a traitor," I murmured. "I'd make passing along secrets part of my routine. Such as Rosalie seeing the vicar's wife or the chauffeur when she goes home to see her husband. Such as going to the WI or up to

London for piano practice or putting on magic shows. Such as you fellows talking to locals while drinking in the Wren and Dragon."

"Why do you think I spend so much time there?"

"Your aunt and uncle really do live around here?"

"I told you. He's the vicar of St. Stephen's in Little Rowanwood," Simon told me. "He and my aunt have looked after me since my parents died."

"You were calling Sir Malcolm that night from the phone box on the village green when you told me you were ringing your parents?"

He laughed. "I told him you'd never believe me, but apparently you did. Actually, I was calling to check up on you."

"Oh, thanks." Nice to know I was a suspect.

"I suppose you did the same with me."

"I did." This was getting us nowhere, and I was chilled. "What's our next step?"

"I intend to spend time in the Wren and Dragon, and the Brick and Board in Bletchley, and see what develops. What are you going to do?" he murmured.

"Keep knitting and talking to people, particularly the ones who don't spend a lot of time in pubs."

"Let's meet at the weekend in the Wren and Dragon and see what we come up with."

"It's a date." With that, a flash of light crossed Simon's face, letting us both know someone was now outside watching us.

Before I could stop him, Simon caught me in an embrace and put his mouth close to mine. "Might as well give her a show," he whispered.

"Um," I replied, turning my head a little. "Call it a night. Let's see if I can catch her."

"Be careful." Simon let me go and I ran back toward the door. I was most of the way up the rise when I thought I saw a second flash of light around the area of the far end of the servants' wing. Had someone else come outside, or had the first person gone back in?

I sped up, hoping to discover who'd also been out in the dark. When I entered our outer door, no one was there. I locked the door and headed for my room. I heard only the soft sounds of people setting out clothes for the next day or climbing into bed. No one pounded on the front door to be let in.

Taking my key, I walked to the door facing me at the far end of the hall. I had assumed it was a broom cupboard and hadn't investigated it before, but I knew the light I'd seen had to originate from some point along this hall. When I tried the door, it was locked. Just as I was about to slide my key into the lock on the door, a voice behind me said, "You have no business being in there."

I turned to find Aileen standing, string bag of toiletries in hand and arms folded.

"What's in there?" I asked.

"None of your business, and none of mine." When I didn't walk off, she said, "Go on. You don't belong in there."

I slipped the key into my palm and walked off. “Good night, Aileen.”

“Good night.”

When I came out of my room with my own string bag of toiletries, she was still standing there, watching me.

I used the washroom to brush my teeth and then quickly readied for bed. Aileen was still in the hallway when I went back into my room. As if she were on guard duty.

Good grief. She’d be watching me now.

As I fell asleep, my last thought was, *How do I find one traitor among so many people?*

Chapter Seventeen

The next day went on as usual. A great deal of work at BP, some knitting, and some friendly chatter that gave me no insight into who our traitor and killer could be. I had no idea if anyone had listened to the conversation in the cold between Simon and me. No one mentioned seeing me kissed by another man. I was grateful for that, at least.

Sarah seemed to be fading from our thoughts as more immediate things, such as rumors of all-out war, U-boat sightings, and military call-ups for friends and family, took up our attention. And at BP, we were pressing forward as quickly as we could to crack the various Enigma codes. We couldn't mention our work anywhere at any time, not even at Bloomington Grove.

Christmas would arrive later that month, and we didn't know if anyone would get leave. I wanted to finish this assignment and get back to London before the holidays, especially if Adam might get leave to come home as the phony war continued.

I finished my frustrating scarf at nearly bedtime the night

after I'd seen the flash of light on Simon's face. While everyone was busy elsewhere, I dropped off my scarf in my room and walked to the far end of the corridor to look around. No one was behind me. Not even the suspicious Aileen.

The doors to the left and right of me led to rooms. Gwen's on the right, Maryellen's to the left. While Gwen was frequently in her room when she wasn't upstairs practicing the piano, Maryellen was constantly in the servants' hall or her sister's room.

The door straight ahead was again locked. I tried my room key on the door and found it fit. I wondered if all of our keys fit everyone else's locks as I opened the door.

Flipping a switch, I shut the door behind me and found myself in a storeroom. The brick-walled space was windowless and very cold. Vegetables and tins were stored in bins and on shelves all around the shallow space. Trunks and crates were stacked three high. A single bulb hung from the ceiling. There was a door a bit to the left on the far wall behind bins of carrots and cabbages.

I slid the bins away from the door, making a great deal of noise as I did. Then I opened the door and leaned out. Any view of the door from the drive was blocked by a row of tall evergreens that ran along the end of our wing. This area must be dark even in daylight, since the evergreens had grown together into a thick hedge along the entire end of our hallway where there were no windows. However, at night when the door was opened, the light from this room would shine through the evergreens and be seen from the drive.

I heard a sound, but before I could turn, a shove sent me flying into the evergreens and a second later, the door slammed behind me. I righted myself, brushing off evergreen twigs sticking to my jumper, and swung around to turn the door handle. It was locked. I banged on the door, again and again, but no one opened the door.

My key didn't fit this outdoor lock.

Any thought that this had been a prank, probably because I'd asked too many questions or used the bathing room at the wrong time, faded as the prankster failed to let me back in. I didn't hear any giggles coming from inside. No taunting. Nothing.

I was glad of my heavy wool jumper and skirt and the shoes I hadn't traded in for house slippers yet as I fought my way free of the imprisoning evergreens at the end of the wing. They snagged and grabbed at my clothes and my hair as I struggled against them in the dark. Once free, I hurried my way across the lawn to the door by the kitchen. It was frigid outside and I hoped someone would let me in quickly when I banged on the locked outer door.

I hugged my arms against my body and then rubbed my hands together, breathing on them for a little warmth before I banged on the door again.

Rosalie opened the door, blinking in surprise as I nearly jumped onto her in my haste to get in out of the cold. "What were you doing outside without a coat? I wish you'd told me you were going out. I almost didn't hear you over the music."

"I wasn't planning to go out. I found a second door that leads outside from this wing." Something kept me from telling the truth about what happened. Why would anyone believe someone on our hall had deliberately locked me outside? Pushed me out from a door no one had mentioned knowing about.

"I got locked out." I shivered and blew on my hands again. "I think all the keys we've been given for our rooms open all the doors on our wing. Something you might want to remember if you bring anything expensive from home."

Rosalie nodded. "Where is this door you found?"

"I'll show you."

No one was in the servants' hall or our hallway as I led Rosalie to the storage room. I imagined everyone else had gone to bed. I used my key to open the door and, in the darkness, once more reached out to flip the switch and turn on the bare lightbulb.

Not very smart of someone if they wanted me to believe I'd stumbled out on my own and was accidentally locked out, because I couldn't have then turned off the light. Fortunately, Rosalie didn't notice. Or at least didn't comment.

"It's cold enough in here. Good on Elsie for using this to store our food." Rosalie looked at the outer door. "Do you think Sarah went out this way the night she died? If she did, then she must have been meeting someone she didn't want the rest of us to know about."

"It would be one way to meet her boyfriend at the army base here, except the night she was killed she was supposed to meet him in an office through a door off the kitchen. Meeting him wouldn't have been the reason she used this door the night she died." I realized Rosalie was frowning. I'd given away that I knew more about Sarah's movements than I should have. "Did Sarah tell anyone about this door?"

Rosalie shook her head. "Not that I know of."

I mentioned the second exit the next morning as we were all trying to grab tea and toast before leaving for the bus. The other young women all denied knowing about the door off the storeroom.

"Oh, that," Betty said. "Anyone who'd been a servant here would know about it. We used it a great deal when there were parties here and loads of servants to feed. No reason to use it since the war began and the house was handed over to the government. We're not feeding that lot in the main house. Thank goodness."

"Anyone here with a relative in service at Bloomington Grove?" I asked.

Betty put a rack of toast on the table. "Gwen's the only one with a relative who ever worked at this place. Miss Ellison was your aunt, wasn't she? You seem to favor her."

"Gwen?" Maryellen said. "You had an aunt who was a maid?"

"No. An aunt who was a governess," Gwen said with a sniff. "But if she knew of any secret exits, she didn't tell me," she added before rising and picking up her plate and cup.

"How is Miss Ellison?" Betty asked. "She was a nursery maid as I remember her."

"She's well, thank you, and living with her family in the West Country." Gwen glared at the maid and stalked off to the scullery.

"She didn't want to talk about any connection to here," Maryellen said, raising her eyebrows at her sister.

No, she didn't. But did it mean anything? I couldn't see Gwen as a killer, although her hands had to be strong to be hitting keys on both the piano and the TypeX machine. "Anyone else with a link to Bloomington Grove?" I asked Betty.

"None that I know of. Of course, you found the outside door and you don't have any connection to the earl and countess or their people."

Betty had put me in my place, but she was right. There was no need to have a connection to the servants here to find the storeroom door.

After a full day's work, I grabbed my finished scarf after dinner in time to walk to the Little Bricton Women's Institute with Fiona, Aileen, Maryellen, and Marianne to hand over our knitted goods. I hadn't traveled that far before in that direction, and all I saw in the dark was hedgerows looming the same as walls until we reached the village.

The Women's Institute building was a larger bulk in the dark than the cottages, houses, and stores we walked past. If there were lights on, the blackout curtains hid them well.

When we opened the main doors, we walked into a brightly lit, large hall with a wooden floor and a high ceiling. Trestle tables and uncomfortable chairs such as we had at BP were lined up lengthwise from the door to the podium. This seemed to be the night to drop off knitted goods so that members could pack them to ship to military units. I felt safe since the room was well lighted and warm compared to the lane outside.

As we walked forward, I trailed the more experienced knitters. Marianne and Maryellen greeted a woman in her mid-thirties and started talking knitting immediately as they turned over their sizable production. Aileen stood by my side, pointing out in wearisome detail how the WI here had organized knitting night. Her collection of caps seemed paltry compared to the Allen sisters' output, but she was still far ahead of me.

A woman of about fifty walked up to Fiona and set her knitting bag on the table. "Still having trouble with those stitches, I see."

"Yes, Mrs. Hubbard, and I'm getting teased about it."

Mrs. Hubbard ran her fingers along the rows of the navy blue scarf. "It's not pretty, but it will keep one of our boys warm." She paused. "It's a good thing, Miss Carter, that you keep your wool loose, so the holes from the dropped stitches won't chill the neck of a sailor."

"I'm doing the best I can. Oh, this is Mrs. Redmond, with her very first scarf."

"Welcome, Mrs. Redmond. You have very tight stitches from holding your needles too tightly, but your work is lovely for a novice," Mrs. Hubbard told me. "Someone will appreciate this in the cold."

"Every time I make a mistake, someone rips it out and gives it back to me to try again."

"Perhaps it will help you learn how to knit," Mrs. Hubbard said with a shrug. "I'm not such a perfectionist, myself."

"That's why she's willing to take mine," Fiona said.

"I would recommend you loosen your grip on the yarn," Mrs. Hubbard said before giving me various tips on knitting faster and more easily.

The older woman then took Aileen's knitting. "You've done lovely work on these caps, Miss MacLeith. They're sure to be appreciated. And your stitches are nearly perfect."

Mrs. Hubbard was still talking when the other two women came past us. "We're walking back now," Maryellen said. "Are you coming?"

I thought of the cold, dark walk ahead. "Yes. Thank you, Mrs. Hubbard." I started toward the door, Aileen following me as she called out thanks in her soft Scottish accent.

"I'll see you next time," Fiona said to the older woman and followed us out.

We walked back along the middle of the lane, all of us hurrying to get back out of the chilly night air. I was trying to hear what Marianne said from her position a little in front of me when I became aware of an engine behind us.

I glanced back and discovered to my surprise a car was racing toward us in the dark, the headlights shielded to keep light at a minimum as ordered by blackout regulations. "Hey, there's a car...," I shouted as I stepped to the edge of the road.

We all scattered as the car roared toward us and then swerved straight at me.

Chapter Eighteen

I jumped off the road and into the hedgerow, flattening against the unyielding branches as the car brushed against my coat and slid by me.

Aileen was the only one on my side of the road. She found a gap to press into, but by then the car had turned back onto the roadway and zoomed off.

Fiona and the Allen sisters rushed over to where Aileen and I were dislodging ourselves from the hedgerow. “That was close,” Maryellen said.

“They’re crazy,” Aileen said. “They nearly hit me.” She burst into tears.

Marianne put an arm around her and began to walk her back to the house.

No. They almost hit *me*. I brushed myself off, Fiona asking if I was all right.

Could the driver see it was me he was heading toward? My coat trim was designed to reflect light. It made me more visible, since it was designed to stand out on London streets to avoid collisions between autos and pedestrians.

I was the only one with this type of coat in the group walking back to our billet, and I was the one the car was aimed at.

I was the target. Equally quickly, I knew I shouldn't say so. "Yes, I'm all right. The driver must be drunk. Or an idiot. He'll end up in a ditch if he drives that fast along these roads." I sounded angry, which I was.

Anger was all right. That didn't give away that I knew I was the target of that attack.

I needed to talk to Sir Malcolm or Simon. No one knew where I was going tonight except the girls at the house, and Betty and Elsie. And none of them had a car.

How could one of them have arranged an attack with an auto?

I was glad to reach the servants' entrance to Bloomington Grove without any more incidents. Or any more attacks. Aileen and Marianne reached the house before me, and the other women had come into the servants' hall to find out what had happened.

"Are you all right?" Rosalie asked me.

I nodded. If anyone could have arranged an attack with an auto, it would be Rosalie. And she knew my plans.

I liked her and Thorpe. I didn't want it to be her.

Gwen was too young, too innocent, to organize a lethal attempt. And Helen? She could arrange things to happen by magic, but I didn't know her well enough to judge whether she could arrange an auto accident.

That car didn't appear by magic.

Aileen was so upset, I doubted she knew about the attack ahead of time. The Allen sisters could probably run someone down with a tractor, but I had no idea where they would borrow a tractor here. Or an auto, which was what someone used.

I'd have to learn more about Fiona before I could guess at her involvement.

I knew little about Betty and Elsie, but I couldn't see either one of them involved with a car. Elsie could arrange a poisoning, I was sure, but neither woman appeared interested in our work. They were too busy caring for the earl and countess to worry about the wider world.

Nine suspects. Or an accident. I knew which one Sir Malcolm would favor. What would Simon say?

By the next morning, Aileen was over her shock but she was now telling everyone about her close call. Betty and Elsie, who'd have gone upstairs before the incident, tut-tutted. Our colleagues on the bus sympathized.

Simon moved to sit next to me. "Were you hurt?"

I glanced back to make sure the seat behind us was empty as well as the one in front. "Missed me by a hair."

He raised his brows.

I lowered my voice. "Came off the road to miss me by what felt the same as a breath. It brushed against my coat. Maybe it was a warning. I don't know."

He put his arm around my shoulders and snuggled up next to me. "Identify the car?" he murmured.

"It was dark down that lane. A sedan, maybe. No idea of

color."

"Any idea who was driving? Or who called them?" His breath was warm in my ear. I wished he were Adam.

"None. Only nine people knew where I was going and when. I can't see any of them being behind this."

Simon studied me for a minute, our noses nearly touching as I turned to look at him. "Are these the nine people who were closest to the scene when Sarah was murdered?"

I felt all the blood drain from my head. He was thinking the same thing I was.

"Are you all right?" he asked.

I took a deep breath. "Yes." Then I whispered, "You are correct."

"Can you move out of Bloomington Grove? It's not safe."

"It would look too suspicious. Plus, I'm there to find a killer. It's the best place I could be. Especially since I was pushed out of the back door and locked out the night before."

"Who did it?"

"I don't know. But now I know someone found the secret exit to our wing. Or the secret entrance behind the evergreens, if necessary."

"You're brave. That's good, but don't do anything too risky. You know you're the target of a killer now."

"No, I don't." I looked him in the eye and shook my head slightly. "Without suspecting anyone, there is no reason to believe I've frightened a killer into attacking me."

"Did Sarah suspect someone?"

"We think she must have, but no one has any idea who."

He took his arm away from the back of the seat as we pulled up to the gate at BP. "Look at me adoringly. It's our best cover."

We were going to scandalize some of our colleagues, but he was right. It was our best cover, and our best way to pass messages back and forth without being overheard.

However, all I managed to give him was a weak smile. We all filed off the bus and through the gates, showing our passes. Another day of decoding and deciphering Nazi messages had begun.

John called the now six women in our room together. In addition to Rosalie, Gwen, Aileen, and myself, we now had a Maeve and a Katie, both of whom were billeted in houses on the other side of Bletchley. We pulled our chairs close around where he sat.

"This is good news, but it'll mean you will all have to work harder. You are not to discuss this news with anyone, either working in this hut or elsewhere. We want this kept to the smallest number of people possible for as long as we can."

We all nodded, most of us looking puzzled.

"While you all slept, Rosalie came in last night to work on some new settings. Two of our mathematicians went to France over the weekend to check on some information from the Polish codebreakers. On the basis of that, they broke into a new code last night. Rosalie demonstrated the settings led to messages in German."

We all patted Rosalie on the back, saying nothing more

than a whispered "Well done."

"After this meeting, Rosalie is going back to her billet for some well-earned sleep. The rest of you will hopefully be doing a great deal of deciphering today." He paused. "Now for the bad news. You'll have to alternate weekends while we get more German linguists in. We expect on the basis of this breakthrough to have a great deal more work to do. A breakthrough you are not to mention to anyone. Even anyone else working in Hut Six."

"Can't you use some of the women from the Registration Room?" Aileen asked. "They could help cover the weekends."

"They don't speak German. That's why they're in the Registration Room where you don't need any language but English, while you women who work here in the Decoding Room need German to do your jobs," John explained to all of us. "No more questions? Good. Remember, don't mention any of this."

I found I was certain that John now thought there was a strong possibility that a traitor worked in this hut among the female staff. He'd been put in the picture by the admiral or Sir Malcolm. Did he know the role Simon and I were playing?

If he knew my dual assignment, he hid it well.

If the traitor was among us, and the killer was one of the residents of Bloomington Grove, what had triggered the attack by automobile the night before? What had I heard? What had I seen?

Could it possibly be Betty or Elsie spying for the earl and countess and broadcasting on a shortwave radio above our heads? Perhaps Betty or even the earl had taken out their auto last night. No one would have thought anything of it. The car was theirs. The garage was theirs, outside the boundaries of the army camp and not visible from the house.

I tried to remember what I'd heard about the earl and countess's political leanings, but all I could recall were the tales of their fabulous parties. From the mid-1930s and continuing until last summer, there were photos in the press of glittering soirees at Bloomington Grove. I had been fascinated by the fashionable gowns worn by the guests.

But who were the guests? Were there any politicians present?

And then I remembered a photo that made the back page of one of the racier newspapers. The earl and countess were greeting their guest of honor, the German ambassador to the Court of St. James, Count von Ribbentrop, who came attired in his German military uniform decorated with swastika emblems.

Were they merely determined to give the most talked-about parties, or were they, the same as so many of the aristocracy, smitten with Hitler?

Chapter Nineteen

With Rosalie back at Bloomington Grove sleeping, I went on the late lunch shift by myself. I was surprised to see George join me as he sat in a wobbly chair across the table from me. After all, my presence had caused a small tear in his relationship with Peter.

"You seem to have turned Simon's head," he said before he dug into his lunch. Today it was a pie with gravy and vegetables and mushrooms, but no meat. At least not in my serving.

"He's just being sympathetic to my nearly being run over last night," I replied and continued with my lunch.

"He's smitten."

"Hardly."

"He's been watching you since he first arrived. You do realize that, don't you?"

I looked at him in surprise. "Really?" Had he known from the beginning I worked for Sir Malcolm, too?

Or was George determined to cause trouble among the staff in Hut Six to slow down our decryption work against the

Nazis? Could he possibly be the traitor? I didn't see how he could have tricked Sarah into coming outside to kill her.

"Everyone's noticed." Then he yawned behind his hand. "Sorry. It was a late night last night."

"I think I heard. Were you working with Rosalie?"

"Yes."

I smiled. "Good work."

"Thanks." He yawned again.

"Patch everything up with Peter? I heard about your argument last Saturday night," I told him.

"It was much of nothing. I consider you a friend, Livvy, and I don't want to hear Peter complaining about perfectly nice people." George shrugged and took another bite of his lunch.

"Found a way to get messages to your girlfriend?" I asked.

"Yes." He smiled. "It's not entirely legal, but it won't do any harm."

"What do you have in mind?" I remembered him saying how they'd used shortwave before. What did he have in mind now?

"That would be telling." He smiled. "I sent a letter to a friend who passed it on to her. We're all set. I can hardly wait to hear from her again."

"Don't get into trouble," I warned.

He continued to smile.

Peter came over and sat down with us, a cup of coffee in his hand. "I heard what happened to you last night."

"You mean someone trying to turn me into a bonnet ornament?" I asked.

"You do have a bad habit of annoying people."

"Oh, I don't think my charming personality had anything to do with it. Probably some drunk, or someone who can't see in the dark," I told him.

"We can hope it isn't a vendetta against BP. First Sarah, now you." Peter took a gulp of coffee. "Just when we're getting somewhere."

"Don't say that to anyone, even in here," I warned him. "Just in case."

His expression turned serious. "There is something to this."

"Maybe," I admitted. I hurried to tell him, "We've been told not to mention anything about improved decoding to anyone, not even anyone in our hut. I think the brass are getting suspicious."

Peter nodded. He seemed to have begun to wonder if there was a problem at BP.

George, on the other hand, laughed. "Just a lot of bad luck," he said.

"Probably. In that case, the next car will try to run someone else down. Maybe you," Peter said. His smile looked a tad evil.

"Must you always be so awful-minded?" George asked. "But you can't ruin my good mood today. I'm going to hear from Anthea. I'll see you later," he said to me and walked off.

I grinned at Peter. "You've annoyed him."

"He deserves it. Do you need Simon and me to keep watch over you?"

"I take it you don't believe Simon is madly in love with me?" I said quietly.

"Not for a moment," he murmured. "What's going on?"

"I can't tell you. Official secrets and all that. But it would be helpful if you kept your eyes open."

"For what?"

"I wish I knew. That's the problem. Anything that doesn't look right."

"Anything inexplicable?"

"Exactly."

Peter nodded. "I'll keep watch." Then in a louder voice, he said, "Ready to go back to work?"

"One more forkful." I quickly finished eating. "Let's go."

We walked back to Hut Six. When we got there, Fiona and Maryellen came out of the Registration Room where they worked, receiving and logging in the intercepted German Morse code messages that arrived from the various listening posts. "We've heard you made a breakthrough," Maryellen said.

"While I was at lunch? Oh, that's good news," I said, looking at them as if waiting for information.

"No. Last night," Fiona said.

"I'm late getting back to work," Peter said and walked off, leaving me with the two women.

"Not that anyone has told me," I said and walked off to the Decoding Room.

How had Fiona and Maryellen heard? Were they listening outside our room when John was talking that morning? Did it mean anything that they were so interested? Or was someone talking in defiance of John's warning?

The success we were having in deciphering some of our messages made the afternoon busier, so time sped by. I never thought to call Sir Malcolm and tell him about the car aimed at me until it was too late. The bus to Bloomington Grove wouldn't wait for me as everyone else was hurrying to climb aboard.

I just needed to be careful until I gave him a call with my suspicions.

We returned to our billet without incident and soon sat down to a porridge supper flavored with honey. It was so tasty, hot, and filling that none of us complained about the simple fare, although Elsie said she couldn't fix us anything more involved since she'd spent the afternoon making little savories to tempt the "poor earl's" appetite.

After dinner, Rosalie turned on the second evening news broadcast while most of us pulled out our knitting. Gwen went upstairs to practice, and I had no idea where Helen had gone.

I actually was able to cast on my second scarf and began the first row to cheers at my success. "Mrs. Hubbard said I need to hold my yarn looser," I told them. "It should make my scarf warmer."

"She's right," Marianne said.

"That's something we've been trying to point out since

the beginning," Maryellen said. "Why are you listening to Old Mother Hubbard and not us?"

"'Old Mother Hubbard'?" I asked.

"A nickname Maryellen gave her," Aileen said, looking annoyed.

"She tends to give advice, whether we need it or not," Marianne said. I could now see the difference in temperament between the "almost twins." She was more placid, while Maryellen was the bossy one.

That made me wonder if Maryellen's more forceful personality was the reason she'd asked about the breakthrough in deciphering the Enigma code made by the men in the Cottage and in the Machine Room. I hoped it wasn't because she wanted to send a message to the Germans. I couldn't believe Maryellen was involved in espionage while Marianne wasn't. And I couldn't believe Marianne was a traitor.

As I knitted, I considered the women sitting around me. Rosalie had been on her own that day after working the previous night on the newly decipherable messages. Fiona and Maryellen had wanted to know what we'd accomplished based on what they'd heard.

And the rest of them? Helen kept to herself, perhaps concerned about this weekend's magic show. Gwen was so wrapped up in practicing the piano that she didn't seem to be totally in the real world. Aileen was deeply religious—and judgmental.

What about Elsie and Betty? Elsie had already gone

upstairs for the night. Betty called out, “Everyone in for the night?”

Several of us called back, “Yes.”

“The door is now locked. Goodnight.” We heard her slow, steady climb up the stairs.

The news ended—I was glad to hear nothing of importance—and a classical music program began. We continued to knit, and one by one the women in our billet headed off to bed. I was one of the last ones in the main room since I had begun to find the repetitive movements of my hands relaxing. I was holding the yarn looser, too.

I was thinking I could keep up this new hobby when I heard a knock on the door. Rosalie, the only other person up with me as she listened to the end of the BBC concert, raised her eyebrows.

Opening the door, I found Simon standing on the tiny porch.

I turned toward the servants’ hall. “Rosalie, could you wait a few minutes to make certain no one locks me out?”

She nodded.

“I’ll get my coat,” I told Simon and rushed off to retrieve it.

In a minute, I had on my outerwear and stepped outside. “What is it?”

Simon led me away from the house. When he must have felt we were far enough away, he stopped and whispered, “They picked up shortwave activity around here earlier tonight.”

"Morse code?"

He nodded.

"In German?"

"In code," he told me, raising his eyebrows. "They're thinking of moving all our work elsewhere."

"They..." I came close to shouting before I dropped my voice to a murmur. "They can't do that. It will give away that we know someone is a traitor. If they change anything, we'll never be able to catch the guilty parties. And the killer."

"The decision is being made far above our heads."

Simon was right, but still... "We have to stop them. If we want to catch the entire spy ring, we have to stay here and let them show themselves."

"How will they show themselves?" Simon sounded as if he didn't believe me.

"I don't know—yet. Oh, blast," I added as I saw a flash of light on Simon's face again. "Whoever it is, they just came out the hidden exit again." I took off, racing up the drive.

Letting myself in the regular entrance, I locked the door behind me.

Rosalie glanced up. "The program just ended. I'll see you in the morning."

"Did anyone else go out?"

"No."

I had seen that flash of light from someone exiting the wing we lived in. There was no other source. "Are you sure?"

"Yes," she replied. "Livvy, what is it?"

In response, I rushed down the hallway and unlocked the

storeroom. The light was off. I flipped the switch and saw no one was hiding among the bins and trunks.

I closed up the storeroom and found Rosalie in the hall behind me. "Nothing." I shook my head. "Just my imagination. I'll see you in the morning."

We walked slowly back to the servants' hall. Rosalie turned off the radio, we doused the lights, and then headed for bed. One thing was certain. Someone speedy was using the other way out of the servants' wing of Bloomington Grove with some frequency.

All I had to do was catch the person spying on me.

The flaw to my logic was whoever was spying on me was not necessarily the killer. More than one person could have found this exit, especially since I asked if anyone knew about it.

I had checked, but no one had been hiding in the storeroom. I went to bed that night feeling frustrated, and not just from missing Adam.

The next morning followed the usual routine. Eight young women rushing around, trying to dress for work and eat breakfast before hurrying down to the lane to reach the stop for the BP bus before it arrived. Everyone knew the driver wouldn't wait for anyone.

I took a sip of tea and said, "I saw a light from the storeroom exit again last night. Someone is using that way nightly to get out."

"We all told you we didn't know anything about any hidden exits," Fiona said. "Do you want that piece of toast?"

With extra chatter about Christmas, we had to run to the stop. The bus picked us up before it stopped in the village and the men climbed aboard. After they nodded to everyone, Simon and Peter sat together, discussing the finer points of darts play.

I'd have to find a time to speak to Simon alone.

It was Friday, so perhaps we could put our heads together at the Wren and Dragon after work. I guessed the women of Bloomington Grove would stop there on the bus instead of continuing home, and that would give us our chance.

I turned to Rosalie, who was looking out the window glumly. "Look at the bright side," I said. "You can go to the Wren and Dragon with us tonight."

"That's the bright side?" She glowered at me.

"It's the only bright side I could think of. I meant well. Sorry."

"Oh, Livvy, you are amazing." I did see a hint of a smile at the corners of her mouth. "Isn't there a telephone box in the village?"

"In the green near the Wren and Dragon."

"I can always use my change to call Thorpe before you buy me a pint." Then she did smile.

"That works." I smiled back. "Since we're both working this weekend, we can stop there every night on our way home and I'll wait while you call home, if you'd like."

"I'd like that. Thank you."

I was glad to see Rosalie looking less morose by the time

we reached the gates of BP.

The morning didn't go well. The messages we received from the listening stations had breaks in them, rendering the words totally indecipherable. "The weather over the channel last night messed up communications," John said. "I hope for everybody, and not just Britain."

We did the best we could, guessing what word or words might be missing and then trying them out against any parts of the message we could decipher.

It was nearly noon when John came over and said softly, "The admiral wants to see you."

What mistake had I made now, I wondered. I threw on my hat and gloves, my coat staying on in the cold room all morning, and ran to the main building through what was now a chilly downpour.

I shook myself off in the front doorway and walked into the room where the admiral's secretary sat. Without a word, she rose and opened the door to his office for me. I walked in to find the admiral sitting behind his desk—and Sir Malcolm leaning against one of the paneled walls.

"Why didn't you tell me?" he asked.

Chapter Twenty

"Tell you what, sir?" I couldn't resist aggravating him.

"About your little accident the night before last," Sir Malcolm growled.

"You've heard that the auto was aimed right at me, away from the other women?"

"Not necessarily. You'd have all just been moving shadows to the driver."

I peeled off my gloves and unbuttoned and took off my coat. "See this trim?" I held up the skirt of my coat. "It reflects any bit of light that might be available. This has cut down on the number of auto and pedestrian accidents in London by quite a lot since the blackout began. Helen Preston, being from London, has this on her coat, too, but she doesn't go to Little Bricton to the WI on knitting night."

"So you were the only one in the roadway when this car came along that has that fancy material on your coat?"

"Yes. Making me a good target," I added ruefully.

"I must warn my agents not to put that fabric on their outer clothes if they're working. It would make it hard for them to follow anyone using stealth in the dark." Sir Malcolm sounded as if the whole incident was my fault.

There was no point in saying anything else about Wednesday night. "We've learned more since then." I took off my hat and sat across from the admiral.

I waited, but Sir Malcolm was willing to wait even longer for me to speak. I gave up and said, "Monday night, Simon came over at ten. Only Rosalie was there to see me go out, but a minute or two later, we saw a flash of light from our wing from an opened door. Someone left, presumably to watch us, and Rosalie said no one went past her. The next night, I found a second exit from our hall that would have allowed Sarah's killer to come and go without anyone being the wiser."

Sir Malcolm stared at me for a moment, considering. "How did you explain Simon's arrival?"

"No one knew it was Simon. And when he saw the light, he tried to kiss me, hiding behind me." I wasn't certain if I was more or less annoyed because he did it to cover his face.

"That was a good way to hide his identity," Sir Malcolm said solemnly with a nod.

"Everyone there knows I'm married, and no one has mentioned seeing anything. We have a couple of women who are devout and would say something if they'd seen me kissing another man. Any other man."

"So, you would rule them out as your peeping Tom."

"Yes, sir, I would."

"This weekend, you need to search that hidden exit and

look for any clues."

I nodded. "It's very close to the spot where I found Sarah's bracelet by the bushes. Also, Simon told me there was a burst of shortwave traffic close to Bloomington Grove last night. Unexplained shortwave traffic."

"There was. The night after you were nearly run down. Do you know any reason why?" He studied me for a minute, waiting for an explanation. When I didn't respond, he said, "Is there any connection?"

"The only one I can think of is that someone has figured out my role here and tried to eliminate me. When the first attempt failed, they've followed this by asking for instructions on how to proceed."

"They know how to proceed," Sir Malcolm said. "No reason to ask for directions. If they know the real reason why you're here, they need to kill you."

That was not something I wanted to hear. "So why did they send out a shortwave message? Was it in code?"

"In code, yes, but not an Enigma code. It was quite long, as if conversing in Morse code, and we could pick up both ends of the transmission. We should be able to break it soon. In the meantime, be careful."

I didn't want to be killed before Adam and I even had our first fight as a married couple. Or our twenty-fifth wedding anniversary. "How would someone have figured out I had another reason to be here besides translating messages sent by the Germans using the Enigma codes? We've all been cautioned not to say anything to anyone."

"I can assure you no one heard anything from my secretary or myself," the admiral said. "No one else here should know anything about your special status. It has to be in your section, Sir Malcolm."

"That would mean either Simon or Olivia herself." Sir Malcolm stared at me.

"No, we're not fools. But having me pulled out of the office repeatedly to see the admiral would make a spy curious. It would me."

"Would you rather I had them send for you to see me?" Sir Malcolm asked.

"No." That was the only thing worse. There had to be a better solution.

Then I had another thought. "What if the message has nothing to do with the attempt on my life? They broke into a big German army code late Wednesday night or early Thursday morning. Maybe the spies found out and told Germany the good news."

"Hardly good for them," Sir Malcolm said, breathing out hard.

"But it would mean very good intelligence by their spies."

"Is it possible the spy is a servant for the earl and countess? If one of you let something slip, or even if you talked in your sleep. How thick are the walls in your section?"

"Not terribly thick, but the construction is good. I doubt you could overhear anything through a door or a wall. I don't think it's the maid or the cook. They are more interested in getting done with their duties and going upstairs to their rooms," I said.

"You don't think they'd come back down?"

"No, sir. You can hear the cook going up and down the stairs— it's painful for her—and the maid is run ragged all day by the earl and countess. By evening, she doesn't have much energy left for sneaking downstairs."

"As I see it, between knowing that you were walking along that lane and what is going on here, there are only ten people who could be the killer, and therefore probably the spy."

"Ten?" I asked.

"The eight of you living there and the two servants."

He was including me. "Thanks." Then I added, "I've narrowed it down to seven. The shortwave radio isn't at Bloomington Grove, because you would have found it faster if it were. Now we have to figure out which of the people here at BP is talking to someone in the area without attracting any attention."

"It can't be your billeting family, since we've ruled out the earl, the countess, and the servants," the admiral said. "The army has had the Haymarkets under surveillance since they set up camp in Bloomington Grove."

None of us had seen, much less spoken to, our hosts, except Gwen when she practiced the piano. "I guess you check on the drivers?" I asked. We saw them daily.

"Yes, and the dining room staff and the messengers and the guards," the admiral said.

"A couple of the women go to church every Sunday, and

we see the women of the Women's Institute to hand in our knitting for the troops," I told him.

Sir Malcolm shook his head. "We don't have the manpower to check out entire congregations or the membership of the Buckinghamshire WI. We'll need something more concrete before we begin checking on anyone. Now, if there's nothing else?"

I took the hint and put on my outer clothes for the nasty walk back to Hut Six. "I'll see what I can find out. Especially concerning use of that second exit."

Sir Malcolm gave a single nod and said, "Send in Simon, will you?"

I found Simon in the hallway outside the dining room talking to Fiona. "What are you two scheming?" I asked with a smile.

"We're talking about a bit of a party at the Wren and Dragon tonight," Simon said and then asked, "Is he free?" meaning the admiral.

I nodded. "What's the occasion?"

"Does there have to be one?" Fiona asked as Simon walked into the secretary's office.

"I guess not. Count me in," I said. "Were you busy arranging parties wherever your pub was before you came here?"

"Portsmouth. Before the war, sailors had a lot more freedom in the town than they do now. We could get a party going in Dad's pub nearly every night."

"Sounds as if it'd be fun."

"It is. My father's pub was always a fun place. Music and darts and singalongs. It was a great place to live. And then the war came. A commander who is friends with my father suggested I apply here for a job doing war work." She gave me a smile. "So now I'm organizing parties at the Wren and Dragon."

"How do your parents feel about you being away from home and not working in the family business?"

"Oh, Dad's fine with it. Mom's not with us anymore."

"I'm sorry."

"Don't be. It was her choice to leave us."

"Then I'm really sorry."

"Mom's much happier now. And I'm glad for her."

I decided every family was weird in its own way. "Is your father's pub, the—?"

"The Anchor and Pelican."

"The Anchor and Pelican, quite similar to the Wren and Dragon?"

"Aren't all pubs similar?" she asked. "My lunch break must be over by now." We headed for the entrance, Fiona putting up her umbrella as we ran.

We dashed into the entrance of Hut Six, slipping slightly on the linoleum that covered every inch of the floor of the building. Fiona went into the first room on the left, one of the Registration Rooms, while I continued to the Decoding Room in the back.

"Everything all right?" John asked as I nodded and sat at my desk to begin typing the next message into the machine.

I watched as the letters appeared on the tape coming out of the machine. The words were in German.

One station told another the weather was foggy.

I hoped it was useful to our military. All I could think was, *Maybe the Nazis will all get lost in the fog.*

After a short time, Rosalie and I were sent to get lunch.

"I've been thinking about your suggestion to call Thorpe tonight from Little Rowanwood, and I think it's a good one. That way he'll know why I'm not coming home this weekend, although my letter should have reached him by now. And he'll get to hear my voice," Rosalie said as she sat across from me at the table.

"Don't forget, you'll get to hear his voice," I added.

She smiled. "There is that benefit." She tasted our lunch of the day, soup, and set down her spoon. "I'm sorry, I'm going on about my problems and you don't know where your husband is."

"It may be better not knowing." It would stop the worst of my worrying. I suspected Adam, with his espionage work, went to other countries and even slipped behind enemy lines. Unless he was tracking traitors within Britain, which could be just as dangerous.

"I hope you hear from him soon," Rosalie told me.

"If he's written, the letters are going to our flat in London, and I won't know until the next time I go home." There was the possibility that Adam was spending a weekend of rare leave at our flat and didn't know where I was. "I think I may telephone the flat tonight just on the off chance he got a bit of leave."

And I would be thrilled if he answered the telephone. I hadn't heard his voice in ages. That was a strong indication that he was out of the country.

"So, we'll both place trunk calls, and maybe we'll both have good luck," Rosalie said.

"And then we'll join the party at the Wren and Dragon," I said.

"They're having a party?" Rosalie asked in confusion.

"That's what Simon and Fiona said. They're both daft."

"What's the occasion?"

"According to Fiona, you don't need one." I shrugged. "I won't see the point of a party until the war is over and Adam is safely home."

"Thorpe says the same thing about me. He does worry so." Rosalie swallowed another spoonful of soup and made a face. "I've been trying to eat this quickly so I wouldn't taste it."

I set my spoon down. "It tastes burnt."

Rosalie nodded with a sigh, no doubt thinking of the wonderful meals being served at her manor house. "I hope dinner tonight is good."

"It usually is," I told her. After all, we had an earl's cook.

As usual, the time spent in our office went quickly, and soon it was time to leave for the evening. "Rosalie and Olivia, you have duty this weekend," John reminded us.

"Are any of the other women working tomorrow?" I asked.

"Maryellen and Marianne," John replied.

"There'll be four of us at the bus stop tomorrow. They shouldn't forget us," Rosalie said.

"We can hope." As Rosalie's mood lifted, mine sank. Adam might arrive home after I tried to call the flat. He might go out for something to eat after seeing the note I'd left on the table, not knowing I would try to telephone. He might be running a bath and not hear the phone over the running water.

The odds were against me, but I'd try to telephone. And then I'd be miserable all weekend.

We all climbed off the bus near the Wren and Dragon except for Gwen and Aileen. Rosalie and I headed for the telephone box while the rest went into the pub.

I let Rosalie call first.

While she was inside, I could hear muffled talking, so I paced around the edge of the green. A dogwalker went past with a medium-sized mongrel and we exchanged greetings. The dog's wagging tail was the last thing to disappear into the darkness.

Rosalie continued to talk. She must have found a source of coins for the telephone from somewhere in BP that day. I heard her laugh and knew things were good at her house.

A bit of jealousy flashed through me. If Adam made it through the war safely, he'd be whole, while Thorpe would still be in a wheeled chair. After the war, Rosalie might be jealous of me.

Or I might end up a widow, and I knew I'd be jealous of

her since Thorpe would still be alive.

Her conversation went on for what felt as if it were a great deal longer, but was probably only a couple of minutes, before she said good-bye as she opened the door to the taped-glass and red metal-framed booth.

"Thank you," Rosalie said as she came out. "Thorpe is sounding much more cheerful now that we've talked."

"So are you."

"I am, aren't I?" She smiled at me.

"Wish me luck," I said as I stepped in and shut the door.

I slipped my coins in the slot and waited for the operator's voice. I gave her the number, she told me what to do for a trunk call, and I followed her directions. Then I could hear the telephone ring.

The telephone was answered on the second ring. I heard Adam's voice, far off, recite our number.

I screamed "Adam!"

"Livvy! Where are you?"

"I have to work this weekend. Out of town."

"How far out?"

"About an hour." It was against regulations, but I didn't care. "Buckinghamshire."

There was a slight pause. Then Adam's voice, sounding puzzled. "What are you doing at BP? Is this for Sir M?"

Chapter Twenty-One

"Yes," I told Adam in a loud voice, certain I sounded as faint as he did to me over the trunk line.

"I'll be there tomorrow when you get off work. What time?"

"You know you can't get in there."

"We can at least go out to dinner when you get off. What time?"

"Six." I was so excited I did a sort of hop inside the telephone box.

"I'll wait for you at the front gate."

We barely had time to say good-bye before we ran out of time on my coins. I bounded out of the glass enclosure and ran straight into Rosalie.

"You spoke to him?" she asked.

"He guessed where I was. He's coming out here tomorrow to take me to dinner. I'll get to see him." I threw back my head and laughed.

"I can see we'll get no work out of you tomorrow," Rosalie said in mock seriousness.

The flash of light as the door to the Wren and Dragon opened reminded me of the flash of light on Simon's face. "You're more familiar with old mansions than the rest of us. Had you guessed there was a second door to get out of our wing of the old manor house?"

"I wasn't surprised. The place is two or three hundred years old. Have you asked Betty if anyone has helped carry supplies in and out of there for Elsie? Betty's lived there a long time, and she's aware of what goes on, the way any good servant is." Then Rosalie smiled. "Planning on smuggling your husband into your room?"

My room barely had enough room for me. At least she drew the conclusion I wanted her to. "Would I do that?" More along the lines of slipping out of my room without anyone seeing me. As Sarah Wycott had.

"Please don't say anything," I added. "I don't want to spend all my time with Adam introducing him to everyone."

* * *

It would be cold in the hut during the weekend and if Adam managed to obtain a hotel room, I wouldn't have room for more than my toothbrush, a comb, and a lipstick in my handbag. I put on my heaviest tweed skirt and pulled on a heavy jumper over my blouse before I went to breakfast.

Time dragged. What felt more than an hour to me was only a minute on the clock. I'd had no luck in catching Betty alone either that night or the next morning. We did nothing of any use in the Decoding Room, at least of no use that I could see, as we tried setting after setting with no luck. And I wouldn't see Adam until six in the evening.

At least Rosalie kept her word. She didn't tell anyone about Adam coming to Bletchley.

True to his word, Adam was waiting outside the gates in the cold and dark at six that evening. I told Rosalie I'd see her later and rushed over to jump into his arms as if I were a giddy schoolgirl.

"I booked us into a room at the Green Donkey for the night. I only have forty-eight hours of leave, so I have to be back by three tomorrow afternoon," Adam said when we both came up for air.

"Booked us?"

"Yes. You don't mind, do you?"

"Not at all. I can stay in Bletchley tonight. And that gives us more time together than just dinner." The joy in my smile must have been evident to everyone around me. However, it was dark out and the only person who could see the happy glow on my face was Adam. And he was the only one who mattered.

"It's not the Ritz, but it'll do." Adam glanced over at the bus, the engine running and the headlamps on, although shielded. "What's he doing here?"

I was close enough to make out Adam's scowl. "Who?"

"Simon Townsend."

I looked where he was staring and saw Simon walk out of the light of the headlamps toward the door of the bus. "Do you know him?"

"More than I want to." He put an arm around my

shoulders. “Let’s get out of here.”

We started to walk toward the train station. “Why don’t you like Simon?” I asked, turning my head toward him and lowering my voice.

“Why? Do you?”

“He’s working for Sir Malcolm. Which means I need to work with him.”

“Be wary of Townsend.” We reached the train station, and I could see in the dim light that Adam was outraged. “I can’t believe Sir Malcolm was foolish enough to keep him on. Good grief. Doesn’t he talk to General Alford?”

I knew General Alford was the army’s equivalent of Sir Malcolm, their counterintelligence chief, but I doubted he was as ruthless as Sir Malcolm. “Why?”

There were people walking around in the station and even more on the pavement as we walked past the station into the town.

Adam shook his head and continued down the main street. “Maybe we can find a good restaurant.” Then he looked down. “What is that on your coat?”

I swung around so he could see the reflective strip on the skirt of my coat. “I had this sewn on in London. It cuts down on traffic accidents in the blackout.”

“Good. I want you to stay safe.” He pulled me in close to his side.

After all the time we’d spent apart since the war began over three months before, my heart was fluttering to finally be this close to Adam.

We found an adequate restaurant. I was so happy to be spending time with Adam I didn't notice the food. We basked in each other's company while we ate quietly and gazed into each other's eyes.

It was too cold and too dark to stroll through the streets of the little town. We hurried back to the Green Donkey, and finding the bar a working-class place, went into the snug. Adam got us each a pint of ale and we sat at an old scarred table in the corner.

There was another couple in the snug, as wrapped up in each other as we were. We nodded to each other and then turned our attentions to our partners.

I murmured into Adam's ear, "Are you going to tell me about Simon?"

"Not here."

"I can't tell you what I'm working on."

He nodded.

"I can tell you we had a colleague murdered near my billet a couple of weeks ago."

Adam raised his eyebrows. Considering earlier investigations I had been mixed up with at the spymaster's direction, Adam must have guessed that was the reason I was here. "Why was she killed?"

"No one knows. Yet."

"But Sir Malcolm has a guess."

"Yes. Which is why I want to know about Simon. He's involved with this, too." We were talking in circles around what we really wanted to say, not wanting anyone else to pick up on our conversation.

"Tonight. It'll make a great bedtime story." His voice was filled with sarcasm.

He wouldn't say anything else about Simon. He did tell me my father "sends his regards." That was as warm as anything my father said to me.

We drank up and went up the narrow stairs to where our room was located. It was small, located under the eaves, and cold. But we had plenty of blankets and each other. This was the first time we'd been together practically since the war began, and we didn't notice the chill.

Eventually, snuggled under the blankets before we went to sleep, I asked again about Simon.

"This was an operation I was on in October." We were so close Adam was practically whispering in my ear. Which was fine with me. "We found a German spy and took him into custody, very quietly, while sending out erroneous information with his code."

He shifted closer to me. "We convinced him to help us and things were going well until Simon led a separate group in to arrest him in a most public manner. Told reporters his work had saved countless British lives and made us all safer, while in truth he destroyed a way we had to confuse the enemy. The Germans then knew their spy's cover was blown and not to believe anything else we sent them from him."

I don't know why I felt the need to be fair to Simon. "He's not the first person to say the wrong thing to a reporter and have them blow the whole thing out of proportion."

"When he first collared this man, I told Simon to keep quiet, that he was our asset. That we were using him for counterespionage. His response? 'Too bad, old chap. He's mine, now.' And he just barged ahead, making sure the papers knew, trying to make a name for himself."

No wonder Adam was angry. "Maybe he didn't understand you were using this German to help Britain."

"He understood, all right. He's determined to make a name for himself. Don't trust him, Livvy. He'll use anyone and anything for his own advancement." He yawned widely. "Good night, my beauty." He shifted a little in the bed, and in a moment he was snoring.

I was still awake. Life was easier when I thought I could trust Simon to help me find Sarah's killer because it was important. Now I had to worry about him taking shortcuts and coming up with the wrong person, or endangering others in our wing of the manor house in his search for a killer who'd struck once already.

As I fell asleep, I wondered how he got involved in counterespionage if he had been a Cambridge mathematics lecturer before the war.

When we finally rose and I was dashing madly about our room to get ready to return to BP on Sunday morning, I asked Adam how Simon got his start working in Adam's field.

"I don't know. I know he's trying very hard not to come to the attention of the military. I guess he went to Sir Malcolm and volunteered. Anyone working at Bletchley or for Sir M are automatically safe from the draft board." Adam pulled on his clothes. "Do you have time for breakfast?"

"Not even a cup of tea." I gave him a hug and a kiss. "It was so good to spend some time with you."

"Give me a minute and I'll walk up to your work with you."

"Don't dawdle." I softened as I watched him tie his shoes. "I love you, Adam."

"I love you, Liv." He pulled on his coat, swung me around in a hug, and we started out.

The bus I normally rode to BP pulled in just as we reached the front gates from the other direction.

Simon glanced over at me, a smile freezing on his face when he spotted Adam. He nearly knocked over some woman I didn't know in his rush to get inside the gates and away from us.

I looked at Adam. "What was that about?"

He grinned. "I may have threatened to knock his block off the next time I saw him. Glad he took me seriously."

"Don't tell me I married a bully." I grinned up at him.

"No. Someone who doesn't enjoy seeing others mistreated. Especially when they've been convinced to help Britain against the Nazis."

I stared into Adam's eyes, wondering at the stern way he spoke.

He murmured into my ear. "The German and our people had made a deal. He wouldn't have been too comfortable, but he wouldn't have been in a dungeon. That was a part of why he agreed to work with us. And he was truly being useful.

Then Simon came along. The German's in a secure prison now, and you know he won't help us again, while Simon got a promotion from some stuffy Home Office type and a safe position here."

"I'm sorry, Adam."

"Don't be. It's not your fault." He gave me a quick hug and a kiss on the forehead. "Everyone's gone in. You'd better get a move on."

"Will you get breakfast?" All these last-minute thoughts came out in one inane question.

"Yes, and I'll get back to my station in time. Don't worry."

"Be careful."

"I will." He squeezed my hands. "I love you."

I squeezed his fingers in return. "I love you. I'll be off duty next weekend if it fits into your schedule."

He smiled. "I'll see what I can do."

"Coming to work today?" a guard asked from a few feet away.

My face heated in embarrassment.

Adam dropped my hands and stepped back a few feet. I gave him a smile that began to wobble and then hurried through the gates, showing them my pass.

When I turned back, he had disappeared.

* * *

Marianne and Maryellen ate lunch the same time Rosalie and I did. They sat down at the table where Rosalie and I were eating and Maryellen said, "Was that your husband?"

"I hope so, since I just spent the night with him in

Bletchley."

The non-twins both laughed. "He's handsome," Marianne said.

"What does he do?" Maryellen asked.

"He's an army captain," I replied. "And yes, he is good looking."

"He's not as handsome as Simon," Maryellen said.

"Well, Simon is all yours," I said.

"I see the way he looks at you. Your husband may have to fight him off."

"Maryellen, your imagination is running away with you. Simon worked with my husband just a couple of months ago. They know each other. There's no reason for fighting."

"Simon said your husband doesn't talk about you very nicely when you aren't around."

I gave her a hard stare. "I don't believe it."

"That's what he said. That, and..."

Marianne elbowed her sister.

I raised my eyebrows. "And?"

"Nothing." Maryellen kept her head down.

"Come on, Maryellen. Simon said something you are afraid to repeat." And from what I'd learned about Simon, it could be almost anything.

"I'm not afraid." Maryellen pouted.

Her sister groaned. "You ought to be."

Maryellen lifted her chin and said, "Simon says your husband has told some of his fellow officers he wants a divorce."

Chapter Twenty-Two

Divorce. The word rang of failure and embarrassment. I felt as if someone had punched me in the chest and knocked the air out of my lungs. "I don't believe it," came out in an angry, gasping cry.

"That's what he said, not me," Maryellen said, rubbing her side where her sister had poked her a second time.

Divorce had been scandalous even before the previous king abdicated so he could marry a divorced woman. Now, instead of just being unwelcome in social circles, avoided as a pariah, and sniggered at behind cupped hands, divorce was now the symbol of a failed reign, a sign of agreeing with the Nazis as the former king and his now wife appeared to do, and a symbol of appeasement.

"Why would Simon say that?" Rosalie asked, looking from Maryellen to me.

"Apparently, when Simon and Adam worked together a couple of months ago, they had a big disagreement." We fell silent as our lunches arrived.

"About what?" Maryellen asked before I could add

anything else.

"Official Secrets Act," I replied, making a cringing face.

"Golly, but I hate that. Makes everything so boring," Maryellen fumed.

"Or mysterious. It must have been quite a disagreement for Simon to be spreading a story such as this around," Rosalie said. "Divorce is such a taboo, especially after Edward abdicated to marry Mrs. Simpson and then compounded his treachery by traveling to Germany."

"Adam and Simon had a major falling-out. If they were countries, they'd be Britain and Germany," I told her.

"Which is which?" Maryellen asked.

Even her sister looked askance at her.

"That's not the point. I just meant they'd be at war."

Marianne and Maryellen looked at each other. Finally, Marianne said, "Simon said you'd say something along those lines. When Simon saw your husband here, he knew your husband would tell you something to discredit him."

"He said you'd tell us not to believe him," Maryellen added.

I shook my head. "I wouldn't have said anything about Simon. He had a work disagreement with Adam that has nothing to do with any of us. But the lie he's telling you, that Adam wants a divorce, makes me think I need to keep a close eye on him. What other lies is he telling us?"

"I don't think he's truly lying," Marianne said. "Perhaps he misunderstood what your husband said. He might have been talking about someone else."

I glared at her. “But Simon feels it necessary to spread gossip about me that isn’t true. Even if it were true, and it’s not, why would he be telling everyone about it? It’s certainly not your business, and it isn’t Simon’s. I trusted him before. I don’t, now.”

“Well, whatever is going on, know that Maryellen and I are here to help you in any way.”

I glared at Marianne. She obviously didn’t believe me.

Rosalie changed the conversation to the weather, that old standby, as we finished our meal. I was furious. I was upset enough about missing Adam and not being at the flat to see him as soon as he arrived on leave. Now I had a liar telling tales about my marriage, taking my mind off the investigation I had to carry out if I wanted to return home.

As I walked back to Hut Six, I thought maybe that was the reason he told his story. He wanted me tied up in knots so he could finish the investigation and take all the credit. Wasn’t that what he wanted when he destroyed Adam’s operation?

Too bad he didn’t realize I didn’t care who got the credit, as long as the investigation was wrapped up satisfactorily, and we found the traitor.

I would have to watch Simon. He didn’t have the knowledge he needed to have tricked Sarah Wycott to come back outside to kill her, and he had no motive. Still, at that moment, I wouldn’t have minded discovering he was the killer.

Mentally shaking my head at my vengeful fantasy, I went back to work, taking out my anger on the keys of the refitted

TypeX machine. It took a lot of effort to press them down, and I had them banging with every stroke.

Unlike most days, Simon didn't make an appearance in the Decoding Room where I worked. He stayed in the Machine Room all afternoon, hopefully keeping his mouth shut. Any deliveries or verifications were done by Peter. Things went smoothly until quitting time.

They took the four of us staying at Bloomington Grove back in an estate car, so Simon and I didn't need to see each other on the way to our billets.

Walking up the drive from the lane, I tried to guess who had used the exit that I had found. Simon had seen it. Had he seen the woman who'd used it? I'd only seen the reflection on his face, a faint light in the vast darkness around us, but it had been enough.

When we entered, it was to hear that we needed to come to the table. Dinner was ready.

I dropped off my coat in my room and then went into the bathing room to wash my hands. When I arrived at the table, there was an uncomfortable silence and Maryellen looked guilty. Elsie had gone upstairs already, and Betty was dishing out our dinners, a potato stew.

"How was your stay in town with your husband last night?" she asked.

"It was splendid. We've only seen each other twice in over three months since the war started, so we had a tremendous time together. My only complaint was it was much too short."

"I'm glad," Betty said, giving Maryellen a dark look.

Oh, terrific. The talk was spreading. Simon had chosen the right person to spread his lie when he told Maryellen.

As soon as we began eating, Betty wished us a good night and headed upstairs. I wouldn't be able to ask her any more questions tonight about the hidden door and if any of us were using it. Oh, well. I'd just have to be practical. Someone knew more about it than they'd admitted.

Gwen cleared her throat. "We all want you to know we're on your side, Olivia. I'm sure you and your husband can work things out. Divorce is such an evil—"

"Aaaah!" I half-shouted. "That is a story Simon made up because he's mad at my husband over a work-related difference of opinion from a couple of months ago. There is nothing wrong between Adam and me."

"And Maryellen knows this because she asked Olivia about it at lunch today," Rosalie said, staring at Maryellen with raised brows. "Apparently, she believes Simon about Livvy's marriage more than she believes Livvy about her marriage."

"And Simon swears he heard this from Adam Redmond's lips. Why would Simon lie?" Maryellen said.

"I can't answer that because of the Official Secrets Act. Believe Simon or don't, but there's nothing wrong between Adam and me." I glared at Maryellen.

"Simon swears it's true. And he has no reason to cover up anything out of pride. Why have Simon and Olivia been whispering together until this weekend?" Maryellen said.

Everyone looked at me. How could I answer that without revealing the real reason Simon and I were here? Especially since chances were very good that the killer was in the room with us.

The best lies were the ones that were close enough to the truth to be believed. "Simon's been making passes at me, just trying it on because he and Adam had a falling-out at work and he wanted to start some mischief. I finally got tired of it and told him off. That's when he started this story about Adam planning to divorce me. Why, if he were going to divorce me, would Adam spend his leave coming out here to spend time with me when he could be enjoying himself in London?"

"She's got a point," Gwen said to Maryellen, who pouted.

Oh, I hoped Maryellen didn't have feelings for that jerk Simon. At least Aileen wasn't at dinner tonight to listen to Simon's lie. Since she was rigorously chapel, she'd have plenty to say to me.

"Where is Aileen this weekend?" I asked, hoping I didn't bring myself bad luck by asking and getting more questions about the state of my marriage.

All I got were shrugs and "She didn't tell me."

After that, we got down to the business of finishing dinner and cleaning up the kitchen, mostly in silence. Then we all went our separate ways, washing out underclothes, or listening to chamber music on the radio, or knitting, or having a bath.

"May I try to unlock your door with my key?" I asked Rosalie when I saw her in the hall.

Rosalie made a sweeping gesture toward her door.

"Is the door locked?" I asked.

"Of course."

I put my key into the lock and turned. The door opened easily.

"Well, that explains it." Rosalie said, her face muscles rigid.

"Explains what?"

Rosalie gave me a considering gaze. "I had five pounds disappear from my room. It was before you arrived. Everyone said I'd dropped it and it wasn't in my room at all, but I knew it was. I'd hidden it in my jewelry case."

"Wonderful." I looked at Rosalie, wondering how she'd take this. "On top of the murder of one of the residents, we have a thief."

"You don't think it's the same person, do you?" Rosalie asked.

"There's no reason to, at least not without some proof. How many people know these room keys are interchangeable?" I answered with a question of my own.

Fiona and Helen were coming up the hallway at that moment, Fiona with her latest scarf full of mistakes and Helen with a book in her hand. They must have overheard, because Fiona said, "Sarah knew."

Chapter Twenty-Three

"Really. How did you find out?"

Fiona laughed. "I locked myself out one day. Sarah used her key to let me in. We discovered our keys were identical, and she suspected there was really only one key pattern and it fit every lock on our floor."

"Makes me feel really safe with a murderer about," Rosalie said.

"Sarah went out to meet him. We're safe enough in here," Helen said. "Just don't go wandering about outside in the dark the way she did. I grew up south of the Thames in London, not in the nicest neighborhood, but I know I'd be safer there."

"Sarah had one boyfriend she was meeting by going out a door from the kitchen into the main house. Does it make sense she was meeting a second one on the same night?" I wondered, more to myself than to the others.

"Where did you hear that?" Fiona asked. The scowl on her face told me I'd better answer carefully.

"I heard a couple of the men talking." I sighed. "And after

I carried on about Simon spreading tales, I certainly shouldn't do it."

Helen raised her eyebrows at me. She was the one who told me about Sarah's boyfriend, but hadn't wanted to admit any involvement.

Rosalie seemed to be considering something else. As the two other women began to walk off, she said, "Did anyone else have anything stolen? Money, perhaps?"

"I lost a ten-shilling note," Helen said. "But that was a while back. And you lost something, too, didn't you, Fiona?"

"A few shillings. And I admit I was hot about it, too. I planned to buy more yarn with that money."

"How's the scarf coming?" As a fellow novice knitter, I sympathized with Fiona's struggles to improve with more help than she could use.

"Fairly well, but you'd not know that from the way the twins keep at me." Fiona knew Marianne and Maryellen weren't twins, but she called them that when she was annoyed with them.

Rosalie took Fiona's scarf and held it up. It was the second time recently I'd been able to see it stretched out. "It's coming right along. Good for you, Fiona. It almost looks as if you've got a pattern going with all your little knots," she said, studying it closely.

"Don't say that too loudly," Fiona said, taking her work back, "or the twins will tell me I'm doing that wrong, too."

"I'm sure it's well appreciated." There was something about Fiona's scarf that reminded me of something. I had no idea what. If I didn't think about it, it would come to me.

I hoped.

"It'll keep somebody warm. That's what's important." Fiona sauntered off with Helen, chatting about Ngaio Marsh's newest story, *Overture to Death*.

Rosalie opened her door and nodded to me to enter. When we were settled, Rosalie on the bed and I on the straight-backed chair, she said, "All those thefts took place a while ago. Before Sarah's death."

"Did she have a need for money? Well, more than the usual?"

Rosalie studied the floor. "Apparently, her family wasn't well off, and she said she felt obligated to make enough money to help them since they'd gone without so she could attend university. Her young man's family was struggling, too, since both fathers are fishermen, and she needed money if they were to marry."

"I can't see someone murdering her because she was a thief."

"No, thieves just get their hands cut off, or some such thing," Rosalie replied.

"Except Sarah was strangled, after sneaking out through the storeroom. This changes my thinking," I told her.

Rosalie studied me for a moment. "I won't ask you why you are so interested, because I'm certain you can't tell me. I also won't ask if Simon is also interested in Sarah's murder for the same reason, because I'm sure you can't tell me that, either."

"The bus comes awfully early in the morning. It's time we both get to bed," I said, rising from the chair. Rosalie was right. I couldn't tell her anything. I wasn't completely convinced she wasn't the killer. She was certainly smart enough, but she didn't have the temperament to murder, nor did she have a motive.

I was almost certain I could trust her.

"Thorpe likes you," she said as I reached the door. "He told me to keep you as a friend and look out for you, because you're much cleverer than most of the people we know. However, he thinks your cleverness may put you in danger."

I turned and said, "I like Thorpe, too. He's more clearsighted and generous than just about anyone I know."

* * *

I didn't sleep well that night, thinking about the hidden door and the possibility that Sarah Wycott was a thief and where that left the investigation. I had finally dropped off when I awoke, sitting upright in the bed.

After a moment, I realized the door to my room was beginning to open. I turned on my lamp, blinking my eyes to adjust to the light and trying to chase the sleep from my brain.

The door silently shut.

It took a moment for me to believe the door had ever opened, but I was certain I hadn't dreamed it. I jumped out of bed and hurried across the icy floor to the door in bare feet. When I opened the door and looked out, no one was there.

I shut and locked the door and rushed back to bed. After I turned off the light and snuggled under the covers, I realized my door had been unlocked. I always locked it before I climbed into bed, and that night was no exception.

Who had tried to enter my room? Listen as I might, I didn't hear anyone moving around.

And then in the early hours Simon's rumor came back to worry me. I knew it was rubbish, but I'd rather have Adam assure me it was a lie. I was certain it was untrue, but Simon had found a way to sneak into my brain with doubts in the dead of night.

In addition, I hadn't had much sleep the night before since I'd finally had a chance to spend time with Adam. After tossing and turning, short on sleep for two nights running, I was tired the next morning.

"Morning, Gwen," I said, sitting down next to her with my toast.

She rose and walked away without a word.

Rosalie looked at me, her eyes wide with shock.

I'd never been snubbed that way before, but I was too tired to be angry. I gulped down toast and coffee and hoped it would wake me up.

That and a brisk walk in the cold morning air to the bus stop did the trick. I noticed Aileen wasn't with us at the bus stop, but it wasn't until I was seated in our cold office that I realized she really wasn't there.

"Where did Aileen go this weekend?" I asked.

John came in and looked around the room. "That's a

good question. Anyone know?"

We all shook our heads.

"When was the last time anyone saw her?"

The five women in the room looked at each other. Friday night at dinner, I thought, trying to picture the table. No empty places, so she must have been there. What about after dinner? I could remember her knitting, but which night was that? They all ran together.

And all I was thinking about on Friday night was seeing Adam.

"She was at dinner on Friday night," I said.

"Aileen was awfully quiet. Not that she wasn't anyway, but she was particularly silent last Friday," Gwen said.

"I can't remember if I saw her knitting in the servants' hall after dinner," Rosalie said.

"I can't remember either," I admitted. Unlike the others, I was supposed to be paying attention. "You might ask the women in the Registration Room who live at Bloomington Grove. Maybe she said something about where she was going to one of them."

John nodded and walked out of the room. None of us started working. We glanced at each other, thinking of Sarah Wycott's disappearance. The two new girls sat watching us, unsure what to do.

John returned a couple of minutes later. "They don't know where she is, either."

"You'll have to notify the police and the admiral," I said somberly.

"Won't we feel silly when she turns up with a logical explanation?" one of the new girls, Katie, asked.

"I'd rather feel foolish than not do something that might help her if she's lying injured somewhere," I replied.

"You need to get working," John said and left the room, pulling his coat on.

We set the three wheels on our TypeX machines and began on the messages we had been given. I didn't feel tired anymore, I just felt a nagging worry, both for Aileen and for Adam. And then I hit a message that was a garbled mess, and I felt the need to scream. I was not in the mood for puzzles.

When I slammed my fists onto my desk and turned my face up to the ceiling, John came over. I hadn't realized he had returned. "Are you all right?"

"This message starts out all right, and then it just becomes impossible." I didn't completely hide a yawn.

John studied it for a minute. "You're right. Let me hand this over to the Intercept Control Room. They can chase down the original transcript and see what the problem is."

At that moment, Gwen ran into the same problem. I looked over John's shoulder and saw the time was nearly identical. "Some sort of interference? That might garble the letters."

"Well, the dots and dashes. What the listening stations are hearing is Morse code. In German," John said, not looking up from the cards containing messages we needed to decode. "Yes, if the weather was bad over the North Sea, it could have rendered reception difficult."

He looked around at us. "Anyone else with messages that become garbled?"

Everyone had at least one. Rosalie and the new woman, Katie, each had two. John gathered them all up and strode from the room.

We went back to work, separating the messages we could decipher from those that were garbled.

John came back a few minutes later and said to continue with what we had. "Yes, there was a storm over the North Sea last night. Do the best you can with these messages. If there's enough to guess at a word, go ahead with your guess and mark it as such. And if the traffic analysis gives a hint, such as which location was broadcasting, use that information, too."

He glanced over his shoulder toward the hall and added, "The Intercept Control Room is going to see if they can match messages copied from two of our receiving locations to find the missing words."

We went back to work, the room completely silent as we redoubled our efforts at figuring out what was missing or garbled. It could be important. It could save lives. And those lives were counting on us.

Aileen still wasn't there, her empty spot an extra weight at the backs of our minds.

By the time last lunch was held, Rosalie and I rose, stretching, from our hard seats. I was so stiff from the cold in the room and sitting hunched over for hours concentrating on the messages that I could barely move.

I couldn't remember ever working so hard, but it was so necessary. In the short time I'd been there, I'd had drilled into me that what we were doing mattered. That what we were doing would save lives. It might be the very thing that saved our country.

And then I thought, nothing would save Sarah Wycott's life now. I wondered, was that why Aileen disappeared? Was she the killer, or another victim?

I pulled on my coat and hat, pushed my gloves over fingers sore and stiff from typing, and followed Rosalie out of the building. We rushed through the rain to the main building and our lunch.

"I thought it was supposed to be dry today," Rosalie said once we were safely undercover. "If it gets any colder, it'll snow."

"I wish it would warm up so we don't freeze while we work," I replied as we walked into the dining room.

Today's lunch was a meat and vegetable stew, meat variety unspecified, and since neither of us got any in our portion, unknown. The room was crowded, so we shared a table with Marianne and Maryellen. Maryellen was her usual chatty self, mostly about Aileen's vanishing act. I was struggling to force myself to eat. I noticed Rosalie was unusually quiet, too.

We were partway through our meal when Simon came over. "Olivia, may I speak with you? Outside?"

"When I finish my lunch, I'll talk to you in the corridor." I sounded haughty, and it earned me a dark glance from

Maryellen. She was definitely sweet on him.

He nodded and walked out of the room.

"You weren't very nice to him," Maryellen said.

"He's been spreading gossip and lies about me and my marriage. If he were doing this to you, you wouldn't like it," I told her.

"He's not lying," she protested.

"It is gossip," Rosalie said, "and quite possibly untrue. It certainly brings him no credit to spread tales about others that are painful and embarrassing whether or not they're true."

"She's right," Marianne said.

Maryellen shot her sister an angry look and walked out of the dining room in the direction Simon had gone.

"She's sweet on him," Rosalie said. "You can't hold that against her."

"Oh, I don't. I just wish she didn't repeat every stupid story he tells to anyone who will listen." I was angry at Simon, not Maryellen. "It's not true, and it's embarrassing. Divorce, indeed."

"Gwen is giving Livvy the cold shoulder because of this gossip," Rosalie told Marianne.

"You can't hold that against Maryellen," her sister argued. "And it might be because Livvy's questions led us to find out Gwen had an aunt in service at Bloomington Grove. In service, of all things." Marianne might warn her sister not to gossip, but she'd defend her against all criticisms.

"For making up the stories, no, I don't hold that against

Maryellen. For spreading them, yes, I do." I finished my lunch and rose from the table. "Now, if you'll excuse me, I need to talk to Simon."

As soon as I reached the doorway, I saw Simon at a distance down the corridor with Maryellen standing in front of him, looking up into his face with rapture. He glanced over, saw me, smiled, and brushed Maryellen aside as he hurried toward me.

She watched him walk away from her, glowering in my direction.

Simon walked up to me, took my arm, and headed us toward the front door. "I'm sorry if what I said has put you in a bad position. I did hear him say something about divorce, and I really believed he was talking about the two of you, but if I misunderstood, I'm sorry."

"You misunderstood, and now your malicious gossip is all over the facility." I stopped and glared at him with my arms folded across my chest, letting him know I couldn't be talked around that easily.

"I should have known better than to say anything to Maryellen." He glanced in her direction with a sour expression. "Anything that goes in her ears comes out her mouth. Not a characteristic I'd want in someone working here, but that's not my decision."

"We could also say that about you. You thought you heard something, misunderstood, and talked about it, making me the subject of pity and scorn. Not a characteristic I want in someone I'm working with."

"All right. I messed up. I'm sorry. Now, can we please get back to the subject at hand?" He sounded more annoyed than contrite.

"And what is that?" I was curious as to why he wanted to talk to me despite my anger at his foolish stories.

"We both know we have a traitor in our midst, and the secret of BP isn't safe as long as this person can let the Nazis know how far we've come toward breaking their codes."

"You believe a traitor killed Sarah Wycott?" Actually, after eliminating Charlie Adler and Peter Watson, I thought so too. I didn't believe she'd been murdered for some petty thieving.

"There's nothing else. And BP isn't safe as long as we might have a spy in our midst."

I raised my eyebrows. "'Might'? Who do you have in mind? And Aileen is missing. Is she a traitor or a victim?"

Chapter Twenty-Four

"Aileen MacLeith is missing? When did this happen?" Simon looked surprised. Perhaps he truly was. I found it hard to believe him about anything.

"Any time since Friday night," I said. "We don't know."

"I barely know her. She never comes to the Wren and Dragon."

"She's a devout chapel-goer. She's Scottish. And she knits."

"Anything else?" he asked.

"She lived at home until she moved here. Lived in Edinburgh all her life and attended university there. Keeps herself to herself." I didn't add that she caught me trying to get into the storeroom. Did she know about the outside door?

"Any chance she's our traitor?"

"I wouldn't think so. But she was a teacher, and teaching is a reserved occupation. She said she gave up her work, and living in Edinburgh, to come here because she felt the need to do more for the war effort. She saw it as her duty to come here and help out."

"So, she could be our traitor."

"No, Simon, she couldn't. She was sincere in her beliefs."

He shrugged. "Have they reported her missing?"

"Yes, first thing this morning," I told him.

"What has her family said about her disappearance?" he asked.

I shook my head. I doubted they'd said anything to her parents.

"I feel as if we should be out there looking for her," Simon said.

"Where?"

"Anywhere they need us. And now that we know George Kester has been transmitting on a shortwave radio, we have our possible traitor. What does Aileen have to do with that?"

"What? No. Are you joking?" I looked at Simon as if he'd lost his mind. George Kester and Aileen MacLeith traitors? Murderers? I couldn't fathom it.

"Do you know where his room is at the Wren and Dragon?"

"If you make one more comment about my morals..." I was already annoyed with Simon and his comments about my nonexistent divorce.

"No, not that," he said, brushing aside my anger as if not worth worrying about. "He has a room facing the back. He has an aerial there that he's run over the kitchen wing. He must have climbed onto the roof one night. And he has a shortwave radio in his room."

Having a shortwave radio wasn't illegal. Sending radio broadcasts out, however, would be if it helped the Nazis in any way. Amateur radio enthusiasts had been asked to completely stop broadcasting for the good of the country, and the BBC had only been able to use two frequencies for their broadcasts since the war started.

"Are you telling me George was the one transmitting on Thursday night?"

"Yes." Simon continued, "I've called Sir Malcolm and told him."

"What did he say?"

"Good work. He's coming out and he wants to see you as well." Simon looked pleased with himself, but he kept his voice down. "He'll be here for the hunt for Aileen."

"How would George know I'd gone to the WI so he could have someone run me down?" I was nearly whispering.

"It was a coincidence. Nothing more. The WI involved in espionage? Don't be silly." I didn't know anyone could scoff and murmur at the same time, but Simon could.

"How did he get Sarah to come outside? Or Aileen? I think you're wrong."

"Think what you want. I'm taking credit for this arrest, but you can come along and see how it's done. Or not, I don't care. I have experience with arresting traitors." His expression grew smug.

I thought about what Adam had told me. "So I've heard."

He ignored my sarcasm. "Hopefully, George will tell us

where Aileen is before any harm comes to her."

Seething, I rushed out of the manor house and over to Hut Six, unaware of the rain until I was back inside. My anger should have made my coat and hat steam from the heat my temper generated.

I went back to work, typing and translating by rote. My mind was busy elsewhere. Could George be the killer? If he was, then he must be the spy, because he had no other reason to kill Sarah. Or Aileen. But how did he get them outside?

He couldn't call them. Did he send a note? Or tap on their windows? How would he know which window was theirs?

If he set up the meeting ahead of time, Sarah wouldn't have been ready to have dinner one moment and disappeared the next.

Could I be that wrong about George? I'd ruled him out almost immediately. He was friendly, kindly, and willing to let all the different personalities at BP have their little foibles without criticism.

Simon's conclusion just didn't make sense to me. I'd tell that to Sir M when I saw him, but who could I suggest in his place? I thought it had to be someone at Bloomington Grove.

If the traitor was there, and Sarah had found out by searching her room for money, that person would have a good reason to murder. Sarah might have tried to blackmail her killer, not realizing she was dealing with a traitor. And that person certainly wasn't George.

Had Aileen seen something that told her who the killer

was? She'd been watching me. Who else was she keeping track of? Had she told the killer to confess? That would be something the upright Aileen...

My mind came back to the present when I felt a hand on my shoulder. "Olivia, the admiral wants to see you," John told me.

I nodded and glanced at Rosalie, who was staring at me with a puzzled look. Slipping into my outerwear again, I marched out of the hut and over to the main building, ignoring the cold rain.

Marching past the secretary, I opened the admiral's office door before she could stop me and walked in.

"Come in, Olivia," Sir Malcolm said. He stood, as usual, behind the door. The admiral sat at his desk, Simon sat on a comfortable-looking chair, and two large, blank-faced men wearing suits stood to one side, waiting.

I shut the door in the secretary's face and walked over to sit in the wooden chair in front of the admiral's desk. And then I waited in silence.

"Townsend says George Kester is the murderer and the traitor."

"I don't agree."

Simon smirked.

Sir Malcolm raised an eyebrow. "Why?"

"Three questions. Why did someone try to run me over when we returned from the WI building, and how did George get Sarah to leave her nice warm billet in the dark of night after a long workday to go out into the cold? And where is

Aileen and why is she missing?"

"That's four questions." Simon gave me a smug smile.

Sir Malcolm turned to Simon, displeasure written on his face.

"We'll find out he worked out some easy method to get both of them outside once we start to question him, sir. And I think Livvy is being paranoid about the incident with the car on a dark road. That was most likely an accident."

"You're certain of this."

"Absolutely," Simon told Sir Malcolm.

"Why would George kill Sarah or Aileen?" I asked.

"They figured out he was a traitor," Simon answered.

The big man nodded. "We'll pick him up at the end of the day. Admiral, can you have him detained in his office for a few minutes? Make some excuse. Simon, Olivia, meet me at quitting time."

"With respect, sir, I'd like to handle the questioning," Simon told him.

"With respect, sir, I won't be there. I'm going to check out another possibility for the murderer and traitor," I said immediately after.

"I was going to say you were excused. You could go home and back to the newspaper," Sir Malcolm said.

As much as it hurt, I had to stay here to finish this investigation. "Not yet, sir. I want to check out another person. The traitor isn't George. And it isn't Aileen."

"How long do you want?" Sir Malcolm stared at me from under his bushy eyebrows.

If I said indefinitely, he'd send me away immediately and the traitor I suspected at Bloomington Grove would get away with murder, not to mention treason. I wasn't certain which person it was. How long could I hold him off? "Until Thursday."

"Why Thursday?"

"Wednesday night is WI night." I thought it smarter not to say any more. I really didn't have any more to tell him.

"Still going on about the car on the dark lane, Livvy?" Simon asked. His tone was patronizing.

"It's another indication. It's not the major factor." The WI had to be involved. Or someone at the WI. But who?

"Until Thursday. I'll expect your report then." Sir Malcolm nodded to tell me I was excused.

"Any news on Aileen MacLeith?" I asked.

"We have everyone we can spare looking for her."

I rose and left the office to return to the Decoding Room.

What had I done? I only had three more days to find a killer.

The rest of the day dragged. I'd type in a message and check to be sure it made sense in German, all the time wondering who the traitor was. And how could I prove it? How were they sending messages to Germany? How much of the secret of BP had they already shared with the Nazis?

Rosalie was the person best placed to be the traitor, but I couldn't believe that of her. She had nothing to do with the WI, but she knew when I'd be on that lane and she had contacts with autos and could arrange for someone to run me over.

Between the TypeX and the piano, Gwen had the strongest hands in Bloomington Grove. I had ruled her out on the fact she was busy even in her off-hours and she was too absorbed in her music. Was I that wrong about her?

We cleared up at the end of the day and headed to the gate, rain coming down in buckets. When we were seated on the bus and started off, I noticed neither Simon nor George were with us.

Peter sat down next to me. "What's going on?" he asked in a murmur.

I began to wonder if anyone would ever say anything to me in a normal speaking voice again. "You'll have to ask Simon or George."

"Or you. You're mixed up in this too."

"No. This time I'm not." We exchanged a look that told me he understood I wanted no part of whatever was going on.

We rode to the village in silence, where he and the others who were billeted in Little Rowanwood climbed down and then rushed to find cover. A few minutes later, the bus arrived at our stop and the seven of us alighted and ran at various speeds to the drive and then uphill to the servants' entrance at the side of the manor house.

Rosalie kept pace with me. "I'll be glad to help however I can."

"I don't know if you can, but thanks." I wasn't certain I could trust her.

"I know a good deal more about knitting than you realize. Than any of you realize."

I stopped, the rain pouring down, and stared at her. Knitting. Had Rosalie found the traitor? Or was Rosalie the traitor?

"Come on. We'll drown. Bring your knitting to my room after dinner."

We both rushed the rest of the way to the door, coming in last in this strange race against the weather.

"Golly. You ladies are slow," Fiona said, setting her shoes in a corner of the kitchen to dry in the warmest room in our area of the house.

"But you're all slow compared to me," Maryellen said, already changed into dry clothes and her house slippers.

"Were you captain of your sports teams in school?" I asked.

"Of course. Field hockey, foot races, anything we did on sports day." Maryellen sounded proud of her accomplishments. "I rowed in the first eight at university."

"It sounds as if you've mastered every sport out there," Rosalie said. "I always sat in the stands."

"I was always ahead of Marianne, although she's a whiz at throwing things. She always won a stuffed animal at those toss games at church fétes," Maryellen said.

"And embarrassed the village lads," Marianne said, carrying out her shoes to dry next to Fiona's. "But I was never a sporting girl the way Maryellen is."

Nosy, argumentative Maryellen was an athlete, capable

of strangling Sarah. As was Marianne. I hadn't thought of two traitors working together. Was that the answer as to how Sarah was lured outside?

"You're all going to be hungry girls if you don't get out of the kitchen and to your places at the table," Elsie announced from in front of the stove.

I took off for my room, quickly hanging up my outerwear and changing my shoes. I wasn't the last to the table, but I only beat Rosalie by about ten seconds.

Dinner was hot and filling. That was all anyone cared about that night as rain hit the windows. We were all glad to be inside. And yet there was the empty chair. Where was Aileen?

"I hope it's not this wet on Wednesday night. I'll have another scarf to take to the WI collection, and I don't want to drown on the way," Fiona said.

"If it is, you can spend the next week taking the knots out of it," Maryellen suggested.

"Rosalie said it almost looks as if it's a pattern," Fiona said with a note of defiance in her voice.

Maryellen and Marianne, sitting along one side of the table, turned as one to stare at Rosalie. She nodded, a slight smile on her face.

A gust of wind rattled the windowpanes and made me shiver. "It must be awful for anyone hunting for Aileen tonight in this weather."

"It's bad enough for the boys in the temporary barracks in back of the main wing tonight. They may not leak, but the damp and the wind must make those temporary quarters uncomfortable," Helen said.

I noticed some of the women at the table looked toward the ceiling and walls and sighed. The cavernous servants' hall seemed particularly cozy and snug that night.

"A good night for knitting," Marianne said.

"And an extra cup of tea," Maryellen said, looking at Betty.

"Bold girl," Betty said, but she went into the kitchen and we heard her begin to make an extra pot.

"How is your latest scarf coming, Olivia?" Marianne asked.

"I've started it, but I've been busy the last few days." I thought of Adam and smiled.

"What did your husband think of it?" Gwen asked.

"I didn't show it to him. We—we had other things to talk about since we only had a short time to be together." Such as Simon seeking honor and glory at other people's expense.

"Will you have it ready to take to the WI Wednesday night?" Fiona asked.

"I hope so." I needed to. The secret had to be at the WI with the knitting. Sarah Wycott was an excellent knitter and took something to the WI every Wednesday. As did Aileen.

Sarah was a knitter. Sarah was a thief. Sarah had a boyfriend at the army school on the other side of the locked kitchen door. No, I felt I could rule out that last as unimportant to the investigation. This whole case focused on Bletchley Park.

Sarah stuck up for her friends, evidenced by her defense of Celia Flowers. I suspected she'd stick up for her friends against a traitor, and that took me back to her knitting for our soldiers and sailors. I idly wondered if she knitted in khaki or in navy blue. No, I told myself. The color didn't make any difference, only the nationality.

We finished dinner and cleared the table. It was Helen and Fiona's night to do dishes. Everyone else headed back to their rooms to get their knitting or a book to bring back to the servants' hall, including me.

Once in my room, I took out my few pitiful inches of knitted scarf and wondered how I could get a complete scarf in two evenings. Even if I didn't sleep, I couldn't get it finished in two nights. I was too slow.

And khaki was a dull color compared to navy blue. Then I remembered Fiona's scarf and the multicolored, patterned lap robe that Thorpe used. A glimmer of an idea came to me.

Just then, I heard someone shout down the hall, "Livvy! The police are here for you."

Chapter Twenty-Five

I headed toward the servants' hall to find two dripping constables standing just inside the outer door. "May I help you?" I asked.

"We were told you may have some idea where we should look for the missing woman, if she's been hurt or met with an accident," one of the constables said.

The other sneezed and said, "Excuse me." Rain soaked his hair and slid off his chin.

"Have you had a chance to look in her room?"

"No, ma'am. We haven't," the first one said.

"Neither have we, except to check she wasn't there." I gestured to them to follow me to where I unlocked her room with my room key and looked in as I flipped on the light switch. The blackout curtains were drawn, so she must have left here at night. Which night was still to be determined, since she was last seen three nights before.

The constables looked under the bed and in the wardrobe. She wasn't there. Her coat, however, still was. I had a bad feeling about this. Worse, there was no sign of a note saying where she'd gone.

"I have another idea." There was little chance Aileen would have left this way, but it would keep the poor men out of the rain for a couple of minutes more. I saw water had soaked their trouser legs to the knees. I turned off the light in Aileen's room and locked her door. Then I led them to the storeroom at the end of the hallway.

Unlocking the door, I turned on the light and showed them Elsie's storeroom. "I think someone has been going in and out of here through that door," I told them, pointing.

One of the constables moved bins out of the way, opened the door, and switched on his torch. He shone the beam of light around for a few seconds before he said, "Blimey," and dashed outside. The other constable followed him as he sneezed again, and I stuck my head out of the doorway.

Beyond the two men I could see a woman's legs lying against the outer wall behind the thick evergreen bushes at the end of the wing. One shoe was half-off her foot and one stocking had a huge ladder in it, possibly caused by the buildup of pine needles on the ground as if her body had been dragged across them.

It didn't appear that she was wearing a coat. She would never have gone outside without one. If she had been conscious.

The first bobby came back in. "I need to use a telephone, ma'am."

"We don't have one. There's one in the main part of the

house used by the army, but we might be able to get in through a door off the kitchen." I swung around to lead him toward the kitchen and found I had to get through the cluster of women around the storeroom door.

They stepped back, and I continued down the hall to the kitchen and then to the door that led to the office in the main part of the house. I banged on the door.

A soldier opened it a little. "You can't come in here."

"Police," the constable said from behind me.

I moved aside. Startled, the soldier stepped back a half step, enough for the constable to push in with his wet cape. He walked over, picked up the receiver, and called the local station.

My task completed, I walked back into the servants' hall and dropped into a chair. Aileen was dead. I hadn't figured out who Sarah's killer was, and now another woman had died. I'd failed them both.

The constable came in and broke into my depressing thoughts. I told him, "Her boss's name is John Wiggins. He's rooming at the Wren and Dragon. He'll have contact information for her family." Shock left my voice a monotone.

The constable wrote in his little notebook with a short pencil. "Did you work with her?"

"Yes." Then I asked, "What happened to her?"

"I really couldn't..."

I held his gaze. "Another girl who lived here died three weeks ago. She was strangled, her body found in the hedgerow down by the lane."

He nodded and took more notes.

Then a heavy knock sounded on our entrance. The bobby answered, and our floor of the wing was taken over by the police. They shed water everywhere.

I slowly walked back to my room and picked up my knitting bag again and walked across the hall. I needed someone's help, and it sounded as if Rosalie was offering.

I needed to trust someone here. She might be the last person I should rely on, but my instinct said she was trustworthy.

Rosalie answered my knock with, "Come in." She took one look at my face and said, "Sit down. I take it they found Aileen's body."

"I think so." I slumped into her chair and added, "If someone had found Sarah's killer, Aileen would still be alive."

She sighed, shutting the door behind me. "Do you feel guilty?"

I held Rosalie's gaze and gave away more than I should have when I answered, "Yes."

"Don't. I was here more than you were, and I never noticed she was missing."

"You were at BP all weekend," I protested.

"So were you. Don't waste time feeling guilty. Just find the blighter who did this to both of our housemates."

I nodded. I only saw one way to find the killer. "I know you knit. My question is, how quickly do you knit?"

Rosalie's mouth rounded in an O. "Thorpe's lap robe."

I nodded.

"That took me less than a week while sitting in his hospital room, waiting to see if he'd live."

It was much larger and more complicated than my simple scarf. "Could you do this scarf for me? Please? I need something to turn in Wednesday evening."

"And you can't tell me why."

"No."

"But I can guess you suspect someone."

"You can." I wasn't certain who I suspected, but I'd narrowed down the list.

She sat down on her bed and waved me to hand her the project. "Do you want me to do most of it tonight, and then have you do the last inch or two tomorrow night in the hall?" she asked, my needles flashing in her hands as they used up yarn.

"I'd just as soon have it done. Does anyone here beside Fiona knit in navy blue?"

"Aileen sometimes. Sarah did, since she came from a fisherman's family. And I've seen Marianne use navy blue." Rosalie frowned at me, the needles never slowing no matter where she looked or what she said.

The information didn't narrow down my list of suspects. It probably didn't make a difference.

"Do you want me to put in a few errors the way Fiona does?"

"Not as many as that, please." I looked at Rosalie in confusion. "What do you mean, 'put in errors'?"

"She'll knit three rows without an error and then one row

will have several errors. Or one row will have some errors on one side, and then two rows later, the errors will appear on the other side. Except they aren't errors. They are actual stitches. The same stitches."

"What do you mean?"

"When I looked at Fiona's scarf, I realized her so-called errors are a specific stitch, or actually, two specific stitches. They aren't just a knot. And they are always the same specific stitches, not random, different stitches each time she has a supposed error."

"Can you demonstrate on mine what you mean?" I watched in fascination as she showed me.

She'd put a bit of a knot in and then two stitches later she'd put in a larger knot. Two more stitches, another knot, two more stitches, another knot.

I looked at Rosalie in amazement. "That's a Y. Or an L, depending on which knots are dots or dashes."

"The scarves Fiona had done before had slipped stitches and only one size of knot, but lately, the scarves she has knitted have two different types of knots and no slipped stitches." The needles flew as she knitted.

"I wish I could study one of them. Unless she's knitting not only in Morse code but in a cypher as well, guessing the meaning would be easy," I admitted.

"You know Morse code that well?" she asked.

"My history teacher at St. Agnes, Miss Weaver, was also the Girl Guides leader. She made sure we were all fluent in Morse code in case we were lost in the wilderness." She was also my favorite teacher and I put effort into anything I did for her.

Now it was Rosalie who looked amazed. "How would that have helped? If you were lost, I mean."

"I don't know, but we practiced Morse code every week for three years."

"I've never been able to remember the letters, even though I was supposed to learn in Girl Guides, too."

"Just the way I can't see a slipped stitch until I actually put on the woolen garment," I told her. "My theory only works if the mistakes actually spell something out." I wondered whether Fiona's scarves spelled out a message or she could only keep her needles working correctly for so long before she began to make mistakes.

But why did she always make the same stitch when she made a mistake?

I knew from trying to learn to knit that once I made a mistake, with the Allen sisters going at me about it, I'd make more. If I kept going, I would soon have a scarf similar to Fiona's. But I thought every mistake I made was different.

Rosalie pulled out the mistakes and began to knit properly again, row after row of even, perfect stitches. I watched her, my mind racing with possibilities. But how to prove or disprove any of them?

Did Sarah's thieving have anything to do with her death? Or was it her expert knowledge of knitting? Did she break in to steal and then look at the knitting? Was it not the knitting itself but a paper message worked into one end of a woolen garment? Were the mistakes only to draw attention to the scarf so someone would know which item held the attached message? Or with all the mistakes in one item, were our eyes drawn away from the hidden message in another knit item taken to the WI?

I needed to make a close inspection of Fiona's knitting without her knowing. That would be the quickest way to prove or disprove at least some of my theories. But how? Unless I broke into her room using my key.

I looked at the scarf that Rosalie was turning out. It seemed to grow by an inch a minute. "I'm impressed."

"Don't be. I don't have to think about this. I had to concentrate on that lap robe. Changing colors and patterns. It's a lot of work."

"I appreciate you knitting this for me."

"My pleasure. I liked Sarah, even if she was a thief, which isn't definite by any means. And Aileen was such a stickler for the rules, she would have confronted the killer, or the traitor, and told them to make amends without realizing she was putting herself in danger. Their killer should not go free."

"No, she shouldn't." I watched her hands for a minute. "Why don't you knit for the WI?"

"What makes you think I don't?" She glanced at me and then back at the scarf. "I just do my knitting for the WI at home. It's expected of me there. Lady of the manor and all that."

We both looked up as we heard a banging and "Mrs. Redmond" shouted in the hallway.

I rose and opened Rosalie's door. "Yes?"

In addition to the constable, there was a plainclothes detective outside my room. "Mrs. Redmond?" He introduced himself as a detective inspector. "Where can we talk?"

His expression said that avoiding speaking to him at that moment was not an option.

Chapter Twenty-Six

Wordlessly, I unlocked my door and flipped on the light. I sat on the side of the bed and let the two men figure out who would get the chair.

The inspector pulled over the chair and said, "What made you think to look in the storeroom?"

"I just discovered a few days ago that any of us could come and go outside from this floor of the wing without anyone else knowing. When Sarah, the first woman murdered, disappeared from inside here and no one saw her leave, I thought she'd found another way out. No one saw Aileen leave. Or perhaps the killer murdered Aileen somewhere in here and had to get rid of the body." I glanced in the direction of the storeroom. "What could be easier?"

He studied me for a moment. "You work at Bletchley Park?"

"We all do."

"But they're not your only bosses, are they?"

I looked at him blankly. "I don't know what you mean, inspector."

"Where do you think Miss MacLeith was killed?"

I was relieved he didn't push the subject of who I worked for, but I decided that meant he had a pretty good idea of who my primary boss was. How did he find out? Did he work for Sir Malcolm, too? "Somewhere in here," I answered, "but if there was any evidence, the killer has had since Friday night or whenever to dispose of it. How was she killed?"

"Strangulation. Same as Miss Wycott. That's not a usual method for a woman," the inspector added. "Women's hands generally aren't strong enough to do that kind of damage."

"Between typing on those—typing and knitting and Gwen's piano playing and Helen's magic tricks, we all have strong fingers and hands," I assured him. "The method doesn't help you at all."

* * *

Sleep didn't come easily that night. I kept waiting for someone to unlock my door and come in. Fortunately, they didn't, and I finally fell into a fitful doze.

The next morning, I was still trying to think of an excuse to see Fiona's scarf in progress when I wasn't thinking about Aileen's murder. At least I didn't have to worry about finishing my scarf. Rosalie had completed it for me before bedtime.

Everyone was somber at breakfast. Elsie was heard to mumble something about "This place is cursed," and Betty's eyes were red from weeping. "That's two now," she muttered to Elsie. Breakfast didn't disappear as quickly as usual.

Perhaps I wasn't the only one to feel guilty for not worrying about Aileen's disappearance over the weekend.

I wondered if Sir Malcolm would help me find the killer. That would depend, I guessed, on what happened with George.

I couldn't wait to go to work.

Neither George nor Simon got on the bus in Little Rowanwood. No one commented on their absence, so I kept my questions to myself. None of the men who climbed aboard in the village had a chance to say anything on the bus or while waiting in line to enter through the gates, with all the talk of a second murder at Bloomington Grove. Had they discussed the absence of two of their colleagues in the pub last night? Probably, but they were closing ranks now. I'd have to ask them later.

I turned to say something to Peter, but he pushed by me in silence.

In the Decoding Room, the now five of us worked on yesterday's leftover translations, with nothing coming in to us from the Machine Room where the men worked their mathematical wizardry. John looked worried as he walked between the two rooms. Every time he heard footsteps coming down the corridor, he would look to see who it was. And every time, his face fell.

After a very long morning, Rosalie and I went to the last lunch serving. When we ran in on a gust of wind, we found Peter at a table by himself. I walked over, Rosalie following, and said, "May we sit here?"

He shrugged, but didn't answer.

We sat. "Are you all right, Peter?" I asked.

"What are you and your friends up to?" he asked in a murmur between clenched teeth.

"If you mean George, that is all Simon's show," I told him, muttering into my plate.

"Couldn't you do anything?"

"No."

"Can't you find out what's going on?" Peter finally asked.

"No. I can't even tell you what happened to Aileen."

Peter grumbled, "Don't tell me George killed her, too."

I could tell Peter was angry with me, but there was nothing I could do. Even if I convinced Sir Malcolm to tell me what was going on, I couldn't tell Peter because of the Official Secrets Act. Rosalie's guesses were already too close to the mark.

We all ate our lunches quickly. I didn't even taste mine. "If you two will excuse me, I'll see you back in the office." I rose, took my coat with me, and left.

I went around the corner to the admiral's office. His secretary wasn't at her desk, so I walked over and knocked on the door.

"Come."

I walked in and shut the door behind me. "I need to phone Sir Malcolm's office," I told the admiral.

He nodded and gestured to the scrambled phone on the right side of his desk. "I am sorry about your colleague Miss MacLeith's death."

I nodded. After dialing, I waited longer than usual for someone to answer. Finally, I heard an unfamiliar voice say, "Hello?"

"Sir Malcolm?"

"Unavailable."

"This is Olivia Redmond. I need to speak to him before Wednesday night. The next message he's worried about is going out through the WI." Why did I say that? I couldn't prove it. I didn't even feel certain about it. How would the Women's Institute—the Women's Institute, for heaven's sake—get a message to the Nazis? "And I hope he's heard Aileen MacLeith has been murdered."

"I'll give him the message. Don't expect an answer soon," the voice said and hung up.

I suspected Sir Malcolm was angry with me because I didn't back up Simon in his stupidity and had told his minions to take a message and nothing else if I should call.

Where else could I go for help?

My boss at the *Daily Premier*, Sir Henry Benton, could have the women of the WI in Little Bricton checked out. I had one, Mrs. Hubbard, in particular, that I thought could be a traitor only because Fiona gave her the scarf when I'd gone to the WI and the older woman had been kind about the mistakes knitted in.

Fiona may have given her scarves to others on other nights. Any of the women at the WI hall could have picked up Fiona's scarf. I had a couple of other names of women who could be involved with getting word to the Nazis.

"May I make a call on the unsecure line?"

Again, the admiral nodded.

I called the newspaper offices, and Sir Henry's secretary passed me right through. "Livvy, how are you? When are you coming back?" Sir Henry's voice boomed out at me.

"I'm fine. I hope to be back soon, but I need your help to make that happen. Can you get someone to do checks on Mrs. Hubbard, Mrs. Linfield, and Mrs. Walker, all of the WI in Little Bricton not far from Bletchley? And the Magnificent Prestons, the performing act. Did they do shows last weekend? When and where, and was Helen Preston part of the act? And I need it as soon as you can."

"Where do you want me to call you?"

"You can't. I'll call you after work. A little after six tonight?"

"Fine. Are you safe, Livvy?" I could hear the concern in his voice.

"Yes. Everything is fine." I tried to sound bright and cheerful, but I sounded false to my ears. Sir Henry would know in a second that things were not going well.

"Be very careful. If anything happens to you, Esther will kill me. Even if it is all Sir Malcolm's fault."

His daughter, Esther, and I had been the best of friends since our school days. Esther was fiercely protective of anyone she cared about, and her father was smart to keep on her good side.

"Give her my love," I said.

There was nothing to do now once I hung up the

telephone, but go back to work and wait to call Sir Henry from the phone box on the green of Little Rowanwood village.

I checked the dining room, but Peter and Rosalie had already left to go back to work. Then I ran back to Hut Six, holding my hat on my head against a fierce wind.

The Machine Room had been making progress while I was at lunch, and there were now plenty of settings to try out on our TypeX machines. The afternoon went quickly, and it felt as if no time had passed before we left for the day.

"I have to make a call from the phone box," I told Rosalie as we waited in line to get out of the gates.

"Do you want me to wait with you?" Rosalie asked. "I wouldn't mind phoning Thorpe to see how he is."

"That would be brilliant."

We told our fellow lodgers we'd walk back from the phone box and got off the bus with the people, not only men anymore, staying in Little Rowanwood. Rosalie let me use the phone first.

Sir Henry picked up after the first ring. "I have something on all of the women you mentioned. We have a good little researcher, a woman, who has proven useful. Very useful."

Was I being told I was being replaced? I hoped not. I liked working on the *Daily Premier.* But I couldn't worry about that at the moment. I had a killer to catch. One who had a key that would open the door to the room where I slept at night.

"First, the Magnificent Prestons. They had shows Friday night, Saturday night, and Sunday afternoon in London theaters. Helen was part of the Saturday and Sunday shows.

"We picked up some gossip there. Apparently, the family is rumored to have used some sleight of hand to help the Foreign Office a time or two extract, shall we say, secret documents from the Nazis."

"The whole family?"

"Yes. It must have been as carefully choreographed as any of their shows. I wish I had seen it." He cleared his throat after that admission. "Apparently, the government was suitably grateful."

"That could explain how Helen obtained her position here." I could take her off my list of possible traitors. "Great. Go on."

"Mrs. Walker of the WI is married, three children, husband works for the railroad. They've both lived in the district all their lives. Don't travel except once a year to the beach on railway passes her husband gets.

"Mrs. Linfield is a widow, lives with her daughter, son-in-law, and two very young grandchildren. She babysits all day while both parents work. She's lived in the same village since George V was in short trousers."

"I suspect this is where it gets interesting," I said.

"Mrs. Elizabeth Hubbard," Sir Henry continued, "moved to Little Bricton to join her sister three years ago. There seems to be some confusion as to where she lived before, her husband's name, whether they had children, anything. The sister died soon after her arrival."

"Natural causes?"

"Yes. Mrs. Hubbard came to nurse her through her final

illness. She died less than a week after Mrs. Hubbard arrived. The neighbors were suspicious, but since the woman was expected to die, sooner or later, no one officially followed up. Is this what you needed?"

"That's what I needed. Thanks."

I got off the phone and waited while Rosalie went in and phoned Lancaster. I could tell it was taking her a while to get through by the faces she made at me while she waited. I could tell when she got through to Thorpe by her big smile. I started to walk along the edge of the lane, the wind trying to push me to the side, when a hand clamped down on my shoulder.

Suddenly, I couldn't move, pinned in place by a strong grip. The kind of grip that could easily strangle me.

Chapter Twenty-Seven

I couldn't move, and I couldn't turn my head enough to see who had trapped me in the dark and cold of the night. I stood in silence, hoping the killer didn't think I was smarter than I was.

"It isn't George. He's not our man." I recognized Simon's voice near my ear.

"I knew that." I reached up and shoved at his hand on my shoulder, unafraid now I knew it was him. He couldn't be Aileen's killer.

"How? He was the one broadcasting in Morse code on shortwave."

"It was in English, wasn't it? George doesn't speak German. And he's too relaxed. Too easygoing. Does that make sense?" I hoped I could explain it. His grip still hurt through my heavy coat. "You'd expect someone hiding something to be tense. Watchful." *The same as you*, I wanted to add.

"Makes sense." He released his grip and I turned to face

him.

"Who was he sending messages to by shortwave?" I asked, although I suspected I knew.

"Some girl in northern England." I could sense, rather than see, his shrug.

"Anthea. But why in Morse code?"

"He thinks it's romantic. No one knows what they're saying but the two of them."

I laughed. "Or anyone listening in. Why don't they just get married?" I knew, but I wanted to know if Simon did.

"Their parents don't approve."

"George told me about her aristocratic family and his religious family not getting along. But they're both of age. Why not marry? Instead, they communicated in code over shortwave and nearly got him jailed. Idiots." I shook my head.

"And made me look as if I were a fool." Simon sounded furious.

"I told you it wasn't George."

"For absolutely no reason."

"Now it's been proven by the death of another woman."

He gave me a hard stare. "Who are you calling?"

I remembered Adam's words about Simon trying to steal the glory on his investigation, and how Simon went ahead and had George pulled in on very little evidence. I didn't need him messing up my investigation and letting everyone escape. "No one. I'm waiting for Rosalie while she calls her husband."

"He's some kind of an invalid."

"Yes." Far be it from me to try to straighten out Simon. I knew I couldn't trust him. I planned to get the evidence I needed and then pass it on to Sir Malcolm. Then I could be done with murderers, spies, and Simon.

Rosalie hung up and came out of the phone box. "Thanks for waiting," she said to me.

"No problem. I'll walk you back, shall I?" Simon said.

Rosalie caught something from my expression. "It's really not necessary. With Livvy here, I'm sure we'll both be quite safe."

"With three you'll be even safer."

"It's going to be a cold walk back," I said. "And it's pretty dark tonight. Who's going to look out for you on the return journey?"

"Oh, I'm sure I'll be fine."

"Then why do we need you?" Rosalie asked, using an innocent tone.

"Because another of your housemates just got murdered?" Simon said.

There was no answer for that. Rosalie and I discussed the weather the entire walk. The weather there, the weather in Lancaster, how different weather felt in London. Simon made a few comments on the weather, asked how her husband was—Rosalie said "Fine"—and then he gave up trying to speak to us.

We thanked him as he turned away near the bottom of the drive. Hurrying, we rang the bell in hopes that someone would quickly let us in. Betty opened the door almost immediately.

"Come in quick now, it's cold out."

We rushed in and shut the door behind us. "It is horribly cold, Betty," Rosalie said. "Thank you for opening the door so quickly."

"I've been keeping your dinners warm. Elsie went up a few minutes ago. And once I get you served, I can go up for the night and put my feet up."

"We appreciate it," I said before following Rosalie down the hall to hang up my outerwear. When I entered the servants' hall, I found the rest of the women had finished dinner already and were now knitting and listening to the wireless. The BBC was reporting the news.

Fortunately, there wasn't any news of interest. News to me would only mean the shooting war had begun.

Dinner, a thick soup of potatoes and odds and ends, was warm, and the bread was crusty. Stale, perhaps, but it was warm and passed for crusty. Rosalie and I ate quickly in silence.

"Are you going to work on your scarf tonight, Olivia?" Marianne asked.

"It's finished. I'll turn it in to the WI tomorrow night." I didn't mention Rosalie had knitted it for me.

"When do we get to see it?" Maryellen asked.

"Tomorrow night. You'll be so proud of me."

"Did you know Simon and George are back? No word of where they were," Fiona said.

"Lucky things probably got a spot of vacation time or

went to a conference in Cambridge," Gwen said.

"Too short for a real vacation," I said, "but I heard there was a conference in Cambridge." There was always a conference in Cambridge. At least when I was a student there.

We'd all gone to Cambridge. Except Aileen who went to Edinburgh, and Fiona and Helen who didn't go to university. And Gwen had attended the Royal College of Music. Did our university backgrounds mean anything?

Six of us had been vouched for by someone at our university, plus who knew who else. Who had vouched for Fiona and Helen? Fiona had said a commander suggested she apply, and Helen was known to someone in the government who'd used her family to help steal Nazi documents. How carefully were the two of them checked out?

"Was it snowing before you came in?" Helen asked.

I jumped as her words broke into my thoughts.

"No, but it felt cold enough," Rosalie told her, taking her bowl and spoon to the scullery.

I finished and joined her before Rosalie dried her dishes. "Need anything else?" Rosalie asked in a murmur.

"Only a chance to examine Fiona's scarf without her looking on. Thanks for not saying anything in front of Simon."

"You don't trust him, do you?"

"He goes chasing off after—ideas, and when they don't lead where he thinks they should, he tries to force them to take him where they don't want to go." I tried to find words that wouldn't say what I suspected we both knew, that Simon and I were in counterintelligence.

"He doesn't follow scientific method and logic," Rosalie said.

I gave her a smile. "Exactly."

Rosalie stopped before she left the scullery. "George is in the clear?"

"Apparently." I had to ask, "Rosalie, does it seem strange to work in the scullery? You're a countess."

"Here I'm just another decoder. Trying to do my bit for Britain." She shrugged as she walked out of the room. I watched her go, hoping she really meant what she said. I wanted to have her as a friend. I wanted to trust her.

I did my washing up quickly and went back to the servants' hall, where Rosalie was leaning over Fiona's shoulder looking at her knitting. "This is really good. I like your pattern," she said.

"A pattern is regular. That is all over the place," Maryellen said, not looking up as she knitted.

"This pattern could be extremely long or spread out. A pattern doesn't have to be every other row," Rosalie observed.

"I just try it when I feel as if I want to," Fiona said, sounding defensive. Maryellen had a talent for hurting people's feelings.

I came over and asked, "What is that stitch called?"

"That's a moss seed stitch," Rosalie said before Fiona could answer, pointing at the navy blue scarf, "and that's a double moss stitch."

"Are they hard to learn?"

"No," said Rosalie and Fiona together. "I'm just a beginner myself," Fiona added, "and I've picked it up."

"I'll try that, too, on my next scarf," I said, sounding brave. Sir Malcolm had said I'd be out of here in another day or two. There wouldn't be another scarf.

I was sorry about that, but I wanted to go home. However not, I told myself, before I caught Sarah and Aileen's killer.

The fancy stitches appeared every few rows. I looked at the end Fiona wasn't working on. She'd tried five of the moss stitch the first time, and a few rows later, three double moss stitches.

If it was Morse code, and the smaller stitches were dots and the larger were dashes, then the first two letters would be F, O.

Then Fiona moved the scarf to fold under itself, and I couldn't read anymore.

FO. Forget? Found? I needed to study that scarf more closely.

I couldn't do it that evening, no matter how much I tried. I hung around, listening to the musical program Rosalie turned to on the radio while the other women in our billet gossiped about people in their hometowns.

Fiona sat there, saying little as her fingers flew. She must have had a great deal more practice than I had, because my hands moved slowly. She didn't walk out of the room and leave her knitting behind at any time. She didn't move until she rose to go to bed along with the rest of us.

I lingered in the servants' hall while Rosalie and Gwen discussed the piano concerto that was performed last on the BBC program. When I saw Fiona go into the bathroom with her string bag of toiletries, I hurried up the hallway to her door. Looking around, I put my hand on the doorknob. Locked.

Just as I was going to put my key in the lock, I heard a throat clear behind me. I turned to find Maryellen behind me.

My pulse went skyward and my face heated. I forced a smile onto my face. "Good night, Maryellen."

"That's not your room." The accusation of theft hung in the air.

"Of course it..." I glanced around. "Blast. I'm losing my mind."

Shaking my head, I walked to the next door on that side of the hall and opened it with my key. Maryellen stood watching from the hallway, her arms crossed.

She hadn't moved as I said, "Good night, Maryellen," and walked into my room and shut the door.

I had less than twenty-four hours to find and read Fiona's scarf, to learn whether it was innocent or traitorous, and nosy Maryellen was now alerted to my actions.

I wondered how she'd react if she had my suspicions about Fiona and her knitting. Probably with self-righteous indignation if she believed me. However, I doubted she would believe someone she now thought was against her wonderful Simon.

I wouldn't believe my suspicions, except I couldn't find anyone besides a fellow resident of our hall who would have been able to get Sarah to go outside, supposedly alone, on a cold, dark night. Or attack Aileen in our living quarters, since there wasn't enough room between the building and the evergreens to strangle anyone.

Now that I knew the person who killed Sarah could have slipped back into our wing through the storeroom, in fact could come and go freely at any time, and had dumped Aileen's body behind the evergreens to the side of the door, I was certain that person was also the traitor. Elsie and Betty weren't aware of what we were doing at BP. The other women I'd slowly ruled out. The only one left was Fiona, and now I suspected how she passed on her messages and who received them next.

I just needed proof.

* * *

The next morning, in the chaos of seven women getting ready for work and racing to meet the bus on time, I had no chance to see Fiona's scarf.

I could, however, catch a moment to talk to Rosalie out of hearing of the others. "I've got to get back here at lunch time, but it's too far to walk and there are no taxis in Bletchley that I know of. Do you have any ideas?" I was nearly whispering.

"Leave it to me. But I'll have to come with you."

Sir Malcolm wouldn't approve, but he wasn't there. "Are you sure you can do this?"

"As Rosalie, no. But for the Countess of Briarcliffe, friend of the Earl and Countess of Haymarket, it should be a piece of cake. Now, go have your breakfast while I work my magic."

I went to the servants' hall to have porridge and coffee. A few moments later, Rosalie spoke quietly to Betty and slipped her a note. Betty gave an abbreviated curtsey. I don't think anyone else noticed, not knowing Rosalie's title.

Rosalie got extra honey on her porridge before Betty went upstairs. I think Marianne and Maryellen noticed that from the look they exchanged. Maryellen's eyebrows went almost to her hairline.

I wondered how often they noticed Rosalie get extra or that Betty cleared up after her when she wouldn't for the rest of us. Most of the time you could explain it away because Rosalie was the last one finished. Unless you knew Rosalie's secret.

Once we were all ready and hurrying out to the stop to be picked up for our morning ride to BP, Rosalie fell into step next to me. "It's all set for one o'clock. Marjory will pick us up." Then she strode ahead.

I wondered who Marjory was.

Marianne looked at the sky with a countrywoman's appraisal and said, "At least it will stay dry. But it's going to get colder."

"Colder than this?" Helen grumbled.

The bus arrived before we all had frozen fingers and toes. I climbed aboard, thinking I didn't care if Britain turned into the arctic, as long as Marjory showed up with a way for us to get back to Bloomington Grove and return to BP without anyone noticing.

Chapter Twenty-Eight

To say the morning went slowly was an understatement. The Machine Room was having trouble finding the right settings and without them we didn't have much to do.

At a little after ten, I was summoned to the admiral's office. After so many summonses, my colleagues didn't seem to notice them anymore. I bundled up and hurried through the bitter cold to the old manor house. The admiral's secretary waved me through as she continued with her typing.

I knocked and entered to find Sir Malcolm in his usual spot behind the door, the admiral behind his desk, and Simon lounging in a chair.

Sir Malcolm said, "You're out of time."

"You said I have until tomorrow. Actually, I should have a discovery for you by this afternoon."

Simon smirked. Sir Malcolm and the admiral ignored him, but I wanted to smack that expression off his face.

"Why this afternoon?"

"It's a matter of proof. I hope to have it by this afternoon. If I do, then I will also know who she is handing off her secret messages to. I planned to phone you this afternoon with the results."

"And what do you expect me to do when you telephone?" Sir Malcolm asked.

"Arrange the arrests of two people."

"You're certain you are correct about the identity of the traitor?"

"And the killer. They're one and the same. I will be certain by tonight."

"I don't want another trip down a rabbit hole the way you two sent me before," Sir Malcolm growled. With his size and his bushy eyebrows, he could look fierce when he wanted.

"With respect, sir, that was all Simon's doing," I told him.

"You were in it up to your—" Simon shouted at me.

I cut him off. "I've said all along it has to be a woman living at Bloomington Grove." I snapped at him, not caring what Sir Malcolm thought of my behavior.

"And this proof?" Sir Malcolm asked, ignoring both of our outbursts. "Where is it?"

"It's in the knitting, sir."

All three men looked at me as if I'd lost my mind.

"I suppose I should let you get back to work. I'll be in my office this afternoon awaiting your telephone call. She may use your phone to call me, I hope?" Sir Malcolm asked, looking at the admiral.

He nodded. "I'm coming back to town with you for a meeting, but I'll tell my secretary to let her into my office."

"Will that do, Mrs. Redmond?" Sir Malcolm asked.

"Yes, sir."

Both Simon and I were dismissed and headed back to Hut Six. As soon as we were out of the secretary's office, Simon said, "What have you found?"

"Nothing yet. That's why there's no proof yet."

"What do you expect to find, then?"

"I'll let you know this afternoon. I don't want to accuse someone unjustly."

He looked ashamed, but I wasn't fooled. "Which I did. I'm sorry. I was so sure it was George. He was broadcasting in Morse code over a shortwave channel."

"I don't want to make the same mistake." I weakened a bit then. "I'll tell you after lunch. Before I call. Will that be all right?"

He stopped just outside the door to the hut. "Yes. And if you need any help..."

"I won't know until I find proof that this person is a traitor." I dashed inside out of the cold into the merely chilly interior of the temporary building.

At one o'clock, it was time for Rosalie and me to go to lunch. We bundled up and hurried out toward the gate. "What am I looking for?" I asked.

"I don't know. Probably a Rolls."

We passed through the gate and then saw where a large black Rolls-Royce was parked down the lane. As we approached, I saw the auto carried a thin layer of dust on the otherwise pristine coat of paint and well-polished chrome.

Waiting in the driver's seat was a thin woman swathed in furs. Her hair and makeup showed understated elegance. I'd never met her, but I suspected this was the Countess of Haymarket, the hostess of Bloomington Grove. She looked somewhat older than her photographs in the newspapers from before the war.

Rosalie opened the door. "Marjory, this is so good of you."

"You hinted at excitement and spies. Tell me all."

Rosalie climbed in the front seat and gestured to me to climb in the back. "This is Livvy. She's in charge of catching spies. We are her minions today."

"Ooh, I've always wanted to be a minion." The countess held out a hand. "Pleased to meet you, Livvy. Is that an alias?"

I shook her hand and gave her a wink. "That would be telling." Up close, Marjory looked as if she'd aged twenty years since her photos appeared in the papers last summer. I guessed that was what wild living or knowing how to pose for the camera did for one.

The countess nodded and started the car. Just as we started to move, Simon opened the door next to me and jumped in. "Oh, are you a spy?" Marjory asked. She missed the shift and the car jerked.

"No, ma'am, I catch them," Simon said as he was jolted across the back seat.

I glared at him. "This is Simon."

As Marjory, Countess of Haymarket, drove down the lane, she turned and stuck her hand over the back of the front seat. “Pleased to meet you. Oh, this is so exciting.”

Rosalie said, “Marjory, you’re driving. Please face forward.” Her voice was devoid of panic, but I noticed she had gone pale.

“Oh. Yes. I must face forward, mustn’t I.” When her actions matched her words, I began to breathe again.

“We have to get them to Bloomington Grove and back in one piece if we’re going to save Britain,” Rosalie said in a businesslike tone.

Since we’d almost gone into a ditch and then swerved to the other side of the road, I was still feeling pale. Simon shot me a look that clearly said he hadn’t signed up for this.

I glared at him. He had no room to complain. No one had invited him.

Marjory ground the gears trying to climb a hill and then coasted too fast down the other side, swinging wide at the bottom and just missing a drystone wall that sat a few feet off the lane. We dodged a few more hazards, mainly large trees and deep ditches, before a long final metallic screech going up the drive to the servants’ wing.

Betty and Elsie were at the door waiting for us.

The Countess of Haymarket led the way into the house, saying in a stage whisper that could be heard in London, “We’re going to find a spy!”

“Well, we hope to.” I led the parade down our corridor and stopped in front of Fiona’s door.

"Are you going to pick the lock?" the countess asked in her booming whisper.

I unlocked the door with my key. Then I walked in and looked for her knitting bag. It wasn't out in plain sight. I checked under the bed. Nothing.

Rosalie looked in her wardrobe as I said, "She wasn't carrying it this morning."

"Her knitting bag's not in here, either," Rosalie replied.

I pulled over her chair and climbed up to look on top. The bag was at the back of the top of the wardrobe. I took it down and looked inside, pulling out the navy blue scarf. "There's a large number of raised stitches," I told Rosalie.

"Morse code?" Simon asked.

"I think so. Rosalie, will you get paper and pencil and write down the letters as I call them out?"

Rosalie did as I asked, while Simon took out his own notebook to write down the message.

When Rosalie was ready, I began. "Five single moss stitches, which I think are dots, so the first letter is F. These next are double moss seed stitches, aren't they?"

Rosalie looked over. "Yes."

"Three double stitches, which we think are dashes, would be an O. Then this would be an R, and this one dash is T—"

"Fort. It's a military message," the countess said loudly.

I glanced over. Behind her, Betty and Elsie stood, wide-eyed.

"—S C H R I T T. That would translate to 'progress.' Next

word, I think," I decided because of the extra wide space between designs, "E N T S C H L Ü S S E L U N G. Can that be right?"

Simon studied his notebook. "Decrypting."

I nodded. "E N I G..." I looked at Rosalie and Simon. "Oh, dear."

"What? What?" The countess was flapping her arms and bouncing on her heels in excitement.

"This is very serious. None of you may ever say a word about this. Ever. You must act as if nothing has happened here today," I said.

"They'll haul you away and put you in jail if you say a single word about this, or even hint that you know," Simon added.

"They can't do that," Betty protested. "I'm an Englishwoman."

"And we are at war. Any hint of anything you've heard or seen today is treason. Saying anything about this could cause Britain to lose the war. If you are a good Englishwoman, you'll forget this ever happened."

Betty looked at Elsie, who shrugged.

"A certain woman won't hear anything from me," Betty said, planting herself solidly in the hallway.

"No one. Not a single, solitary person anywhere can hear about this," I told Betty.

She nodded.

"Who won't? What is it?" the countess asked.

"It's a secret, Marjory. I'll tell you when it's safe for you to know. We can't go endangering the earl, can we?" Rosalie said.

"Oh, dear." She seemed even more dithery than before, waving her bejeweled hands about. "They won't come after us and murder us in our beds, will they?"

"Not if you keep your mouth shut," Simon told her with menace in his tone.

"Oh. Oh. I'm going to hide upstairs," the countess exclaimed, turning and scurrying away.

"Marjory!" Rosalie used a commanding voice I'd not heard from her before. "You need to drive us back to the station."

She stopped. "What if they come after me?"

"Let's do this quickly, before anyone knows we were here." I carefully folded the scarf and put it in the bag to put on top of the wardrobe. "Simon, can you drive?"

"Yes."

"You can drive us and the countess back to Bletchley. Then she can drive back here without us, and if anyone is watching they'll think nothing of it." I hoped that would reassure her.

I put the chair back, made certain everything matched the way it looked before, and pushed Simon out of the room ahead of me.

When I reached the hallway, I asked, "Rosalie, do you have navy blue wool here?"

"No."

"Well, there goes that idea."

"I have a couple of skeins of it," Betty said.

"Could we have it, please? For the sake of Britain's future?" I wasn't too proud to beg.

Her chin lifted. "Of course."

"Okay, Rosalie, this is what we need..."

When I finished writing out the details of a navy-blue scarf, Rosalie said, "I'm a fast knitter. I'm not that fast."

"Since you've suddenly taken ill, you'll have all afternoon. I'll take it down to the WI and switch it for Fiona's tonight." I gave Rosalie a big smile.

Betty retrieved the yarn from her room. Meanwhile, Rosalie put an arm around the countess and led her toward the car. I didn't hear what she said, but her voice was soothing.

I pulled Simon toward the car. "No foolishness, now. It's a Rolls."

"I know." He appeared to have stars in his eyes. "I'm going to drive a Rolls."

Betty and Elsie were waiting by the door. "It's his lordship's auto. No messing about," Elsie warned.

"I won't, ma'am." He sounded surprisingly reverential.

I was skeptical. Elsie looked as if she'd box his ears if he harmed the earl's car.

"Remember, not a word to anyone. It would endanger the earl and countess as well as Britain," I warned them as we left the wing of the manor house.

"You were never here," Betty replied.

"Good." As we reached the car, Simon said, "All right,

your ladyship. I'll drive us over, if you'd like."

"Stop before you get to the gates. I don't want anyone seeing you with me," the countess said, slumping down to hide in the back seat with Rosalie sitting next to her.

I sat in front with Simon as we drove quickly and smoothly back to BP. When we arrived, he swung the auto around so the Rolls was aimed toward home at the top of a grade. He put on the handbrake and climbed out. "It's been a pleasure, ma'am. Just start the car and release the handbrake, and you can take off easily."

As he opened her door, she said in her carrying voice, "Why thank you, young man. And you can trust me not to say a word about you being a spy."

Simon cringed.

Rosalie opened her door herself and looked at me with an expression of relief mixed with disbelief. "While you go make your phone call, I'll try to get us back to Bloomington Grove in one piece."

"See that you do. Please! We need that fake scarf tonight." I thanked the countess for her aid and hurried toward the gates.

We passed the guards with no problem and hurried to the main house. While Simon went toward the dining room, I went to the admiral's office.

His secretary was nowhere to be seen. Her typewriter was covered and her desk locked for the night. When I tried the admiral's office door, it was locked. I needed to get hold of Sir Malcolm immediately. He needed to make arrests.

I pulled out a hairpin I kept in my coat pocket and began to work on the lock.

"Stop right there," came a male voice from behind me.

Chapter Twenty-Nine

I stopped and turned to find a man in the British army uniform of a colonel standing behind me, blocking my way.

"I need to get in to make a phone call. The admiral gave me permission before he left to go to London. His secretary was supposed to be here to let me in."

"She's not here, is she?"

"Where is she? It's important I get this message to London immediately."

"She left half an hour ago. And the only place you're going is the conference room by the front door while we straighten out your attempt to break into the admiral's office. Come on. March."

I put away my hairpin and strode out into the hall. Simon watched me as the colonel forced me down the hall toward the main door with a firm grip on my arm. "Call Sir M," I shouted.

Simon stood looking shocked as I was quickly herded into the small room to the side of the front entrance.

We entered the tiny conference room where I was

ordered to take a seat in a wooden folding chair as if I were a criminal. "If you'd just—"

"Name?" he barked.

I tried to remain calm while I used an upper-class attitude to tell him, "Olivia Redmond. Here's my pass."

He snatched it away. "It could be stolen."

"Well, it's not. I want to spe—"

"Quiet," he snarled at me.

If this was an example of the quality of people Adam had to work with, I felt sorry for him.

A man dressed in civilian clothes came in and my jailer nodded to him. "Who's this?" the new man asked.

"Olivia Redmond," I answered.

"Do not speak unless you are directly spoken to." The colonel then relented. "Where do you work?"

"Are you supposed to ask that? There is the small matter of the Official Secrets Act."

The man in civilian dress said with an air of patience stretched to the limit, "We just want to clear this up and get you back to work."

"Hut Six."

The two men exchanged a look that clearly said *Another of those nutters.* "Go over to the hut and get someone in charge to come down and verify her identity." The colonel sounded annoyed.

The civilian left, taking my pass with me, and I sat, staring angrily at the colonel. That did me no good, since he never once looked in my direction.

Minutes ticked by on the clock over the doorway. I began to picture ever-worse disasters occurring, with secrets being leaked, spies escaping, and the Countess of Haymarket, Betty, and Elsie being murdered. And now that I had time to sit and think, I realized I was hungry from having missed my lunch.

I was becoming impatient and wanted to ask the colonel to call the admiral's secretary when John burst into the room. "Olivia, what is going on?"

"I was supposed to call London this afternoon using the admiral's phone. The admiral's gone to London, but his secretary was supposed to let me in. She—"

"She was sent to London with papers for the admiral a short time later. But why are you here?" John asked.

"Not finding the secretary, I tried to open the door by an alternative method—"

"Alternative method?" John asked.

I tried to look innocent, but I'm sure I failed. "—so I could use the telephone and this colonel saw me and dragged me in here. And he took my pass."

"I have your pass. Let's go and stop wasting the assistant director's time." John stared at me. "Or mine. We are a woman down."

"Two women down. Rosalie went home ill."

"Do you verify that she is one of yours?" the colonel asked with a note of distaste in his voice.

"Oh, good grief," I muttered.

The colonel was still ignoring me. John assured him I was

part of his staff and the colonel told him to maintain better discipline in his office. Neither showed any interest in introducing me to the colonel. John handed me my pass and we walked out of the room.

As I began to head toward the admiral's office, John said, "Simon already called in whatever it was you were supposed to tell someone."

"Then I need to talk to Simon."

We walked to Hut Six and I went to the Machine Room. When he saw me, Simon headed toward me, pulling on his coat. "Outside," he muttered as he passed me.

I followed him, while John shook his head as he went into the Decoding Room.

"Did you call Sir M?" I asked once we were far enough outside the building that I wasn't worried about anyone hearing me.

"Yes. He wants you to call him."

"That's what started this confusion. Where did you call from?"

"The admiral's office. By the way, his secretary had to go to London with papers for her boss."

"I heard. How did you get in?"

"I picked the lock." He gave me a smug smile.

"That's what I was doing when I got caught by some colonel."

"Well, I wasn't daft enough to get caught." He smirked at me.

I really wanted to choke him. I restrained myself enough

to say, "Come with me. Let's make sure this call goes through."

We crossed over to the main house quickly and walked into the secretary's office. Simon immediately unlocked the doorknob to the admiral's office with a small piece of metal and stood holding the door open for me.

I went inside and picked up the receiver of the phone on the far side of the desk to make my call, knowing the conversation would be encrypted. Simon followed me in and leaned against the door.

When Sir Malcolm came on the line, I said, "I know who the traitor is and I think I know why she killed Sarah Wycott and Aileen MacLeith."

"Go on," he said.

"It's Fiona Carter. She's putting her messages in Morse code into the stitches of the scarves she's giving to the WI. One of the WI ladies, Mrs. Hubbard, wasn't known in the village until a couple of years ago. She sends the scarves or the message on somehow. You'll have to find out the next step from her."

"And Miss Carter? How much does she know?"

"Quite a bit. She works in the Registration Room in Hut Six. The message on the scarf she's going to hand in tonight is 'Progress deciphering Enigma. Possible broken codes.' In German," I added.

"Blast."

"Yes, sir." My feelings exactly. "The Countess of Briarcliffe, who also works in Hut Six, is knitting a replacement scarf with the message 'Failed deciphering Enigma. Closing down unit,' in German."

"Where will you make the switch?" Sir Malcolm sounded intrigued.

"If all goes well, at the WI tonight. Will you be sending people out to make the arrests?"

"What time will Miss Carter be at the WI handing off the scarf?"

"We always get there about eight."

"We'll be there then to make the arrests after she is clear of the WI." Sir Malcolm hung up without saying good-bye. As usual.

I told Simon what Sir Malcolm said and we went back to our workstations after relocking the admiral's office door.

Now that I knew everything was in place for this evening's arrest and I would soon be going home, my mind kept wandering from my work. I finally took a deep breath, told myself not to be so silly, and got down to work decrypting messages.

At the end of the day, we all packed up and headed for the gates and the bus, which at least made a decent windbreak even if it wasn't warm. We rode back to Bloomington Grove in good spirits, although the walk from the stop to the top of the rise to enter the servants' wing was dark and even colder than before due to the wind.

No one would be outside who could help it. However, tonight was the night we turned in our knitting to the WI in Little Bricton, necessitating a long, cold walk along a dark lane.

And I had to keep an eye on Fiona and her scarf if I was to make the switch.

All of us, including Rosalie, sat down to dinner soon after we entered our billet. Elsie made certain our vegetable stew was hot, which was welcome, and flavored with a beef bone, which was delicious. There was no bread, but there were enough potatoes in the stew that it filled us up.

Fiona was sitting across the table and up one from me, and when I looked in her direction, she was watching me. Did I put something away wrong in her room? Did someone tell her what we did today? I finished my mouthful and said, "It's going to be cold walking to the WI tonight."

She shrugged and continued eating her stew.

"When are we leaving for the WI?" I asked when we rose from the table.

"I still have to finish my second sock," Maryellen said. "Won't take but a minute."

"Don't dawdle," her sister said. "Get started and I'll do your washing up."

I followed Marianne into the scullery with more dishes.

"I don't know that I want to go back out in that cold," Marianne said.

"What do we do about Aileen's knitting? Did she have anything finished to turn in?" I asked.

"I think she had a cap or two finished. Can we check her room to see about getting them?" Marianne said.

"Our keys fit each other's rooms. We can get in there and

get the caps and lock her room up again. Who's boxing everything up to send to Edinburgh?"

"Probably Betty. She was the one who cleaned out your room after Sarah was murdered." Then Marianne looked at me and said, "I can't believe we're talking about it so—so matter-of-factly."

"If we didn't, we'd all go crazy." Actually, I was constantly walking around with guilt over Aileen's death on my shoulders. That I couldn't admit it made it worse.

Marianne handed me another bowl and more utensils to put away in their spot in the scullery. "Come on, Livvy. If we hurry, we'll stay warm."

With much fussing and bundling up and promises from Betty of hot tea when we returned, we were ready on time. I tucked the scarf Rosalie had finished that afternoon around my neck so I could avoid mistaking it for anything else we were turning in to the WI.

"Where's Fiona?" Maryellen asked, her socks finished and her coat on.

"I don't know. Go find her," Marianne said.

Two minutes later, Maryellen returned. "She's not in her room or the washroom or the loo. Has anyone seen her?"

We all shook our heads. It was only seven-twenty and Sir Malcolm wouldn't be here until eight. I walked over to Betty and spoke very quietly. "Did you or anyone else say anything to Fiona about this afternoon's activities?"

She looked at me, wide-eyed. "No. We know our duty." Then she released a long breath. "She seemed to be watching us all tonight. I think something caught her attention, warned her that something wasn't right. But Elsie and I didn't tell her," she whispered. "Nor did anyone else."

"The countess?" I was sure she was the weak link.

"Never comes down here." Betty shook her head. "Wasn't one of us."

"Maybe she's already left," I suggested when I returned to the knitters.

"Did anyone see her leave?" Marianne asked.

Shrugs and shaken heads were the only reply.

"We might as well go," Maryellen said. "Maybe we'll meet her on the way."

I deliberately stayed between the Allen sisters while the three of us walked down the lane. It was at least a half-mile to Little Bricton down a dark, hedge-shrouded road. I felt vulnerable the entire walk, no matter how fast we moved in the chilly wind. The hedges shifted, but was it from the wind or because someone was lurking there?

We crossed the village quickly and entered the WI hall as a group. I immediately looked around for Fiona, but I didn't see her. I also couldn't find Mrs. Hubbard.

When it was my turn to hand in my scarf, I asked, "Have you seen Miss Carter?"

"No. Didn't she come with you?"

Something had definitely warned Fiona that we were on to her, since she hadn't arrived to deliver her knitting. "Where is Mrs. Hubbard? I wanted to show her my scarf, since she was so helpful with a few hints the last time I was here."

"She told Mrs. Linfield she wouldn't be able to make tonight's meeting. Some friend came to pick her up shortly afterward and they drove out of the village."

"Toward Bletchley?"

"Now that you mention it, yes."

Mrs. Hubbard could be escaping by train or by auto. Either way, she had whatever secrets Fiona had passed to her. I wondered if that car was the one that had taken aim at me.

And where was Fiona? Had she escaped with her? That was what I would do if I knew I'd soon be arrested for treason and murder.

If Fiona had run off, that meant she wouldn't be here to attack me in the lane on the return journey to Bloomington Grove. I really hoped she had left the district. But how could we exchange the scarves?

"Could you see how many people were in the car?" I asked.

"How many people—? I don't pay that much attention to my neighbors' comings and goings." She gave me a quizzical look. "I'm not that nosy. And it was far too dark to tell anything."

"Of course," I said.

"Olivia, we're ready to go," Maryellen called out. Already, Marianne was heading out the door.

I thanked the woman and raced after my colleagues, seeing on the hall clock that it was seven forty-five. By the time I left the hall, the Allen twins were halfway across the village.

No matter how much I hurried, Marianne and Maryellen, both athletes, widened the distance. In the dark, I soon lost sight of them, and by the time I left the dark shapes of the village cottages behind, I no longer heard the echo of their footsteps on the road or their voices in the wind.

I hurried as much as I could while I tried to keep watch all around me. I hoped Fiona had left with Mrs. Hubbard. She was a killer and I didn't want to suffer the same fate as Sarah Wycott and Aileen MacLeith.

As I came up to the bend in the lane where Sarah's body had been found, my steps started to slow. It wasn't much farther to safety, but the cold air I was dragging in with every breath was now burning my lungs. I took two long breaths and then started to speed up.

That was when a figure sprang out from the hedgerow.

Chapter Thirty

I spun around and took two steps backward. I was ready to try to fight my assailant, my back toward Bloomington Grove. If I wanted to survive, I had to fight my way free.

When she stepped closer, I could make out Fiona's features. "What are you doing out here in the cold?" I asked her, still moving backward.

"Waiting for you."

Her tone told me she knew what I'd learned. "Why, Fiona?" I edged away from her.

"You ask me why? Why do you follow a king? Why do you follow a medieval order of society in the middle of the twentieth century? This government run by old aristocratic simpletons needs to be wiped away. Replaced by a new order. The order of the superior race." As she spoke, she walked toward me.

I backed up the lane in the direction of the drive to the manor house. "The House of Commons, the political power in this country, isn't all old fools and isn't made up of the aristocracy."

She stalked toward me, taking larger steps than I could in reverse. "You're a bigger fool than they are. You believe that nonsense."

I sped up my shortened steps, no longer noticing the cold. The wind, however, blew me and my words backward as it blew Fiona toward me. "And you believe you'll be rewarded in Berlin? You're the biggest fool of all."

"It'll keep my brother safe if you never solve the riddle of the codes. He's serving on a U-boat. Silly boy, but he loves his work for the German navy."

"How did your brother end up on a U-boat?" Keep her talking, I thought, as I kept stumbling backward toward where someone from the house might see us.

I recognized that as a dream. No one would be looking out in the cold and dark, just as they hadn't when Sarah was killed. There was no one around to hear us. I had to rely on myself.

"He's German. My uncle Oscar and I came here several years ago and bought the pub with money from the Reich. We said we were a father and daughter from Essex. No one ever questioned us. Not even the naval commander who told me to apply to BP on his recommendation."

"Is your name really Fiona Carter?"

"Of course not. How naïve you are. My uncle and I both went to the government school to learn to sound and act English. As soon as we finished, we were sent here as sleepers to wait for the day that we were needed for the Fatherland."

"Why did this commander recommend you for a job

here?"

"Anyone who buys him a drink is his friend, and we own a pub. After several drinks, he'll tell all sorts of British naval secrets. As soon as he told us about the possibility of working deep inside the government on codebreaking, we knew I needed to apply."

If I got out of this alive, I'd tell Sir Malcolm to have them tighten up their recruitment for Bletchley Park.

Fiona was almost to me now. I had to know what happened, and I had to keep her talking. "Why did you kill Sarah?"

"Sarah broke into my room to steal from me and took the opportunity to look closely at my knitting pattern. On the other hand, Aileen figured out what I was doing just from sitting next to me one evening. They both spoke German and had learned Morse code as girls, so they could translate the code on the scarves."

"You must think we're all stupid. I figured out your code, and I'm just a beginning knitter."

"You're the smartest of the bunch of weaklings here. But it won't save you, any more than it saved them."

"How did you get Sarah to come down here? She wouldn't ordinarily walk to Little Bricton except on WI night. Wednesday night. But she was killed on a Monday."

"The little fool followed me," Fiona said. Her footsteps had slowed, but mine hadn't. "I went out to meet Mrs. Hubbard at her house, and Sarah saw me go into the storeroom. She still had her coat on, so she decided to be a hero and find out where I was going. She wasn't very quiet about it, so I stepped into the shadows in the bend in the road and waited to see who was there.

"As soon as she appeared, I knew. I moved next to her and said, 'Following me?' She jumped a foot. She finally admitted it, as if she thought that would save her."

"And Aileen?" I asked.

"She came to my room late Friday night and accused me. Of course, then I had a dead body in my room. Your questions let me know you thought Sarah was killed by someone in the servants' wing, so when everyone was asleep in the middle of the night, I dragged Aileen out through the storeroom and left her outside. Nothing could be easier. I was surprised no one searched for her earlier, but you were busy with your husband that weekend, and Simon is a fool."

She lunged at me, her hands grabbing at my neck, but I darted to the side and then pivoted and ran.

I made a half-dozen steps before she grabbed me from behind and we both fell into the hedgerow. The branches scratched my face and legs and clutched at my clothes.

I managed to roll onto my side and push my gloved hand into her face. She tried to grab me around the neck, but the scarf tucked inside my coat, the replacement scarf with the fake message, proved to be a barrier she couldn't overcome.

I got my hand under her chin and shoved upward, forcing her halfway off of me and scraping her against the hedgerow branches.

Somehow, she forced her knee into my chest and pushed

me onto my back. I couldn't breathe in while she crushed my ribs.

She kept her upper body high enough above me that I couldn't reach her face with my hand, although she was squishing me. Was this how she overpowered Sarah?

I tried to wiggle out. I tried to shove her to the side. Nothing worked. I couldn't breathe. Darkness closed in. I was losing the battle.

Then I heard footsteps. A torch shone in my eyes. Fiona was lifted off of me bodily as she pushed once more against my chest, screaming and struggling the whole time.

I gasped and rolled on my side, clutching my stomach. Hands lifted me to a sitting position. Then Simon said, "Can you stand?"

Rosalie snapped at him, "Don't be daft. Olivia, it's all right. Simon, George, and Peter are here. They have Fiona. You're safe."

"The scarf," I groaned out.

"Scarf?" I heard Sir Malcolm at a distance as more footsteps approached.

"She's given it to Mrs. Hubbard. She left," was all I could get out before I tried to catch my breath again.

I could hear questions thrown at Fiona, but she didn't answer.

"Left in a car. Neighbor saw." I was doubled up in pain now, barely making any sound.

Simon rushed over to Sir Malcolm, leaving me with Rosalie. Then the other four women from the servants' hall came down to check on us. They helped me up, and with Marianne on one side and Maryellen on the other, they assisted me one halting step at a time the entire distance to the entrance to our wing.

As we reached the door, Simon rushed up to us. "Is there anything else Sir M needs to know?"

"He needs to find Mrs. Hubbard and the scarf," I whispered. "Exchange." I took off my scarf, the one Rosalie had knitted, and handed it to him before I was half-carried inside.

I was dropped by Maryellen and set down more carefully by Marianne at the table in the servants' hall, where Rosalie and Gwen took off my coat and hat while I struggled to pull off my gloves. Someone set a hot cup of tea in front of me and I picked it up with two shaking hands.

I could barely swallow.

"That's quite a mark on your neck," Helen said.

"Did she try to strangle you?" Rosalie asked.

I nodded and tried again to swallow some warming tea.

"The same as Sarah," Marianne said, looking at her sister. "The same as Aileen."

"How was I to know?" Maryellen said. "Fiona was always nice to me."

"She was nice to me, too," I whispered, "until I learned the same thing Sarah Wycott did. And then Aileen became suspicious."

"What?" Maryellen asked.

"Those errors in her knitting you wanted her to fix were

stitches marking dots and dashes in Morse code. Mrs. Hubbard sent or took the scarves to someone who got them to Germany. She was telling them about our progress at BP."

"No. I mean, why would she?" Maryellen's face reddened.

"She's German. Her brother is on a U-boat. That's her country. At least, that's what she told me." Maybe I wasn't supposed to tell them, but they deserved to know. They were her friends here in Bletchley.

Maryellen was scowling now. "She told me she didn't speak German."

"Her scarves contained Morse code in German. She spoke German. And she had to be able to knit well to manage something that complex."

"What was your role in all this?" Gwen asked.

I looked around me. Everyone was staring at me. Could I tell them?

"Be honest with us, Olivia." Helen looked stern.

"I was sent here to learn if Sarah was killed because of a grudge someone had against her, or if she'd found a leak. A traitor."

Women dropped into chairs around me, looking as if I'd knocked the wind out of them. Rosalie alone didn't appear surprised. "Thank you," she murmured.

"How did you get Simon and the other men here so quickly?" I asked her.

"I called them."

I looked at Rosalie in surprise. There was no telephone

here.

"I went upstairs and used the earl's telephone to call the Wren and Dragon." She winked at me.

"Thank goodness. You saved my life."

* * *

It was a solemn six of us who ate breakfast and hurried down to the bus stop the next morning. If anyone had a good night's sleep, it didn't show on our faces.

Simon, George, and Peter must have told everyone about the events of the night before, because the men from the village nodded to me but otherwise didn't speak.

We started on our usual work when we arrived at BP, but I kept listening for someone to say I was wanted in the admiral's office. I knew Sir Malcolm would appear at some point and take me away, with or without an explanation.

Finally, at ten-thirty, Simon came in and signaled me to come outside with him. I had kept my coat and hat on. Wrapping my own scarf around my still-sore neck and pulling on my gloves, I walked with him to the main building.

Sir Malcolm was waiting for us in the admiral's office, but the admiral was not there. Instead, Sir Malcolm was seated behind the desk. "Sit down, both of you."

We peeled off hats and gloves and scarves and then sat.

"Mrs. Hubbard, not her real name, you understand, was apprehended with a man as they boarded a fishing trawler to sail to the Netherlands on a regular voyage for the fishermen. We don't yet know which of the fishermen are working for the Nazis, but rest assured, we will find out. Mrs. Hubbard still had Fiona's scarf in her possession. Neither she nor the man have talked. Yet." Sir Malcolm sounded as if he had high expectations.

"Mr. Preston, Helen's father, went with my men to the boat with the scarf you provided, and while the arrests were made, switched it for Fiona's scarf. The scarf with its phony message has probably reached its intended recipient in the Netherlands by now, with no one being the wiser."

"The scarf worked? It will help keep Bletchley Park safe?" His news made me want to cheer. "And it was Helen's father who did the switch?"

"Yes. You remember this isn't the first time he has helped us with his sleight of hand." He turned his head to stare at me. "We have no evidence, but I believe Mrs. Hubbard's accomplice was the driver of the auto that tried to run you over. They were afraid you were getting too close to the truth."

Before I could say anything, he added, "I take it you learned to knit?"

"A little. Most of what I used to catch Fiona was learned from some of my billet mates who are talented knitters." I wanted to give them credit. I couldn't have found a traitor without them.

"It was well spotted. Miss Carter has begun to talk, at least to assure us that she is a loyal German, as is all of her family. She says she never would have been certain you had picked up on her loyalty to the Fatherland if you hadn't disturbed the dust on top of her wardrobe." Sir Malcolm shook his head as if he couldn't believe I was so careless.

"Oh, good grief." I'd tried to be careful, but obviously not careful enough.

"Fiona hid her knowledge of German, which kept her away from the most vital work. Thank goodness she outsmarted herself there. She didn't seem aware of efforts to decipher Enigma messages until recently. With luck, our work on Enigma here at Bletchley will escape the notice of the Nazis now that we've sent them the phony message in the scarf by their own code."

"And now, Sir Malcolm? What are our next assignments?" Simon asked.

Sir Malcolm smiled, which immediately put me on edge. "I've been told what an asset you've been using your mathematical knowledge to help break the machine settings. You're staying here for the remainder of the war."

"What?" Simon came close to shrieking. "No, sir. I need to be out there, finding spies."

"As you did with George Kester? As you did with the army's double agent? No, Townsend, you stay here where you can be of the greatest use to your country."

Simon glared at Sir Malcolm. I suspected he was already considering avenues that would get him back into the business of hunting spies, and doing it badly.

"And me, sir?" I asked. I tried not to cross my fingers that he'd let me go back to London and the *Daily Premier.*

"Your time here is finished, Mrs. Redmond. You are to go back to Sir Henry and his newspaper until we need you again.

Get your bag from your office and come back here, quickly, please. We'll take you by Bloomington Grove to collect your belongings and then we'll give you a ride back to London."

"Thank you, sir." I was leaving the office as I pulled on my hat and wound my scarf around my neck.

"Don't thank me, Mrs. Redmond. You're going to have to keep quiet about this for the rest of your life."

I glanced at Sir Malcolm as I left the room. His lips were smiling, but his eyes were cold.

As I entered the Decoding Room, all eyes turned toward me. "I'm off to London," I told them. "Doing something less useful than your work. I wish you all the luck and success in the world."

They each shook my hand, John included. Rosalie was last. "You were a huge help. Thank you," I told her.

"If you ever need me again, just call me. And thank you for letting me be part of..." She stepped back and took a deep breath. "And Simon?"

"Simon is staying in the Machine Room for the duration."

There were smiles. "George will love that," John said, shaking his head.

I nodded to them, turned in my pass, picked up my bag, and left.

In the car on the way to Bloomington Grove, I asked Sir Malcolm, "You're really not going to keep Simon here for the rest of the war?"

"We've finally found something Townsend is good at. Of course he's staying here. We can't chance him serving overseas and being captured. He knows too much."

I hoped his desire for fame would find an outlet in BP.

When I rang the bell, Betty answered the door. "What are you doing here so early?" After her experiences the day before, she sounded dubious.

"Leaving. I'm being sent back to London."

"And the," she stopped and thought, "difficulties?"

"All sorted out. Fiona will be leaving, too. We'll both be replaced."

"So, it's safe now? The countess has been afraid to get out of bed this morning."

"As long as she never says a word about the difficulties. And that goes for you and Elsie, too."

She looked me straight in the eye and said, "What difficulties?"

I packed up my two suitcases in record time, gave Betty my key, said good-bye to Elsie, who was just beginning dinner, and went out to the car.

It was certainly more comfortable riding to London in Sir Malcolm's auto than on the crowded train. He dropped me off at my building, and Sutton, our doorman, took me up in the lift, telling me about the adventures of various tenants and that Captain Redmond had been home a week or so ago.

I unlocked my door, carried in my cases, and sighed as I shut myself in my home. I walked from room to room, smiling. It would be a shame to have to cook again, especially with my cooking, but on balance, I was glad to return. I picked up the mail and glanced through it. Nothing from Adam. Oh, how I wanted to see him.

Christmas was nearly here, the first year of the war was ending, and the shooting hadn't begun. I really hoped Adam would be able to get leave for Christmas. I looked around the flat again. I needed to decorate for the holiday. Make our home look inviting and cozy.

Then I picked up the telephone and dialed a number I knew so well. "Sir Henry," I told the familiar voice that answered, "I'm back in London and ready to get back to work."

I hope you enjoyed Deadly Cypher. If you have, please be sure to read the rest of Olivia's adventures in The Deadly Series. And go to my website www.KateParkerbooks.com and sign up for my newsletter. In exchange, you'll receive links to my free Deadly Series short stories you can download from BookFunnel onto your ereader of choice. Or check out www.TheDeadlySeries.com for articles about Britain and World War II. You can sign up for my newsletter there as well which will give you the links to those free short stories.

Acknowledgments

I was lucky enough to visit Bletchley Park before everything was shut down for the pandemic, and I found the place fascinating. I knew right away that Olivia had to be involved in the work there. The bookstore on site provided me with many nonfiction volumes that made it possible for me to check details while I was writing Deadly Cypher.

I made a conscious decision not to mention any of the actual Bletchley Park staff or local villages in this work of fiction. While I drew on real people, events, and locations, I have fictionalized and combined them so that while the flavor of their everyday lives and work is accurate, I made certain not to have made any individual's life or contribution less than it really was. These were remarkable people doing extraordinary work. I hope I have done them justice.

There was a disagreement in the sources I read about the name of the transcription machine Olivia typed on. Variously written as Typex, typeX, typex, and TypeX, I chose one and stuck to it.

The details I write about at Bletchley Park took place between early September, 1939 and early April, 1940, the period of the phony war. While there were shortages in the shops, rationing began in early January, 1940, the same time that Hut Six was first occupied. For fictional and pacing purposes, I condensed the events of the phony war and used late November until mid-December, 1939 for the time this story takes place.

I'd like to thank Eilis Flynn, Jen Parker, and Jennifer Brown for their editorial help, and Les Floyd for replacing my Americanisms with Britishisms. As always, any mistakes are my own.

I thank you, my readers, for coming along with Olivia on this journey. I hope you've enjoyed it.

About the Author

Kate Parker grew up reading her mother's collection of mystery books by Christie, Sayers, and others. Now she can't write a story without someone being murdered, and everyday items are studied for their lethal potential. It had taken her years to convince her husband she hadn't poisoned dinner; that funny taste is because she couldn't cook. Her children have grown up to be surprisingly normal, but two of them are developing their own love of literary mayhem, so the term "normal" may have to be revised.

For the time being, Kate has brought her imagination to the perilous times before and during World War II in the Deadly series. London society resembled today's lifestyle, but Victorian influences still abounded. Kate's sleuth is a young widow earning her living as a society reporter for a large daily newspaper while secretly working as a counterespionage agent for Britain's spymaster and finding danger as she tries to unmask Nazi spies while helping refugees escape oppression.

As much as she loves stately architecture and vintage clothing, Kate has also developed an appreciation of central heating and air conditioning. She's discovered life in Carolina requires her to wear shorts and T-shirts while drinking hot tea and it takes a great deal of imagination to picture cool, misty weather when it's 90 degrees out and sunny.

Follow Kate and her deadly examination of history at www.kateparkerbooks.com

and www.thedeadlyseries.com

where you can sign up for her newsletters

and www.Facebook.com/Author.Kate.Parker/

and www.bookbub.com/authors/kate-parker

Made in the USA
Monee, IL
02 September 2021

76989423R00174